Preface to Murder (Large Print)

An Oxford Murder Mystery

Bridget Hart Book 6

M S Morris

Published by Landmark Media, a division of Landmark Internet Ltd.

CHAPTER 1

The golden stonework, tall arched windows and elaborately vaulted ceiling of the Bodleian Library's Divinity School made a lofty setting for a literary event. Bathed in the warmth of the late evening sunlight, the audience seated inside the medieval hall clapped politely as the spokesperson for the Oxford Literary Festival – a rather formidable lady in a tailored black trouser suit – concluded her health and safety briefing and welcomed the writer and interviewer to the podium.

Michael Dearlove – greying but still rakish in appearance, and well known for his award-winning articles in *The Guardian* and other left-leaning publications – was arguably the more famous of the two people now ascending the platform, but it was the writer and academic, Diane Gilbert, that everyone had come to hear. Dearlove's task this evening would be merely to pose questions and steer the conversation around her debut book. No doubt the audience was hoping for an interesting and thought-provoking discussion.

From her vantage point standing at the back of the fifteenth-century hall – the oldest part of Oxford's world-famous university library – Detective Inspector Bridget Hart had a good view of the academic who was now making herself comfortable in one of the two chairs placed at forty-five degrees either side of a low table on which the festival organisers had arranged two glass tumblers and bottles of mineral water.

Diane Gilbert crossed her long legs and leaned back in her seat, surveying the audience from on high. She was one of those exceptionally tall women who made Bridget acutely conscious of her own diminutive stature. At almost six foot, surely Diane didn't need to wear those towering heels that only served to elevate her even more above her fellow humans?

Bridget estimated the writer to be about sixty years of age, but so well groomed that she would cast many a younger woman into the shadows. Her hair, coloured in shades of dark blonde with subtle highlights, was cut into a layered bob. Her cheekbones were sharp, her eyebrows plucked professionally to perfection, and there was no sign of that sagging jawline that betrayed the age of so many women in later-middle life. Bridget strongly suspected the work of cosmetic intervention in keeping Diane's glowing skin so ice-rink smooth. The woman looked as if she worked out regularly too, her lithe and supple figure displayed to advantage in the understated designer dress she wore with effortless elegance.

Another reason for Bridget to dislike her.

The New Year was now far from new, and three months on, Bridget's well-intentioned resolutions to eat less and exercise more had been consigned to the realm of wishful thinking. A healthy diet and regular visits to the swimming pool seemed incompatible with the job of police detective. At least that was her excuse, and she wasn't afraid to use it.

But it wasn't simply Diane's lithe figure and immaculate presentation that made Bridget feel so uncharitable towards the woman. She wasn't so small-minded as to resent an attractive woman. Nor was it Diane's height, since almost everyone Bridget encountered was taller than her. No, the fact was that in her brief meeting with the writer before the talk, Bridget had found her to be rather cold and supercilious, not to mention surprisingly ungrateful that two members of Thames Valley Police were giving up their evening to "watch over her" as Chief Superintendent Grayson had put it to Bridget earlier in the day.

'She's received a death threat,' Grayson had told her that morning when he'd summoned Bridget into his office and inquired if she had any plans for the evening. As it happened, it was the school Easter holidays, and Chloe, her teenage daughter, was visiting her father – Bridget's ex-husband, Ben – in London. Jonathan, Bridget's boyfriend, was away in New York on business.

Was "boyfriend" the right word to use when she was in her late thirties (she had turned thirty-nine the previous month, but was still in a state of denial) and Jonathan already in his forties? It was Chloe who now had a boyfriend, yet another state of affairs that Bridget was still trying to get used to. As for Jonathan, "friend" didn't convey the true nature of his relationship to Bridget, and "partner" suggested some kind of professional acquaintance. "Romantic partner" sounded altogether too pretentious. If Bridget had been more daring, she might have referred to Jonathan as her "lover", but that would have made her sound like a character from a cheesy romantic novel. She would just have to stick with "boyfriend" and try not to look embarrassed whenever she said it.

'Plans, DI Hart? Hmm?' pressed Grayson, and Bridget realised that her thoughts were wandering. She had fully intended to spend her evening alone catching up with a boxset on Netflix and finishing off a half-drunk bottle of Moscato and a slice of chocolate gateau from the patisserie on Banbury Road, but she didn't think the Chief Super would regard that as a pressing engagement. 'No sir, no plans at all.'

'I'm assigning you to watch over her,' said Grayson, and Bridget got the impression that his response would have been much the same whether she had answered yes or no. 'The Deputy Commissioner thinks we should take this threat to her life seriously, and assign a couple of plain clothes officers to the task, at least until the literary festival is over.'

'Why would someone want to kill a writer?' Bridget asked. Diane Gilbert wasn't exactly a household name. At least Bridget hadn't heard of her before.

Grayson drew his eyebrows together, nodding gently as if he had asked himself the same question. But he was clearly under pressure to carry out the wishes of his superiors. 'Apparently her newly-published book has attracted some controversy. I suggest that you familiarise yourself with its contents before the talk begins.'

'Yes, sir.'

Bridget had so little time to read these days that the prospect of burying her nose in some obscure academic's latest publication held little appeal. But attending the Oxford Literary Festival sounded like a better gig than many of the jobs she was required to do as DI. At least she would be indoors, in the gorgeous surroundings of the Divinity School, and hopefully very far from any likely criminal activity.

She had considered going to the literary festival with Jonathan when the programme had been released earlier in the year. She'd almost booked tickets to go to the Sheldonian to see an award-winning, best-selling author of historical fiction who had just published the long-awaited final instalment of her trilogy. But she'd been too busy at work, and when she finally got round to visiting the festival's website, all the tickets for that event had sold out. Now here she was, and although she was technically working, and the event wasn't one she would personally have chosen, the venue was very much to her taste. She would never tire of Oxford's glorious university buildings, and the Divinity School was surely one of the jewels in its crown. Now, with the last light quickly fading outside, she allowed her gaze to roam over its incredible ceiling. Gothic in style, and five centuries old, it was a masterwork in stone – a mass of soaring arches, intricately interconnected swirls and hanging pendants. The uplighters located around the edge of the hall accentuated its curved forms with light and shadow.

Standing at her side, Bridget's detective sergeant, Jake Derwent, shifted his weight from one foot to another and clasped his big hands behind his back. Even Diane Gilbert with her stick insect legs and her stilettos couldn't compete with Jake's six-foot-five frame.

Bridget had asked him to accompany her to the literary festival for no better reason than he was good company. Unlike her, Jake seemed genuinely to have had no plans for the evening, other than "a beer, a curry and a game of football on the telly", and they were now positioned together at the back of the hall. Standing head and shoulders above her, and with his thick ginger beard, the young sergeant had attracted a fair amount of attention, especially from the ladies in the audience. Diane Gilbert, too, had seemed slightly less dismissive of Jake than she had of Bridget, and the tips of the young sergeant's ears had turned a delicate shade of salmon when she referred to him sarcastically as her handsome protector.

Nearby, a table piled high with glossy hardback editions of Diane Gilbert's book was being staffed by a team from Blackwell's bookshop, who were obviously hoping to sell a large number of copies to the festival-goers. Bridget wondered whether they were being over-optimistic with their teetering display of hardbacks. Bridget had picked one up and scanned the blurb on the back of the dust jacket while waiting for the talk to begin. The book was titled *A Deadly Race: How Western Governments Collude in Sales of Arms to the Middle East* and purported to lay bare the shameful facts of the British and American governments' dealings with countries such as Saudi Arabia. Bridget noted that Michael Dearlove had provided a quote for the cover. *'This book will make you rethink everything you know.'* But at nearly five-hundred pages long, Bridget wasn't sure she had the time or the patience to reconsider anything, especially not matters of national security. It wasn't the security of the nation that was Bridget's responsibility, merely the safety of one person. Besides, the densely-packed words had seemed to blur as she flicked through the book's many pages. She blinked and tried to focus on the narrow typeface, but it was no good. She wasn't even forty – surely she didn't need reading glasses already!

She had returned the book to the pile, obviously disappointing the eager young man from Blackwell's who had hoped to make a sale. But unless Diane Gilbert presented her with a signed copy as a mark of gratitude – and there seemed scant chance of that, judging by the dismissive reception the academic had given her – Bridget didn't think she'd be adding this particular publication to the ever-increasing pile of books she intended to read, one day, when she had more time.

Soon, she promised herself. *And the exercise and the diet too.*

The applause died down and Michael Dearlove opened the proceedings by introducing his guest. Diane Gilbert was a lecturer and researcher at the Blavatnik School of Government in Oxford and although this was her first book, Dearlove seemed to think that it was of considerable importance to the public debate.

Bridget kept one eye on the proceedings, while simultaneously checking out the room for threats. A ruthless killer at the literary festival seemed unlikely indeed, and there were no obvious candidates amongst the largely middle-aged and middle-class audience. The notion that one of the Blackwell's staff might be a trained assassin with a concealed weapon was equally preposterous. Bridget thought regretfully of the chilled Moscato and chocolate gateau waiting for her back in her cottage in Wolvercote. Her evening in front of the TV, though not exactly life-improving, appeared to have been wasted for nothing. Jake, too, seemed distracted. He shuffled his feet and rubbed his nose – both giveaways that his mind was elsewhere. She prodded him gently to refocus his attention on the task in hand.

On stage, Dearlove was asking Diane about the motivations behind her latest work. 'Why did you choose to write this book, and can you tell us why you think it's so important to tell this story right now?'

Diane responded in cool, measured tones, although her views were certainly controversial. In her opinion, the current conflicts in the Middle East were due largely to the failure of western governments to show respect for Arabic culture, and of the greed of those same western nations in enriching themselves through the sales of arms. Continued instability in the region was in the interests of the British and the Americans because it kept the arms trade alive.

Bridget began to wonder who might have sent the death threat. But the details of the talk didn't engage her attention for long. Instead she found herself thinking of Chloe and what she was doing right now. She'd gone to London to spend a couple of days with Ben, and – this news had rocked Bridget's boat and left her feeling out of sorts for quite a while – his *fiancée*.

9

Bridget still couldn't quite believe it. Ben and his girlfriend, Tamsin, had swanned off to the Maldives for Christmas and had returned in January to announce their engagement and their plans to marry in the summer. That was certainly one way of solving the problem of what to call your significant other half. *Fiancée!* Bridget was putting a brave face on it, but the news had left her reeling. It wasn't that she wanted Ben back, far from it. Her marriage to him had been a disaster, the only good thing to come out of it being Chloe. And besides, she loved Jonathan dearly. But the idea of Ben marrying Tamsin – who Bridget still hadn't met but imagined to be more glamorous and attractive than her, and certainly younger and slimmer, not to mention taller – left her feeling bruised.

The fact that Tamsin had asked Chloe to be her chief bridesmaid, and that Chloe had accepted with eager enthusiasm, hadn't softened the blow. The main purpose of Chloe's current visit to London was to attend a fitting for her dress. This, together with the bridal gown, was being designed by a dressmaker who, according to Chloe, made outfits "for celebs". Bridget worried that under Tamsin's influence her daughter was becoming too fixated with celebrity culture and her appearance. The almost certainly svelte Tamsin couldn't possibly be a healthy role model for an impressionable teenager. Whilst Bridget would gladly have shed a few pounds herself, she didn't want Chloe becoming anorexic. The pressure to look good for a wedding, and to fit into a tight dress could be immense, especially for a growing girl. Jonathan had reassured her that Chloe was absolutely fine and showed no signs of developing an eating disorder. But it didn't stop Bridget from worrying.

Forty minutes or so after it had begun, the main part of the interview drew to a close and Dearlove invited the audience to ask questions. At first no one put their hand up, perhaps too intimidated by the writer's haughty demeanour to venture an opinion of their own or risk displaying their ignorance. Then a man on the front row raised his hand and Dearlove, with an obvious look of relief, invited him to speak. A young woman with a microphone rushed over to him.

The questioner was middle-aged and somewhat portly, dressed in a tweed jacket. Bridget couldn't see his face, but the man's hair was silver. 'Ms Gilbert, you have written a very interesting book,' he began. Diane accepted the compliment with a smile and the faintest inclination of her head, but Bridget sensed a "but" coming. The man continued, his voice growing in confidence as he framed his question. 'But don't you think that what you've revealed may be harmful to the security of the United Kingdom?'

A frisson of excitement ran through the audience. People had paid good money to come and listen to a controversial writer and now it seemed they were going to get their money's worth.

Bridget swept her gaze across the crowd, immediately on heightened alert. Next to her, Jake shifted his position as if he too sensed possible danger. Diane Gilbert had received a death threat after all. When the questioner's hand strayed to his jacket pocket, Bridget felt herself tensing. He pulled out a handkerchief, and she exhaled with relief. The man dabbed his forehead as if being the centre of attention was proving to be rather stressful.

Bridget gathered from Diane's somewhat dismissive response that she had little sympathy with the man's concerns. But the first questioner had evidently lent courage to the others, and more hands now went up. Michael Dearlove deftly gave as many as possible a chance to ask their questions, each of which Diane Gilbert answered in her rather brusque fashion.

Finally, and much to Bridget's relief, Dearlove announced that there was only time for one more question. A woman attempted to lighten the mood by asking Diane if she was planning to attend any events at the literary festival herself and, if so, which ones. Diane smiled – rather condescendingly, Bridget thought – and replied that she would have liked to attend the talk by a bestselling novelist but his event had sold out as soon as tickets went on sale. Fiction, she declared, was far more popular than serious books like hers would ever be. Few members of the public had the intellectual capacity or curiosity to read in order to improve themselves. A nervous titter went around the room, but on balance the audience seemed pleased with her performance and gave Diane a more enthusiastic round of applause than she and Dearlove had received at the start of the evening.

This time, Bridget and Jake joined in, relieved that the event had come to an end without incident.

The formidable lady in the black trouser suit took to the stage once again, thanking the two speakers for a "simply fascinating" evening, and informing everyone that Diane would be signing copies of her book at the table set up for the purpose at the side of the podium. At least half the audience then reached into their bags and produced copies of the book which they must have purchased earlier, possibly from the Blackwell's stand at the back of the hall. Maybe a few of them had even managed to wade through its five-hundred-odd pages. They started to form an orderly queue at the table and Bridget realised that the danger was by no means over. None of those bags had been security-checked before their owners had taken their seats. Death threat or not, the Oxford Literary Festival simply wasn't that sort of event. To Bridget's knowledge, no writer had ever been attacked while appearing at the festival and she was determined to keep it that way.

'Come on,' she said to Jake.

They made their way to the front of the hall and positioned themselves unobtrusively behind the table where the writer was already starting to sign copies of her book with a gold-nibbed fountain pen. Up close, the strong scent of Diane's perfume was quite distracting.

Bridget studied each reader closely as they presented their book for signing, but none of them looked remotely like a killer and none behaved in any way suspiciously.

After the final book had been signed, only a handful of people remained in the hall. The team from Blackwell's began packing the unsold hardbacks into boxes. The festival organiser cleared away the glasses and empty bottles of mineral water and realigned the chairs ready for the next day's event.

Dearlove came over to Diane to say goodbye. 'You were fabulous,' he said. 'Your book deserves to be huge.'

'You know this isn't about book sales,' said Diane. 'That's for other people to care about.'

Admirable detachment, thought Bridget. Still, that level of haircare didn't come cheap, and neither did those clothes and shoes.

'I don't suppose you've got time for a drink?' Diane asked Dearlove.

'I'm afraid that I have to get back to London tonight.'

'Another time, then.'

Bridget waited while Dearlove took his leave of

Diane, kissing her warmly on both cheeks. She stepped forward to make her presence known just as Diane stood up from her chair, rising to her full height. Diane glanced down at Bridget as if only just remembering that she was under police protection.

'Oh, Inspector. You're still here.'

'Yes,' said Bridget patiently. 'As I explained earlier, we'll be escorting you back to your home.'

'Oh, yes, of course. Well, while you're here you may as well meet my team. These are the people who make all this possible.' Diane smiled with a modesty that Bridget found somewhat insincere. Throughout her talk, Diane had done her utmost to portray herself as a single-handed campaigner, fighting against the all-powerful and sinister forces of the state. But obviously a book didn't publish itself, and publicity events like this evening's talk didn't happen by magic.

The writer's entourage gathered around like bees to a honeypot, and Diane introduced each one in turn.

'This is my publisher, Jennifer Eagleston.'

A large, boisterous woman in her mid-fifties thrust herself forward and shook Bridget's hand with a firm grip. A huge red tote bag was looped over her shoulder and she wore matching lipstick. 'I do want to thank you for everything you're doing to keep Diane safe. It's really appreciated.'

The publisher sounded genuinely grateful for

the trouble the police were taking to protect Diane, which was more than could be said for the writer herself. 'Not at all,' said Bridget warmly. 'All part of the job.'

'We wouldn't want anything to happen to her,' continued Jennifer. 'Especially not during the week of the book launch.'

'Quite,' said Bridget, wondering whether Jennifer's comment revealed a dark sense of humour, or naked self-interest. The expression on her face offered no clues.

Diane motioned to the second person in the trio. 'This is my agent, Grant Sadler.'

A rather awkward man dressed in an uncoordinated combination of skinny jeans, white T-shirt and smart jacket acknowledged Bridget with a nod of his head, but unlike Jennifer didn't offer his hand. He was in his thirties or forties, Bridget guessed, but couldn't pin down his age more precisely. He stood aloof, and thrust his hands into the back pockets of his jeans, as if striving for a youthful pose. He had a habit of bouncing up and down on the soles of his Converse trainers. Was he nervous for some reason?

'Great evening, Diane,' he said to his client. 'Your talk went really well. It should help to shift some more copies.' He was closer to forty-five, Bridget decided, but looked like someone desperate not to grow up. 'There were some good questions at the end, too.'

'You think so?' said Diane sharply. 'Not

everyone seemed to appreciate what I was saying.'

'You mean the guy who thought you were a threat to national security?' Grant sniggered. 'Old reactionaries kicking up a fuss like that will help to generate more free publicity. Let's hope he writes a strongly-worded letter to *The Telegraph* about it.'

Diane's upper lip curled in distaste. It was impossible to tell whether her reaction was prompted by the prospect of a letter in *The Telegraph* or by Grant's flippant attitude towards the incident. He looked embarrassed, and stood sullenly to one side.

Bridget looked to the third and final member of the group, a woman wearing a long woollen coat covered in dog hairs, and whose thick-soled boots looked better suited for a country walk than a literary festival. Bridget couldn't guess what her role in the world of books might be. 'Do you work in publishing too?' she enquired.

'Heavens, no,' said the woman. 'I'm a teacher. I don't have anything to do with all of this' – she waved a hand vaguely in the direction of the empty podium – 'I've just come along to support Diane.'

'This is my younger sister, Annabel,' explained Diane rather dismissively. 'She hasn't even read my book, she's just here to be polite.'

'I have read it,' said Annabel, although Diane had already turned away from her sister and was busy quizzing her agent about something.

'Well, I'm sure that Diane appreciates your support,' said Bridget.

The medieval hall was now empty of visitors, and the festival organiser was hovering by the arched doorway that led out of the building, casting meaningful glances at her wristwatch. The talk had finished half an hour ago at nine o'clock. The leaded windows of the Divinity School were now black.

The publisher, Jennifer, tapped Diane on the arm. 'I'll be picking you up at six-thirty sharp tomorrow morning. Don't be late.' She turned to Bridget. 'Diane's doing an interview on Radio 4's *Today* programme. She needs to be at BBC Radio Oxford by seven on the dot.'

'Yes, I'm well aware of that,' said Bridget. 'I'll be attending too.' That had been part of Grayson's brief to her this morning. *Watch her until the festival is over.*

'I'm pleased to hear it,' said Jennifer, 'So, in that case, I for one am going to call it a night. Early start in the morning.' She air-kissed Diane on the left cheek then adjusted the tote bag on her shoulder and strode from the hall, her heels clipping briskly on the stone floor.

Diane gazed around at the now almost empty hall. 'How dull. Annabel, do you want to join me for a drink? How about you, Grant?'

Her sister shook her head. 'Not for me, thanks. I need to get home to see to Oscar. He's my Jack Russell terrier,' she added for Bridget's benefit.

Grant bobbed up and down on his shoes. 'I

18

think you should take Jennifer's advice and turn in. It's an early start tomorrow.'

Diane scowled at their lack of enthusiasm, but Bridget felt a strong sense of relief. Attending the literary festival was one thing, but the prospect of following the writer into a crowded pub and watching out for potential threats wasn't an appealing one.

'So,' said Grant, 'I'll say goodnight.' He embraced his client awkwardly, then left the hall, pulling out his phone and thumbing the screen as he went.

Now only Diane and Annabel remained.

'Can we give you a lift?' Bridget asked the writer's sister. It seemed only polite to offer, although her brief was solely to ensure that Diane Gilbert got home safely.

Annabel shook her head. 'Thanks, but don't worry about me. I've got my bicycle with me. I always cycle everywhere.'

Outside, the enclosed quadrangle of the Bodleian was all dark. Although it was just after Easter and well into spring, the air was growing chilly under the clear skies. The bronze statue of the library's founder, Thomas Bodley, glinted in the moonlight. Bridget paused for a moment, stealing a quick glance up at the darkened windows of the upper reading room. As an undergraduate, she had spent countless hours researching and writing her laboriously handwritten essays either here or in the even older library of Merton College – already centuries old when Thomas Bodley founded his eponymous institution. She recalled the archaic declaration she had been obliged to make on first becoming a reader, including the promise "not to bring into the Library or kindle therein any fire or flame." Happy days. How little she had known of life back then, despite all those hours of learning.

Diane was striding across the quad towards an archway, and Bridget hurried after her. She caught up as Diane skirted the outside of the festival marquee next to the Sheldonian Theatre. The marquee, fitted out with bookshelves and tables piled high with shiny new titles, was a book lover's paradise. Bridget resolved to return and spend some time there when she could grab a spare half hour.

Once Diane Gilbert's whirlwind publicity tour is over. Just two more days.

On Broad Street, the two sisters hugged and said their farewells. Annabel unlocked her bicycle and cycled off, her coat flapping somewhat precariously as she went.

Bridget had managed to leave her car right opposite the Sheldonian, her trusty police parking permit strategically employed. Her car, a red Mini convertible, suited her five-foot-two frame perfectly. Jake, on the other hand, always had a little trouble squeezing himself inside, and Diane was going to find the car equally awkward. They should probably have brought a larger vehicle, but Jake's bright orange Subaru seemed singularly inappropriate for the task.

Gentleman as he was, Jake managed to squeeze himself into the back seat of the car, while Diane tried awkwardly to fold her long legs into the front, fiddling with the controls in a futile attempt to increase the legroom.

Bridget watched her struggle with a certain satisfaction. 'Sorry,' she said cheerfully. 'The seat's already pushed back as far as it will go.'

Now that the talk was finished and the period of greatest danger was over, Bridget's mood began to lighten, even though the scent from Diane's perfume was almost overwhelming in the confined space of the car. At this time of the evening it wouldn't take long to drive the short distance up the Banbury Road to Diane's house, and with any luck there would still be enough time for Bridget to watch at least some of her boxset. As for the gateau and wine, she felt she'd earned them.

'You live alone?' she asked Diane as she turned the Mini out of Broad Street, passing the King's Arms where the pavement tables were packed with drinkers braving the cold evening.

'Yes,' said Diane. 'It suits me.'

I'm sure it does. Diane didn't appear inclined to pursue the conversation, and Bridget didn't feel that the rewards from making small talk with the writer were likely to be worth the effort, and so they drove in silence up Parks Road and the Banbury Road before turning left into St Margaret's Road.

'It's just here,' said Diane, indicating a house on the right.

'Yes,' said Bridget through gritted teeth. 'I already know.'

Diane seemed to have no appreciation of the amount of work and planning that went into an operation of this type. She seemed to be under the impression that Bridget and Jake were just casually hanging out with her for a few hours and had nothing better to do with their time. *Gateau*, thought Bridget wistfully.

She drew the car to a halt outside a large, detached Victorian house set well back from the road behind a high brick wall crowned with a hedge. A marked police car was stationed in front of the house.

Diane scowled when she spotted the car. 'Is that for my benefit?'

'Two police officers will be out here all night for your protection,' Bridget explained.

'Is that really necessary?'

Bridget was asking herself the same question. But the Deputy Commissioner certainly thought so, or he wouldn't have allocated so many resources to the operation. Bridget still wasn't sure what Grayson's personal opinion on the matter was, but he had no choice other than to bow to his superior's request, just as she was bowing to hers.

The two uniformed officers left their car and approached the Mini. Both were young, but seemed keen enough. Bridget got out to greet them.

'We've already checked the garden and garage,' said the taller of the two, a local lad with a warm Oxford burr to his voice. 'All clear.'

'Thank you.' Bridget didn't envy the two men having to spend the whole night sitting in a car outside the house. At least they were unlikely to encounter any trouble. The leafy street was so quiet it was hard to imagine anything untoward happening in this tranquil setting.

Diane ignored the two policemen and marched up the driveway, her sharp heels sinking into the gaps between the gravel chips, and Bridget followed in her sensible low-rise shoes.

The house was grand, built over three floors, with tall chimneys just visible in the darkness, and decorative stone work set against red brick, illuminated by a pair of outside lights. Three stone steps led up to the front door. Diane turned her key in the lock and pushed it open to reveal a generously-proportioned entrance hall.

Once inside, Jake made his way up the stairs while Bridget went through to check each room on the ground floor. The house seemed far too big for just one person, and Bridget wondered how Diane could afford it on a lecturer's salary. It wasn't as if her book was an international bestseller.

The house looked as if it had been decorated by an interior designer. Everything was of the highest quality, fitted and coordinating, but the overall effect left Bridget feeling cold. As she ran her hand over the granite worktop of the ultra-modern kitchen with its chrome fittings and stainless-steel appliances, she decided that Diane Gilbert was welcome to the place. Bridget preferred her small, cluttered cottage any day.

Jake met her back in the hall. 'All clear upstairs,' he confirmed.

Diane was standing by the lounge door. 'Well, Inspector, Sergeant,' she said. 'I suppose I'll be seeing you both again in the morning.'

Bridget would have preferred not to have to get up quite so early, and could probably have delegated the job to one of her juniors, but she was making a concerted effort to be a better boss this year, and that included doing her fair share of drudge work so that Jake and the rest of her team got the time off they deserved. It was the only one of her New Year's resolutions to have made it past the end of January. 'I'll be here at six-thirty,' she informed Diane.

'If you must.' Without a word of thanks or farewell, Diane ushered them out through the front door and locked it behind them.

Bridget crunched crossly across the gravel back to the car, Jake at her side. 'What a woman,' she muttered. 'I'm quite tempted to kill her myself.'

'I expect that's against regulations, ma'am,' said Jake drily.

'No doubt.'

'You don't think the threat's serious, then?' he asked.

'Well, she doesn't seem to be taking it

seriously. But it's not for us to question why. We simply have to do our job.'

'Yes, ma'am.'

'Anyway, can I give you a lift home?'

He took a moment to consider her offer, then shook his head. 'Thanks, but a walk will do me good. It'll clear my head after listening to that talk.'

'You won't be rushing back home to read her book then?'

'I think I'll pass.'

They wished each other goodnight, and after speaking once more to the uniformed constables, Bridget drove the short distance to her small house in Wolvercote, just north of Oxford.

Ten minutes later she was curled up on the sofa with a glass of wine and a plate of gateau balanced dexterously in one hand. It was a well-practised manoeuvre. With her free hand she pressed play on the remote and settled back to enjoy an episode of the glamorous American soap she'd recently become addicted to. Just what she needed after a long and tiring day. But twenty minutes into the show she found her eyelids too heavy to keep open. Admitting defeat, she crawled upstairs to bed. It was going to be an early start next morning.

*

The alarm woke Bridget rudely at five-thirty am. She groaned and rolled over, then forced herself out of bed before sleep could reclaim her. It seemed unnecessary to be calling on Diane Gilbert quite so early, but this was the job she'd been given so she might as well get on with it. However, once the morning's appointment at the BBC was done, she fully intended to speak to Grayson and tell him that baby-sitting the writer was a waste of everyone's time. It wasn't as if the woman even showed any gratitude for all the trouble the police were taking on her behalf.

She showered, then spent several agonised minutes peering in dismay at the grey strands ("silver", according to Jonathan) that seemed to be slowly but steadily replacing her dark brown hair. She would have to try and fit in a hair appointment before Jonathan returned from New York. Leaving the bathroom, she stopped by the kitchen to have a quick slice of toast and a coffee, then drove back to the writer's house on St Margaret's Road.

All seemed to be in order. The two uniformed constables were still sitting in their car outside Diane's house. Bridget tapped on the driver's window to let them know she was back. The window rolled down.

'Morning, ma'am.'

'Quiet night?' asked Bridget.

'Dead as a dodo,' said the officer, then blushed at his unfortunate turn of phrase.

'Let's hope it's not that quiet,' said Bridget grinning. 'I'll just check on her, then you two can be off.'

They gave her a grateful smile. She crunched across the gravel and rang the bell beside the gloss-black front door. The bell chimed deep inside the house, but there was no answer. Bridget peered through the large bay windows to the side of the door, but the curtains were still drawn. If Diane had slept in after Bridget had got up so early, she would be annoyed. Mystified, she stepped back onto the driveway and looked up at the window belonging to the master bedroom. The curtains were drawn there too. She pushed the bell once more, holding it down with her thumb for half a minute, and when there was still no answer, walked round the side of the house to the back door.

The sight that met her stopped her in her tracks.

The back door to the house hung open, swinging on its hinges in the early morning breeze. In the kitchen beyond, shattered glass covered the floor, sparkling in the first light like spilled diamonds.

Bridget sprinted back to the front of the house as fast as she could. The two officers saw her coming and jumped out of their car.

'What is it, ma'am?'

'She's not answering the door. And there's been a break-in at the back.'

They paled at the news. 'You want us to break down the front door?'

'It's too solid,' said Bridget. 'We'll go in the

back way. One of you come with me, and one of you stay here.' She looked expectantly at the taller of the two, wishing that Jake was with her.

She made her way round to the back of the house again, the big policeman right behind her. This was a crime scene now, but there was no time to worry about contaminating the scene. A woman was in danger. Being careful not to touch anything, Bridget stepped carefully over the broken glass and made her way into the kitchen, calling out, 'Diane!'

No answer.

She continued on into the house. After quickly checking that the downstairs rooms were empty, she and the constable made their way upstairs. The house was silent.

The door to the master bedroom stood ajar. Bridget pushed it fully open with her gloved fingertips and crept into the room.

The bedroom was dim with the curtains closed, but light enough for Bridget to make out the shape of Diane Gilbert lying in her king-size bed.

'Dr Gilbert? Diane?'

The woman appeared to be fast asleep. But something wasn't right. She was too still. There was no rise and fall of the duvet to show that she was breathing. Bridget touched two fingers to Diane's neck, but felt no pulse. Her skin was cool to the touch.

The writer who had been unafraid to tackle controversial subjects and who had scorned the death threat she had received, was dead. And she had been killed while under Bridget's protection.

CHAPTER 2

'Anything yet?' Bridget demanded impatiently.

The forensic medical examiner, Dr Sarah Walker, was beginning her investigation of Diane Gilbert's body to determine the likely cause of death. Meanwhile, the head of the SOCO team, Vikram Vijayaraghavan – Vik to his friends – and the other Scene Of Crime Officers were busy combing the house and gardens to gather evidence. Bridget knew that the process would take many hours to complete and couldn't be rushed, but she was itching for one of them to give her some initial clue as to what had happened to Diane Gilbert.

After all, this had taken place while Bridget was in charge of the writer's safety and security, even though she hadn't personally been present when the woman was murdered. It was only a matter of hours since she and Jake had escorted Diane home and made sure that everything was in order before bidding her goodnight. Two officers had searched the grounds of the house and had remained on guard all night. And yet someone had broken into the house, murdered its sleeping occupant and escaped without anyone hearing or seeing anything. What had they missed that had allowed such a tragedy to occur?

'We've only just got started,' said Vik.

Sarah shook her head. 'I'll let you know when I've made my preliminary assessment.'

Unable to contain her energy, Bridget stomped outside, taking care to use the front door this time to avoid having to step over the broken glass in the kitchen.

The officers who had been on duty overnight, PC Sam Roberts and PC Scott Wallis, were in the front garden smoking. They hastily stubbed out their cigarettes when they saw Bridget approaching.

'Let's run through this again,' she said.

She had already heard their story once, but a retelling would do no harm. Perhaps there was something she – or they – had missed the first time.

The two constables exchanged glances. They were both clearly distraught at what had happened, and no doubt fearful of the prospect of facing a disciplinary hearing, but right now Bridget was less interested in assigning blame than in finding out what had happened. However much she may have personally disliked Diane Gilbert, she was still Bridget's responsibility. More to the point, a fellow human being had lost their life.

The officer who had accompanied her into the

house – PC Sam Roberts – was the first to speak. 'It's like we said last night, ma'am. We arrived about fifteen minutes before you did yesterday evening. We walked all around the property, checking that the doors and downstairs windows were locked, looking in the garage, and searching the grounds. There was no one here, and no signs of any disturbance.'

'And you didn't fall asleep or leave your post at any time?' She knew from experience how easy it could be to snatch a quick shuteye when on an all-nighter, especially when the job in question appeared pointless.

'No, ma'am,' said the other officer. 'We were here the whole time, and we had a clear view of the house and the driveway. No one entered or left. I swear.'

Bridget studied the two men's faces. From their haggard appearance she was inclined to believe that they really had stayed awake all night.

The only entrance to the property was via the gravel drive that led from the street. A tall side wall separated the house from its neighbours.

'If no one came through the front entrance,' mused Bridget, 'could they have gained access from the rear of the property?'

Scott shook his head. 'No, ma'am. There's a door in the rear wall at the back of the garden, but it was locked last night, and it's still locked now. No one came in that way.'

'Then could they have been hiding in the

garden last night?' The garden was large and the shrubbery extensive.

'No,' said Sam. 'We searched the grounds thoroughly before you came. If there had been anyone there, we'd have found them.'

'But somebody got inside, murdered the occupant, and then escaped again. They even broke the glass in the back door without you hearing anything.'

The two men paled further, if that was possible. But the story they told was the same as before, and Bridget didn't think they were concealing anything from her.

'All right, you can go home. I'll need a written report from both of you. But get some sleep first.'

There was no need to throw a ton of bricks at them. She would soon have Grayson doing that to her, no doubt. She had already had to deal with the flak from Jennifer Eagleston, the publisher, who had inconveniently arrived within five minutes of Bridget discovering the body. Initially, Jennifer had been thoroughly shocked by the news, although not, Bridget noted, as visibly upset as she might have been. Perhaps Bridget wasn't the only one to have felt a personal animosity towards the dead writer and academic.

But on learning what had happened, the publisher's shock had very quickly given way to anger, all traces of the gratitude she had expressed to Bridget the previous evening burned away by outrage. 'I thought you people

33

were supposed to be keeping her safe! Wasn't that the point of all this police protection?' She waved an accusatory hand in the direction of the police car still parked on the street in front of the house. Her nails were painted the same crimson shade as her lips.

It was perfectly understandable that Jennifer was angry, but not entirely fair to place the blame for everything at Bridget's feet. 'We'll be conducting a full enquiry into what happened,' she said, 'but I can assure you that uniformed officers remained on duty outside Diane's house all night.'

'For all the good it did!'

Bridget waited for Jennifer to calm down a little before asking any questions. 'Can I ask if you've noticed anything unusual about Diane recently?'

'Apart from her receiving a death threat, you mean?'

'Apart from that. Has there been any change in her behaviour?'

'Well, in truth I didn't know Diane all that well,' conceded Jennifer. 'Not personally, I mean. Obviously, we'd met a number of times, and had plenty of telephone and email discussions, especially in recent months as we neared publication. But no, I hadn't noticed anything odd about her.'

'Did she talk to you about the death threat?'

'She showed me the letter when it arrived, but she didn't seem unduly worried about it.'

'What did you talk about, then?'

'Her book. She was passionate about it, and there's a lot for a writer and a publisher to discuss when a new book is launched. The type of book Diane writes is never the easiest to sell. That's why it's so important to get the marketing right.' She checked her watch, as if remembering where she was supposed to be. 'Oh God, BBC Oxford are waiting for us to arrive. What am I going to tell them?' she asked, as if Bridget might have any bright ideas.

Well there certainly wasn't going to be an interview on Radio 4 now, although the airwaves would have plenty to talk about once news of Diane's death was announced. But that was the last thing Bridget wanted to happen. It was always a sensitive time when a body had only just been discovered, the cause of death not yet established, and the next of kin still to be informed. Bridget urged Jennifer to be discreet for now and to tell the BBC that Diane was indisposed.

The publisher nodded her agreement while rummaging in her capacious tote bag for her phone. She had already dialled and had the phone glued to her ear by the time she reached the end of the driveway. Bridget let her go. She had more immediate matters to worry about.

The most vexing question was how anyone could have gained access to the house without Sam and Scott noticing. Leaving Sarah to continue her work in the master bedroom and

Vik to examine the break-in at the back door, Bridget made her way back inside the house. She climbed the stairs to a guest bedroom that overlooked the rear garden. If, as Sam and Scott swore, the intruder hadn't gained entry to the house from the front, then logically they must have approached from behind.

The large garden behind the house was mostly laid to lawn with neatly clipped bushes along both sides. It looked like the sort of place where nature was never allowed to get the upper hand, unlike Bridget's own tiny garden which had long since turned into a wildlife habitat. She wouldn't have been surprised if several endangered species had made it their home.

A line of paving stones led across the grass to a door in the tall brick wall that surrounded the garden. From here, it looked as if the door led out onto a narrow lane at the back. Sam and Scott had sworn that the door was locked both before and after the murder. Since the glass in the kitchen door had been broken to gain entry to the house, it was unlikely that the intruder had a key for the garden door. Bridget tried to estimate the height of the wall. Could someone have climbed over it? Bridget could never have managed it herself, but she supposed it was just about possible for someone who was taller and fitter than she was. She went downstairs and put the idea to Vik.

'Let's take a closer look, shall we?' he suggested.

They went outside together, Bridget following him along the line of paving stones that led to the end of the garden. The air was still chilly, and early morning dew glistened on the grass to either side. The wall that enclosed the area stood well over six feet tall and was topped with a layer of moss and lichen.

'If someone had scaled a wall of that height,' said Vik, 'you'd expect to find signs of disturbance – footprints in the soil where they jumped down, or the marks from a ladder – especially when the ground is soft like it is today. There's been a lot of rain recently. But there's nothing out of the ordinary as far as I can see.' He crouched down, examining the ground in front of the back wall. 'Unless they jumped with cat-like accuracy and landed on the paving stone right in front of the gate.' He stepped back and viewed the top of the wall above the gate where the moss was at its thickest. 'It doesn't look as if anyone has disturbed that part of the wall, but I'll get someone to climb up with a ladder and take a closer look.'

'It was just an idea,' said Bridget. 'They must have reached the kitchen door somehow.'

'From a neighbouring property?' suggested Vik.

'It's possible,' said Bridget, but the walls that separated the garden from the houses either side were just as tall as the rear wall.

She and Vik walked around the perimeter of the garden, checking the ground carefully for tell-tale marks, but at the end of their perambulations, Vik stopped and shook his head. 'No one has climbed over these walls in the past few days.'

'Could someone have been hiding in the garden shed?' asked Bridget. They walked over to the wooden structure, but the door was securely padlocked and when Bridget peered through the window, she saw that there was barely enough room for the lawnmower and other gardening equipment, never mind for someone to hide.

'I guess not,' said Vik.

Still puzzling about how the intruder had gained access to the house, Bridget followed him back inside. Since Vik had no answers for her, she returned upstairs, hoping that Sarah Walker would have some by now. When she poked her head around the door to the master bedroom, she found the medical examiner kneeling by the bed, peering closely at Diane Gilbert's exposed torso. Sarah must have heard her enter, because without turning she said, 'Come and take a look at this.'

The room still smelled of Diane Gilbert's rather cloying perfume, lingering on even after her death. The scent brought the woman vividly back to life and made it hard to think of the body on the bed as no longer living.

Sarah pointed to a spot just below the victim's left breast. 'Can you see that?'

Bridget edged closer, stooping to examine the

body. A tiny red dot was visible on the exposed skin. 'It looks like a pinprick.'

'Not a pin precisely,' said Sarah. 'It's a mark from a hypodermic needle.'

'A needle? Could this be what killed her?'

'We'll need a full toxicology report. But it's possible that she was given a lethal injection. I can't find anything else wrong with her. There are no stab wounds or strangulation marks, no bruising or signs of a struggle. I can't rule out natural causes, but for a woman of her age she's in very good shape. At least she was until she died. Roy will get to the bottom of it, I've no doubt.' She turned away from the corpse and began to peel off her surgical gloves.

A lethal injection, if that really was how Diane was murdered, raised all kinds of worrying possibilities. But Bridget's interest was also aroused by Sarah's casual reference to the senior pathologist, Dr Roy Andrews, by his first name, rather than by title and surname. She knew that Sarah and Roy had spent Christmas Day together, and Sarah had divulged the fact that Roy was a very good cook. Bridget's nosy half wanted to quiz Sarah further about the nature of their relationship and how it had developed since Christmas, but the reserved medical examiner was never the easiest person to talk to, especially about her private life, and now really didn't seem like an appropriate time.

'I'll get her bagged up and sent to the morgue,' said Sarah.

'How quickly do you think Roy will be able to do the post-mortem?' asked Bridget. 'Do you know if he's working this weekend?'

Sarah regarded Bridget's clumsy attempt to elicit further information about Sarah's knowledge of the pathologist's movements with faint amusement. 'I'm sure he can be persuaded to put in a few extra hours on your behalf. Roy never says no to a corpse. But why don't you ask him yourself?'

'I will,' said Bridget. But first she had another job to do – one that she dreaded even more than the prospect of attending a post-mortem. To notify the victim's next of kin.

CHAPTER 3

Marston had once been a separate village located some two miles northeast of Oxford, but it was now encompassed by the ring road and subsumed into the wider city. Its name was said to derive from "Marsh Town" on account of the River Cherwell's habit of flooding the low-lying pasture land in winter. Not good for house insurance, Bridget supposed, but charming nonetheless.

The village was only a few minutes' drive from Diane's house on St Margaret's Road, but as Bridget turned off the Marston Ferry Road she felt as if she were leaving the city far behind and entering a rural idyll surrounded by fields and farmland.

It had not always been this peaceful. From her time as a History undergraduate, Bridget knew that during the English Civil War, King Charles I had used Oxford as his capital, and when the Royalist stronghold fell to Oliver Cromwell's Parliamentary forces, the treaty of surrender of the city was negotiated and signed at a house on Mill Lane in Marston.

The old manor house that had witnessed that historic event was still standing, and was situated just a few doors away from the house that now belonged to Diane's sister, Annabel Caldecott. The old stone cottage, one of a row of four, appeared very similar in age and style to Bridget's own modest dwelling in Wolvercote. Both properties would have fitted comfortably inside the floorplan of Diane's capacious Victorian villa with room to spare. The tiny front garden was abundantly planted and although it was still early in the season, was putting on a colourful show. Bridget was a very casual gardener, more inclined to admire other people's efforts than to make any herself, and couldn't have named half the plants on display if her life depended on it, but she did recognise some tulips and hyacinths alongside the fading daffodils. Some large hydrangea bushes were just coming into bud and would no doubt put on a spectacular display when summer arrived. She pushed open the garden gate with a squeak, knocked on the wooden door of the cottage and waited.

There was no answer, and she was about to try phoning Annabel's mobile, when she heard the barking of a small dog. She looked up and saw Annabel returning from a walk.

'Inspector Hart, what brings you here?' Annabel was dressed as before, in long overcoat and boots. Her dog, a Jack Russell terrier with smooth white and brown fur and very muddy legs, trotted through the open gate to sniff at Bridget with great interest. When he looked as if he was about to jump up and plant his paws on Bridget's coat, Annabel tugged on his lead. 'Down, Oscar.' The dog obeyed immediately, looking abashed. 'I'm so sorry. I've just taken him for a walk down the lane and around the field and there's been so much rain recently it's all very muddy down there. Oscar can't help but get covered in it.'

'Yes,' said Bridget, eyeing Annabel's muddy boots.

'Just a moment,' said Annabel, as if she'd only just remembered something. She reached into a deep coat pocket and pulled out a small plastic bag knotted at the top. Although Bridget applauded responsible dog owners who cleaned up after their pets, she preferred not to see the results. Annabel popped the poop bag into a grey wheelie bin and turned back to Bridget. 'Did Diane send you?'

'In a manner of speaking,' said Bridget. 'Do you mind if we go inside?'

'Oh, no. Of course not.'

Annabel fished a key from another pocket and opened the door. 'Would you like to wait in the sitting room? I'll just shut Oscar and his muddy paws in the kitchen.'

Freed from his leash, the dog darted enthusiastically through the door at the end of the hallway and Annabel went to deal with him while Bridget let herself into the front room. The dog's dirty feet would be the least of Annabel's worries once Bridget had broken the news to her of her sister's untimely death.

The sitting room was furnished in a homely style, maybe a little outdated, but comfortable and cheerful. A bookcase in one of the alcoves next to the fireplace was stacked with well-thumbed paperbacks, their spines cracked. Bridget recognised some bestselling thriller and crime writers, as well as a generous helping of classics including Dickens, Austen and Hardy. *A Deadly Race: How Western Governments Collude in Sales of Arms to the Middle East* was nowhere to be seen, but the coffee table was strewn with old copies of *Gardeners' World* and *Your Dog* magazines.

Assorted photographs in wooden frames adorned the mantelpiece. One holiday snapshot showed the two sisters looking relaxed and happy in wide-brimmed straw hats, somewhere hot and sunny. Another picture was of Annabel and her husband on their wedding day – not a formal shot captured by a professional photographer, but one snapped on a pocket camera, the couple waving at their friends just before stepping into a Volkswagen Beetle decorated with balloons and ribbons. But there was no sign of a man's presence in the house. No coat or shoes in the hallway, only Annabel's brightly-coloured hats and scarfs hanging on pegs, and a pair of pink wellies caked in mud.

Bridget perched on the edge of a sofa draped

with a patchwork quilt thick with white dog hairs. The bright yellows, reds and blues of the quilt seemed to encapsulate the feel of the room – ramshackle and patched together with mismatched accessories. Curtains, rugs and cushions were all joyously uncoordinated. If it wasn't for the fact that she had the worst news in the world to break to Annabel, Bridget would have felt much more at ease here than she had in Diane's meticulously styled and coordinated house.

When Annabel reappeared, she had removed her overcoat and changed out of her walking boots into a pair of slippers. Bridget waited until she was seated in an armchair before breaking the news as gently as she could.

For a moment Annabel said nothing, but threw her hand across her mouth in stunned disbelief. 'Are you sure?' she asked at last. 'It was my sister?'

'Yes,' said Bridget. 'Although we will need a family member to make a formal identification.' She wondered if Annabel would be in a fit state to identify the body herself.

Annabel stood up, then rushed from the room uttering an incoherent cry. Bridget followed her into the hallway, but Annabel had locked herself in a downstairs cloakroom. Through the door Bridget could hear the sounds of sobbing.

When Annabel emerged some ten minutes later, her eyes were red and puffy, her face blotchy. She held a scrunched-up roll of toilet paper in her hands.

'Shall I put the kettle on?' asked Bridget.

Annabel nodded dumbly and Bridget went to the kitchen in search of tea, milk and sugar. As soon as she opened the kitchen door, Oscar dashed out. Bridget didn't try to stop him. The dog would be a comfort to Annabel, muddy paws and all.

Teabags and sugar were on the counter by the kettle and Bridget found some colourful, mis-matched mugs on the draining board. When she returned to the living room bearing two mugs of strong, heavily sugared tea, Annabel was hugging the dog to her like a child, her face buried in the soft fur on the top of his head.

Bridget placed the tea on the table and resumed her place on the sofa.

After a minute Annabel recovered her poise enough to speak. 'How did Diane die?'

'We're not sure at the moment,' said Bridget. 'There was evidence of a break-in at the back door, so we're treating her death as suspicious.'

'Murder?' Annabel breathed the word as if not daring to speak it aloud.

'I'm afraid we'll have to wait for the post-mortem report before we can say with any certainty.' Bridget knew how much grieving relatives craved answers to help them make sense of their loss, but she knew too of the dangers of jumping to conclusions or engaging in speculation. She would say nothing about the pinprick until she knew her facts. 'Did Diane

46

suffer from any medical conditions, such as high blood pressure or heart problems?' It was still possible that the shock of discovering an intruder in her house had caused Diane to suffer a cardiac arrest.

Annabel shook her head. 'Diane? No. She was always fit as a fiddle. She hardly suffered a day's illness in her life.'

Annabel seemed to be getting over her initial shock and Bridget gauged that it was safe to ask a few more questions. 'Are you aware that your sister recently received a death threat?'

Annabel's face fell. 'Yes, of course, she showed me the letter. She wouldn't have done anything about it, if it wasn't for me. She didn't think it was worth taking seriously but I told her not to be so stupid. I don't think she would have listened to me alone, but Jennifer, her publisher, and Grant, her agent, both agreed with me, so that's when she took it to the police.' She cast her eyes down at the dog. 'Not that that did any good. She still ended up dead.' Her shoulders began to tremble again.

'I'm truly sorry about that,' said Bridget, 'and I can assure you that I will do everything in my power to find out what happened to your sister. Besides yourself, is there anyone else we need to inform about her death?'

Annabel put a hand to her forehead. 'God, what am I thinking of! It must be the shock, making me so forgetful. Diane has a son in London. His name is Daniel. He'll need to be told, and Ian too.'

'Ian?'

'Ian Dunn, Diane's ex-husband. He lives in Oxford. He's a consultant at the John Radcliffe hospital.'

'I see. What sort of relationship did Diane have with her ex-husband?'

Annabel frowned at the suggestion implicit in the question. 'Oh, don't start imagining that Ian might have killed Diane. He's a good man and their relationship was perfectly amicable. He and Diane divorced around ten years ago, and he remarried a few years back.'

'I'm sorry,' said Bridget. 'But I do have to ask these questions. What about Daniel? Did he get on well with his mother? He lives in London, you say?'

'He's grown up. But he still sees – saw – Diane regularly.'

'Will anyone else need to be notified?'

'University colleagues, I suppose. But no other family. Our parents passed away some years ago.'

'And what about you?' asked Bridget, glancing up at the wedding photograph on the mantelpiece. 'Is there anyone who can provide you with some emotional support?'

Annabel's gaze followed Bridget's, then returned to the dog sitting on her lap. 'It's just me and Oscar now,' she said, patting the dog's side. The animal's ears twitched at the mention of his name. 'John died five years ago.'

'I'm sorry.'

'There's no need to be. It was a blessed relief. He had Huntington's, you see.'

'That's a degenerative disease, isn't it?'

'Yes, it's a genetic disorder. John inherited it from his mother. The first symptoms started when he was in his early thirties. At first it was just little things – being clumsy, forgetting things. He tried to make a joke of it, but we both knew it was bound to get worse. Ian encouraged him to get a diagnosis and after that he just went downhill really quickly. During the final few months, he was completely bed-ridden and I had to nurse him. Eventually he wasn't even able to speak and had problems swallowing and breathing. In the end, death came as a release.'

'I can understand that,' said Bridget. 'You don't have any children?'

'We might have done, but after John was diagnosed, we decided not to. There's a fifty-percent chance of the Huntington's gene being passed on, you see, and we didn't want to take that risk.' Tears were once again welling up in Annabel's eyes. 'Now I wish we had. I lost my husband, and now I've lost my sister too. Oscar's all I have left.' She hugged the dog tightly against her chest.

Bridget finished her tea and put the mug back on the coffee table beside a gardening magazine. 'Do you have any idea who might have sent the death threat to Diane?' she asked gently. 'Did you discuss it with her?'

49

'Diane refused to talk about it. She was convinced it was just some crank. But I was worried. Diane wasn't afraid to write about topics that annoyed certain people in powerful positions. Her academic work was one thing, but her book will bring those matters to the attention of a much wider audience.'

'Yes, I can see that,' said Bridget. 'I'll need you to give me the contact details for Daniel and Ian, if you don't mind.'

'Of course,' said Annabel, wiping her tears away. 'But do you mind if I speak to them first? I think this news would be better coming from me.'

Bridget had no objection to Annabel contacting Diane's son and ex-husband. In fact it was a welcome relief and would make her job much easier when she did speak to them if they were already prepared.

Annabel looked as if she was about to cry again. 'My sister was a good person, Inspector,' she said. 'She wasn't always an easy person to like' – at this, Bridget felt Annabel's eyes boring into hers and she shifted uncomfortably – 'but she was my sister and we were very close. She supported me through some difficult times, especially after my husband died. You will find out who killed her, won't you?'

CHAPTER 4

Bridget knew that before she could begin the job of assembling her team and getting on with solving the murder, she was going to have to face Chief Superintendent Alex Grayson. There was even a risk that Grayson wouldn't want her to head up the investigation, given the mess she'd made of preventing Diane Gilbert's death in the first place. She braced herself for an onslaught as she entered his glass-walled office, aware that Jake and the other members of the department were all watching closely, although doing an excellent job of appearing not to. Surveillance training could be a double-edged sword.

The Chief Super sat in his high-backed swivel chair, tapping a fountain pen on the surface of his immaculate desk. It was always a bad sign when he held a pen in his hand. And an empty desk also spelled trouble.

'Sir, you wanted to see me,' said Bridget, determined not to let him have the first word.

'Sit down,' said Grayson, rotating the pen in his hand to indicate the chair in front of his desk.

Bridget perched on the edge of the chair,

sitting bolt upright in an attempt to bolster her stature by a much-needed extra inch. A photo of Grayson holding up a golfing trophy looked back at her from the desktop. Neither the Grayson in the photograph nor the one in real life was smiling.

'Please explain to me, DI Hart,' said the Chief calmly, 'how Diane Gilbert could possibly have been murdered on our watch.'

She noted with a glimmer of hope that he'd said "our watch" and not "your watch", but she didn't fool herself into imagining that Grayson would readily accept any of the blame for this fiasco himself. Nor did she want the hapless Sam and Scott to be made into scapegoats, assuming that they had told her the whole truth about what took place. Bridget didn't play games or office politics. If she had to shoulder responsibility for the failure of the operation, then she would. But she wouldn't go down without a fight.

'Sir, I can categorically state that when Detective Sergeant Jake Derwent and I left Diane Gilbert at home on Thursday evening, there were no intruders in the house or grounds of the property. The back door and ground floor windows were all securely locked, and we heard her locking the front door as we left the house. The gardens and garage were searched, and the officers on duty overnight have stated that no one entered or left the premises while they were on duty.'

'Well, someone clearly got in and out,' said

Grayson. 'How do you account for that?'

Bridget swallowed, knowing that she had no satisfactory answer to the question. 'They broke in through the back door of the house, but we don't yet know how they gained entry to the grounds. The scene of crime officers are investigating whether someone could have climbed over the rear garden wall.' She didn't add that she and Vik had already taken a look and seen no signs of any disturbance.

The fountain pen tapped rhythmically against the desk. 'Is that likely?'

'It's a possibility.'

'In that case, why wasn't someone assigned to watch over the rear of the property?'

'Sir, with respect, I only had two officers available. They were stationed at the front of the house. How was I supposed to cover the rear entrance with the resources I had been given?'

Bridget knew that she was stepping into dangerous territory by invoking resources and budgets. This was firmly Grayson's area of responsibility.

Tap. Tap. Tap. 'We don't have unlimited resources to babysit every person who says something controversial and puts themselves at risk. Whatever the Deputy Commissioner might think.'

This was the closest the Chief had come to taking Bridget's side. But her relief was short-lived. Grayson closed his fist hard around the fountain pen. 'Having said that, this was a monumental cock-up of the first order. The murderer sent a letter in black and white saying what they intended to do, and still we failed to stop them. You can consider yourself very fortunate that you have only me to answer to, and not the Deputy Commissioner. Now, the two officers who were on duty outside the victim's house last night have been suspended while an enquiry is made into their conduct during this operation. Give me one good reason why I shouldn't also suspend you and assign Baxter to lead the murder investigation.'

'Sir? You can't do that!' Bridget was dismayed to learn that Sam and Scott had been suspended from duty. Her gut feeling told her they had been telling the truth about what happened. But the prospect that she might also be suspended was even more alarming. Taking her off the case now and putting her arch rival within the department, DI Greg Baxter, in charge of clearing her name was an appalling prospect.

'Can't I?' The tone of Grayson's question conveyed a clear warning.

Bridget knew that telling her boss what he could or couldn't do was likely to put her head on the block. But her sense of injustice seemed determined to ride roughshod over her common sense. 'It's just not fair, sir. I have a right to lead this murder enquiry.'

Grayson's already furrowed brow darkened further. He raised the pen and jabbed it in the air. 'Let me make this clear, DI Hart. You have absolutely no rights here whatsoever.'

'An obligation, then, sir. I owe it to the victim and her family to find out who did this. And I'm the person best placed to lead this investigation.'

'Or the one least likely to take an objective view of the situation.'

Grayson raised his hand to stop her saying anything more. He stared up at the ceiling tiles, tapping the pen gently against his desk while he mulled over his decision. It didn't take him long. Grayson was never a man plagued by doubt. 'Well, Inspector Hart, you spectacularly failed to stop Diane Gilbert from being murdered, so you can bloody well make up for it by finding out who killed her. Consider this a penance, not a reward.'

The fountain pen had survived its ordeal and so had Bridget. 'Thank you, sir,' she said, relieved that she wasn't about to be reassigned to policing petty crime on the Blackbird Leys estate in East Oxford. But she knew that her future hung in the balance. If this went badly, her career might be in jeopardy.

'Tread carefully,' warned Grayson. 'No more mistakes. And given the nature of this book of hers, I want to be informed immediately if there is any hint that Diane Gilbert's death may be linked to matters of national security.'

'Yes, sir. Of course, sir.' Bridget rose gratefully to her feet. 'You'll be the first to know.'

CHAPTER 5

Bridget left Grayson's office taking care to close the door softly behind her. Everyone in the department seemed suddenly to be very busy, staring intently at their screens, flipping pages of the reports that lay open before them, dashing off urgently to make tea or use the bathroom. Bridget felt a spotlight shining on her, even though not a single face turned her way. They must surely have heard Grayson's angry tirade. She made her way to her desk, then refusing to bow to her humiliation, immediately stood up again.

'Team meeting, two minutes, sharp.'

There was only one way for her to redeem herself, and it was by moving forward, not looking back.

Team meetings were apparently unendurable without the fortification of tea and coffee, so Bridget waited patiently in the incident room for her team to assemble.

Detective Constable Ffion Hughes was first to appear, bearing her usual Welsh dragon mug, from which dangled a string attached to a herbal teabag. Ginger, judging by the pungent aroma. The smell recalled gingerbread men that Bridget had baked with Chloe when she was little. The memory was comforting, and helped to soothe Bridget's nerves. Ffion had thoughtfully made Bridget a mug of normal tea in one of the office mugs.

Bridget treated her to a smile. Ever since Ffion had returned to visit her family in Wales for a few days after Christmas, Bridget had noticed a marked softening in the young detective's normally prickly manner.

'Everything all right, ma'am?' asked Ffion, placing the mug on the desk.

'Good, thanks.' It was a relief to know that whatever Grayson might think, at least one of her team still backed her.

Next to enter was Jake, balancing a mug of builder's tea with a chocolate bar and a packet of crisps, closely followed by DS Ryan Hooper bearing a Starbucks coffee and a chocolate brownie. DS Andy Cartwright and DC Harry Johns were the last to appear, carrying a coffee and an energy drink respectively.

Once they were all seated, Bridget wasted no time in starting the briefing. A killer was at large, and Bridget was determined to catch them.

'Diane Gilbert,' she said, pointing to a photograph she had pinned to the whiteboard. It was the official press photo taken from inside the dust jacket of Diane's latest book, and showed her in an arty black polo-neck jumper, gazing at the camera with a thoughtful expression on her face.

'Sixty years of age, an academic at the Blavatnik School of Government, and author of *A Deadly Race: How Western Governments Collude in Sales of Arms to the Middle East*. She was found dead in her bed this morning. The cause of death isn't yet known, but a pinprick was discovered immediately below the victim's left breast which could have come from a hypodermic needle.'

Bridget took a deep breath before pressing on. 'As you no doubt already know, Diane was under police protection following receipt of a death threat.' There was no need to remind everyone that Bridget had been responsible for that protection. They were already well aware of the delicacy of the situation. 'I delivered her safely to her home last night shortly after ten o'clock. A marked car was in place outside her house all night, and the property was searched before Diane was left alone in her house.'

Bridget locked eyes briefly with Jake, whose face immediately drained of colour. He was obviously feeling just as bad as her about what had happened. She flashed him a quick smile of reassurance before moving on.

'Her body was found this morning when I arrived at the house to collect her.' Bridget pointed to her next photograph, showing the open back door of the house. 'The intruder gained access by smashing a pane of glass in the kitchen door to open the lock. Diane was still in her bed when I found her. There was no sign of any violent struggle.'

Ffion's hand immediately went up.

'Yes?' prompted Bridget.

'If the glass in the back door was smashed, why was the victim still in bed? Why didn't she wake up and go to investigate the noise?'

'Good question. I don't have an answer to that yet. Diane may have been a particularly heavy sleeper.'

'Might she have taken sleeping pills?' suggested Ryan.

'We'll need to find out. Whatever the reason, it would seem that she was unaware of the break-in, and the intruder was able to attack her in bed while she slept.'

'How did they get access to the house at all?' asked Ryan. 'I thought we had a couple of uniforms keeping watch outside.'

'We did,' said Bridget. 'SOCO are examining the possibility that the killer climbed over the garden wall. Although it's not an easy wall to have scaled and there are no obvious marks like a footprint in the soil.'

'Maybe the guys in the panda car had forty winks or sloped off for a kebab,' said Ryan.

'I don't think so,' said Bridget. Although if it turned out that Sam and Scott had lied to her, she would have their guts for garters.

'The needle mark in the victim's chest,' said Andy, 'does that suggest the use of poison?'

'It's too early to say.' Bridget recalled what

Sarah had told her. 'We'll need a full toxicology report as well as the post-mortem, but the initial signs are that there were no physical injuries to the body and no indications of a struggle.'

'Consistent with the victim being killed in their sleep,' noted Ryan. 'She couldn't just have had a heart attack, could she?'

'We can't entirely rule it out, but we have to bear in mind that an intruder entered the house. And then there's the matter of the death threat.' Bridget tapped the whiteboard where a photocopy of a handwritten letter was pinned next to the picture of Diane. It was written in blue ink on a piece of cheap stationery. The words, penned in a rather elaborate hand, read:

You think you are clever when you write about guns and bombs. But did you know that words can be just as deadly? Cancel your book, or it will be the last thing you ever write. We will cancel you.

'We have to ask ourselves whether the person who sent this is our killer, and if so, who might that be.'

'It's a bit old-fashioned, isn't it?' said Ryan. 'Don't people just send their death threats on Twitter these days?'

'Not if they're serious about carrying them out,' said Ffion. 'And most of the abuse on social media tends to be illiterate. This is all correctly spelled and punctuated.'

'I bet that had her worried,' quipped Ryan.

'What's scarier than a killer who can wield grammatically correct sentences?'

'Well, whoever sent this was clearly very serious about their intent,' said Bridget. 'So finding out who wrote it is a top priority. The original letter is still with forensics. All I can tell you for the moment is that it was sent to the writer's home one week before her death, and carried a London postmark.'

'What exactly was her book about?' asked Andy.

'Arms sales to the Middle East,' said Bridget. 'In particular, to Saudi Arabia.'

Andy made a note in his notebook. 'So if the death threat was related to her work, we need to look at the interested parties.'

'A Middle Eastern government,' said Jake.

'The British government,' said Ffion.

'The American government,' said Ryan.

'MI5,' said Harry, looking pleased to have finally made a contribution.

'Arms manufacturers,' said Andy.

Bridget wrote all the suggestions on the whiteboard. It was quite a formidable list of adversaries. Could one of these really be responsible for murdering Diane Gilbert? If so, they could be looking at the work of a professional assassin.

'The letter refers to "we",' said Andy. 'That certainly seems to imply a group or an organisation of some kind.'

It occurred to Bridget that if Diane's murder

really was linked to the publication of her book, she was going to have to wade through the five-hundred plus pages of *A Deadly Race* herself – an appalling prospect. She saw the book's turgid prose in her mind's eye, its narrow letters wavering before her, and shuddered.

'Whoever sent the death threat,' said Ffion, 'must have wanted to stop Diane publishing her book. So why wait until the book was already published before sending her the letter?'

'Perhaps they didn't know about it until then,' said Ryan.

Ffion continued as if Ryan hadn't said anything. 'And surely they should have realised that when news of the murder gets out, sales of the book will probably go through the roof. Everyone will want to know what was so controversial about her writing that she had to die for it.'

'True,' said Bridget.

A lot of things weren't adding up in this case. But the main question now was where to start. She would have to wait for the post-mortem and the toxicology report, as well as Vik's SOCO team to complete its investigations. The examination of the death threat letter was still being undertaken by forensics. In the meantime, all Bridget had at her disposal was good old-fashioned detective work.

'Andy, I'd like you and Harry to start making door-to-door enquiries in St Margaret's Road. Find out if anyone saw or heard anything out of the ordinary last night.'

'Yes, ma'am.'

'Ryan, coordinate with Vik and organise a team to carry out a fingertip search of the garden and the neighbouring properties. Look for anything that might indicate how the intruder gained access.'

'I'm on it,' said Ryan.

'Jake, you and I are going to pay a visit to the Blavatnik School of Government and speak to Diane's colleagues. And Ffion?'

'Yes?'

Bridget passed her a copy of *A Deadly Race*.

'You want me to read it?' Ffion didn't seem at all daunted by the prospect. She picked up the heavy book and flicked through it, her green eyes darting lightly across the dense text. 'Just over five hundred pages. I can give you a summary by the end of today.'

Bridget beamed at her.

CHAPTER 6

The Blavatnik School of Government occupied a starkly futuristic building on Walton Street. Bridget recalled that the uncompromising design of the building in the heart of historic Oxford had attracted both praise and protest. The glass façade of the circular structure reflected the elegant stone columns of Oxford University Press directly opposite, and it stood in striking contrast to the adjacent neoclassical church that was now Freud's café-bar and which had featured in one of Bridget's recent cases. Modern architecture wasn't truly to her taste, but the Blavatnik School was certainly a dynamic and exciting addition to Oxford's university buildings. At least, Bridget mused, if you didn't appreciate the appearance of the Blavatnik itself, you could always admire the reflections of the more traditional architecture in its glass windows.

She and Jake were met in reception by a tall, good-looking man of Arabic appearance. His neatly-combed hair was black and flecked with grey, his dark olive skin was clean-shaven, and his confident manner and smart, sober suit gave the impression of someone at the pinnacle of their career.

'Detective Inspector Hart.' He bowed gravely as he took her hand and for a brief moment Bridget thought he was about to kiss it. 'I am Professor Mansour Ali Al-Mutairi and it is my honour to welcome you to the Blavatnik School of Government, although of course I wish it could have been in happier circumstances.' He turned to Jake, giving him a more vigorous handshake. 'Sergeant, welcome. Shall we?' He gestured towards a wide spiral staircase with smooth stone sides that reminded Bridget of a toboggan run. As they climbed, she found herself gazing up at the glass-fronted upper storeys and through the huge window that commanded a view over Walton Street.

'This is a very impressive building,' she said.

'Indeed,' said Professor Al-Mutairi. 'It has been designed to facilitate collaborative working' – he gestured to one of the many seating areas where small groups were gathered around tables – 'but it also borrows heavily from Oxford's architectural traditions and heritage.'

'Really?' said Bridget, who had failed to spot any obvious similarities with the city's historic buildings.

'Just so. The circular shape reflects that of the Sheldonian Theatre,' said Professor Al-Mutairi. 'And the vertical spacing of the glass panels is identical to the spacing of the stone façade of the

Bodleian Library.'

'Fascinating,' said Bridget. She risked a look at Jake, who appeared nonplussed by this comparison of what, to a casual observer, might seem to be three strikingly different buildings. Professor Al-Mutairi's private office – more glass and stone – was located on the third floor with an excellent view of the eighteenth-century Radcliffe Observatory on the far side of an empty plot of land. Professor Al-Mutairi followed Bridget's gaze to the beautifully-proportioned building with its octagonal tower.

'Ah yes, the Radcliffe Observatory. Built to enable men to turn their gaze to the stars and planets. A worthy occupation, continuing the long tradition of astronomy pursued by Muslim scholars in the medieval world.'

'Quite.' Bridget shifted her attention to a row of tall, bushy plants growing in ceramic pots along the inside of the windowsill. The shrubs were not particularly attractive, being mainly bare, with tiny spiky leaves, and stood in marked contrast to the clean lines of the building. But every stem was adorned with bright yellow flowers, each one like a miniature sunburst. 'I see that you're quite green-fingered, Professor Al-Mutairi.'

'*Rhanterium epapposum,*' said the professor fondly. 'In Arabic we call it Al-Arfaj. It is the national flower of Kuwait, and reminds me of my home. Actually, it is not so difficult to grow. I feed the plants once a fortnight, otherwise they like to be left alone. My greatest challenge is persuading the cleaning lady not to keep watering them.'

A smile crinkled his face, and he took his place behind a large, tidy desk and gestured for Bridget and Jake to make themselves comfortable in a pair of leather chairs. Jake took out his notebook and pen, ready to take notes.

'Perhaps we could start with a little background about the Blavatnik School?' said Bridget. She'd noticed on their way up the sweeping staircase that the building didn't contain the usual fresh-faced undergraduates that you found in the colleges. Everyone here was older. There was a seriousness about the place.

Professor Al-Mutairi nodded briefly, carefully removing the smile from his face before speaking. 'Our mission here is a grand one, but essential in this day and age. It is, quite simply, to improve the quality of government and public policymaking throughout the world. To that end we offer a one-year Master's course and a three-year Doctorate degree. We also conduct research with the aim of finding solutions to public policy issues and global challenges.'

'And what was Diane Gilbert's position here?'

'Dr Gilbert taught one of the modules in the Master's degree, but her main area of work was research.'

'I see. Can you tell me how long you've known Diane?'

'Dr Gilbert and I have been associated for the

past five years.'

Associated. It seemed a curious word to use, as if the professor was keen to place some distance between himself and the murdered woman. His unwillingness to use her first name suggested an aloofness between the two.

'And your association was what, precisely?'

'A purely professional one. As Dean of the Blavatnik School, I was technically her manager, although Dr Gilbert was not a woman who could easily be managed. She was too headstrong for that.'

Professor Al-Mutairi's characterisation of Diane Gilbert chimed with Bridget's own impressions, but the professor's response seemed to indicate a strong personal dislike of the dead woman.

'Did you and Dr Gilbert clash?'

The professor sighed, and rubbed the bridge of his nose with his thumb and forefinger. 'Our personalities were very different, and so were our opinions. But the Blavatnik School is a broad church. We welcome diversity of all kinds.'

'If you don't mind me saying, professor, that doesn't really answer my question.'

A smile twitched his lips and lit up his dark eyes. 'In truth, Dr Gilbert and I did not see eye to eye. She possessed – how can I put this delicately? – an unhelpful appetite for courting controversy, even danger. Where Dr Gilbert was concerned, the more controversial her ideas, the better. And she was only capable of viewing the world through the distorting prism of her own political views.'

'Those views didn't align with yours?'

'They did not. I desire a world where free trade between countries leads to increased cooperation, understanding and rising standards of living. For Diane, nothing but a socialist revolution could make the world a better place.'

'Were you aware that Diane received a death threat shortly before her death?' asked Bridget.

'I was.'

'And did you take any kind of action to protect her from danger?'

Professor Al-Mutairi smiled wryly. 'Excuse me, DI Hart, but I was under the impression that was the job of the police.' Bridget flinched at the reminder of her own sense of culpability over Diane's death, but the professor quickly moved on. 'In any case, Dr Gilbert herself showed scant regard for any threat to her person. I can say with all honesty that I admired her courage. She would never allow herself to be cowed by any kind of threat.'

'Do you know if she had any enemies?'

Al-Mutairi's brow creased in consternation. 'Enemies? That is a very strong word, if you don't mind me saying. Dr Gilbert was a university academic, not a soldier on the battlefield. In the intellectual world, there exists rivalry, certainly. But we do not have enemies, merely colleagues following different paths to the truth.'

'There may not always be one truth,' said Bridget.

The professor's frown was quickly replaced by a grin. 'Oh, there is always one truth, Inspector. But not everyone can see it.'

'What did you think of her latest book?' asked Jake.

Professor Al-Mutairi nodded as if to acknowledge the pertinence of Jake's question. 'Arms sales to the Middle East. It is an important area of policy, of legitimate concern. It is only right that it should be researched and discussed. And yet...'

Jake looked up from his notebook. 'And yet?'

The professor's lip curled down in disapproval. 'As always, Dr Gilbert allowed her personal biases to infect her work. She was unable to view any topic from a dispassionate perspective. This latest book is a prime example of that.'

'Her book wasn't sanctioned by the School?' asked Bridget.

'Certainly not, and I fear that it will drag our good name through the mud.'

Bridget was beginning to wish now that she had read Diane's book after all. It would be helpful to have a few pertinent facts at her disposal. She cast her mind back to the talk at the Divinity School, but she had been too busy concentrating on security concerns – and, admittedly, some personal matters – to pay much attention to what Diane had said.

'What exactly is it about the book that you

object to, Professor?' she asked politely.

A shadow passed across his face. 'Dr Gilbert approached her work with a very particular mindset. She firmly believed that the Americans and the British were wrong to involve themselves in the affairs of the Middle East. She accused them of acting out of cynical self-interest and greed for oil.' He paused briefly before continuing with a rising passion. 'But she did not grow up in Kuwait, like I did. She did not see her own father gunned down and murdered by Saddam Hussein's rampaging troops when they invaded my country in 1990. She did not see her mother weep and her sisters cower in fear. She did not feel for the region here, like I do.' He thumped his hand against his chest, covering his heart with his fist.

Bridget waited for Professor Al-Mutairi to calm down after his emotional outburst. It was clear that Diane Gilbert wasn't the only member of the Blavatnik School who had trouble viewing the world impartially.

'Forgive me,' he said at last. 'You must understand that this is a matter of profound personal significance to me. The Americans and the British came to the rescue of my country, liberating it from its invaders, and putting it under their protection. According to people like Dr Gilbert, they were warmongers and colonialists. She could not have been further from the truth.'

'You didn't like her.' Bridget made it a

challenge, not a question.

Professor Al-Mutairi laid his palms flat on the desktop. When he spoke again, it was with his emotions carefully in check. 'Inspector, far be it for me to speak ill of the dead, but Dr Gilbert was a difficult and opinionated woman who went out of her way to court controversy, indifferent to the effect that might have on her colleagues.'

'Are you glad that she's dead?' asked Jake.

Al-Mutairi turned the full power of his gaze upon the young sergeant. 'Dr Gilbert was a respected member of this School, and naturally I regret her passing. But I will shed no tears at her graveside.'

CHAPTER 7

When Bridget returned to Kidlington, she found Ffion engrossed in *A Deadly Race*. She had already devoured a hundred pages of the book and was going strong. Bridget toyed with the idea of asking for a quick summary, but decided to leave Ffion to her task.

She sent Jake off to get on with the task of entering the details of their conversation with Professor Al-Mutairi into the HOLMES database while she looked up the website of Grant Sadler, Diane Gilbert's literary agent. She had no idea how long Diane's writing and publishing contacts would be staying in Oxford during the literary festival, and she wanted to catch up with as many as possible before they left town. She hoped that in the case of Grant Sadler, she wasn't already too late.

She found his number on his website which announced that he was "currently open for submissions". Scanning through the list of authors he claimed to represent, Bridget didn't recognise a single name, save for that of Diane Gilbert, who was given pride of place on his homepage, and she wouldn't have known that one two days ago. She wondered how well business was going for the agent.

Grant picked up on the third ring. 'Hello? Who is this?' He sounded on his guard, and Bridget divined that he had already heard about his number-one client's untimely death. No doubt Jennifer Eagleston had informed him of the news.

'Grant Sadler? It's Detective Inspector Bridget Hart from Thames Valley Police. I was wondering if we could meet for a chat?'

'To talk about Diane? Jennifer phoned me first thing this morning to tell me what happened. My God, I can't believe it.'

'Are you still in Oxford?' As the agent had been in no hurry to get away the previous evening, Bridget assumed that he had stayed in the city overnight. 'Where are you? I'm happy to come to you.' She doubted that inviting him over to police headquarters in Kidlington would help to put him at his ease.

Grant hesitated before replying. 'I'm staying at the Travelodge on the Abingdon Road,' he said at last. He didn't sound particularly happy about it. 'There isn't really anywhere here we can talk.'

Bridget pictured the budget hotel next to the Redbridge Park & Ride in the south of the city and wasn't surprised that Grant felt uncomfortable admitting that he was staying there. She had pictured the world of book publishing as altogether more glamorous and imagined him installed in a suite at the Randolph Hotel, but she was clearly being naïve. Maybe high-profile events like the Oxford Literary Festival gave a false impression of the amount of money to be made from books. Writers who went from living on welfare to being worth hundreds of millions were clearly the exception rather than the rule. She began to feel a little sorry for the apparently hard-up agent.

'Why don't we meet in town?' she suggested. 'Do you know the Queen's Lane Coffee House? It's on the High Street opposite University College.'

Bridget hadn't had anything to eat since leaving home that morning, which seemed like eons ago. The Queen's Lane Coffee House was one of her favourite lunchtime haunts, and was said to be England's oldest coffee house – although to be fair, the same claim was also made by the Grand Café on the opposite side of the High. Whatever the truth of the matter, food at the establishment was plentiful and not over-priced. Perfect if the agent was on a tight budget.

'I know it,' said Grant. 'I'll catch a bus and meet you there in half an hour.'

★

The Queen's Lane Coffee House was packed with hungry clientele when Bridget arrived, rather out of breath after hurrying all the way from St Giles' where she had left her car. She checked her watch and saw that she was late. When suggesting the coffee house as a meeting venue, she had forgotten to factor in Oxford's dreadful traffic and lack of parking spaces in the town centre. With hindsight – or perhaps a little more foresight – one of the pubs on St Giles' would have been a smarter choice.

Her route had taken her along Broad Street and past the Sheldonian Theatre and the marquee of the Oxford Literary Festival. Judging from the huge number of people queuing to enter the grand seventeenth-century building, a big-name author must be appearing. She remembered then that it was the historical novelist she had hoped to see herself. It was just as well she'd been unable to buy a ticket, as the murder case would have quashed any chance of her going along.

On entering the coffee house, Bridget discovered that despite being late there was no sign of Grant Sadler. *Damn it.* Had he already been and gone, or had he not turned up at all? She had just removed her phone from her bag and was redialling his number when his familiar face appeared at the door.

If on the previous evening the literary agent had been attempting to cultivate an edgy, cool image, this morning he looked simply haggard. His hair stood up on end, he hadn't shaved, and his eyes were smudged as if he hadn't slept a wink all night. Perhaps the phone call from Jennifer Eagleston had woken him rather earlier than he was used to.

'Sorry I'm late,' he said. 'The bus took ages. I keep forgetting how awful the traffic is in Oxford.'

Bridget smiled, taking pity on him. It seemed that she and Grant shared an aversion for Oxford's road congestion and traffic restrictions. Perhaps they would get on well together. 'There's one last table over in the corner,' she said, pointing.

They grabbed it just before it was claimed by a couple of Japanese tourists who were clearly uncertain whether they were supposed to sit down first or order food at the counter. Bridget felt slightly guilty when she saw them turn and leave the shop, but then her stomach rumbled, quickly dispelling any lingering sense of remorse.

'Lunch?' she enquired cheerfully.

'Yeah, I guess,' said Grant. He took a seat opposite hers, his right knee bouncing up and down beneath the table. If anything, he appeared even more nervous than he had done the previous evening.

Bridget quickly perused the menu and when a young waitress came over to their table, she placed her usual order: Queen's Chicken Royal – a fillet of chicken in ciabatta served with chips – and a bottle of mineral water. It was at least fifty per cent healthy by her reckoning.

'Just a coffee for me,' said Grant.

The waitress vanished into the kitchen, and Grant turned to stare out of the window. He watched as passers-by hurried along the pavement, but didn't seem to see them. Bridget realised that he was in a deep state of shock. Eventually he seemed to recall that she was with him.

'This might seem a silly question,' she asked, 'but what exactly does a literary agent do?'

'Oh, right.' The question had the desired effect, bringing him back from his faraway thoughts to focus on the present. 'I suppose it isn't necessarily obvious to people outside the industry. Agents act as the grease in the machine, making the whole publishing industry work. Or, if you don't like the grease metaphor, you could think of us as glue, bringing authors and publishers together.'

'So did you work on behalf of Diane?'

'She was my client, yes. I negotiated to sell her manuscript to publishers.'

'And she paid you for your services?'

He shook his head. 'Her publisher paid me a percentage of her advance.'

'Her advance?'

'Sorry. Advance payment. It's an amount that the publisher agrees to pay the author in return for the publishing rights to the manuscript.'

'I see. And how long have you been Diane Gilbert's agent?'

'Three years.'

'As long as that? I thought that *A Deadly Race* was her first book.'

'It is.' When Bridget gave him a puzzled look,

he elaborated. 'The cogs of the publishing world don't turn quickly. Getting a first book into the bookshops is a long haul. First the author has to find an agent, which isn't easy. Most authors never even make it that far. The agent makes submissions to publishers and, if successful, negotiates a contract. Then the completed manuscript goes through several rounds of editing and proof-reading before its final publication.'

'I see. So how much contact did you have with Diane during those three years?'

'Well, quite a lot initially, mostly by phone and email. Then not so much for a long while. But I spoke to her more in recent weeks, in the run-up to the book launch.'

'And what did you think of her?'

'Seriously? Diane was an incredible woman. As soon as she wrote to me, I knew she was an author that I wanted to represent.'

'Why was that exactly?'

'Diane was a highly-regarded academic and a fearless writer. She didn't care if what she wrote got her into trouble, she just wanted to get her words out there and have them read. She was already well known within her field, but her book will bring her work to a much wider audience. If there's a silver lining to this tragedy, it's that her book will garner a lot more publicity than it would otherwise have done.'

'I suppose so.'

Bridget waited while the waitress brought the

food and drink to the table. She took a quick bite out of the chicken in ciabatta before continuing with her questioning.

'What do you know about the death threat that Diane received?'

Grant stared mournfully into his coffee. 'I already told the police all I know.'

'Perhaps you could tell me again?'

'All right. Diane told me about it when I was up in Oxford to make arrangements for the literary festival. I went to see her at the Blavatnik, and she showed it to me there. It had arrived by post that morning.'

'At her work or her home address?'

'At home.'

'What did Diane think about the letter?'

'Not a lot. She was used to getting a ton of hate on social media. To be honest, I think she might secretly have enjoyed it. Some of her tweets – well, it was almost as if she was inviting people to send her abuse. Like I said, she was fearless.'

'Had she ever reported the abuse to the police?'

'Not Diane. It wasn't really in her nature to ask for help.'

'But she decided to contact the police about the letter?'

'She wasn't going to. But her sister, Annabel, was worried, and when she showed it to me, I was concerned too. This didn't seem like just your usual internet troll. The fact that it had been delivered to her home address showed that the sender knew where she lived. Who would have access to that kind of information?'

Bridget chewed at her chicken. 'Who do you think might have sent it?'

Grant took a sip of his coffee, drinking it black and unsweetened. 'I would have thought the answer to that was obvious.' He cast a nervous glance around the coffee shop and leaned in close to Bridget, lowering his voice. 'Diane Gilbert was a pain in the British government's backside. My guess is that they instructed the security services to do away with her.'

'Is that a serious suggestion?'

'Absolutely. Have you read her book?'

'Not all of it,' said Bridget, thinking of Ffion back at the office, diligently speed-reading her way through the enormous tome. 'It's quite long, isn't it?'

Grant shot her a slightly scornful look. 'I think you'll find it's detailed and meticulously researched. By the time you reach the end, you'll come to the same conclusion as me.'

Bridget would have to wait for Ffion's synopsis of the book before she could possibly take a view on the plausibility of Grant's allegation regarding the security services, so she decided to try a different tack.

'What did you do last night after the literary event finished?'

'Me? Why are you asking? I thought you invited me here to talk about Diane.'

'I did,' said Bridget. 'But I'm investigating her

81

murder. So perhaps you wouldn't mind telling me what you did.' When he remained silent, she sought to reassure him. 'It's just a routine question. I'll be asking everyone I speak to the same thing.'

'All right,' he said eventually. 'I didn't do very much. After the talk finished, there didn't seem much point in hanging around, so I had a quick pint at the White Horse and then went back to my hotel and watched rubbish TV for the rest of the night.'

The White Horse was a tiny pub situated directly opposite the Sheldonian Theatre on Broad Street and next to Blackwell's bookshop. 'Did you meet anyone you knew in the pub?' Bridget asked.

'No,' said Grant with a scowl.

'And what time did you get back to the hotel?'

'I don't know.'

'Did anyone see you return?'

He gave a bitter laugh. 'I don't know if you've ever stayed in a Travelodge, but it's not the sort of establishment where a gloved and suited porter welcomes the guests at the front door and bids them goodnight. But maybe the receptionist will remember me coming back. They might even have CCTV footage of me. All part of the surveillance state.' He drank the rest of his coffee and replaced the cup on the saucer with rather a loud clatter. 'Look, are we done here? I have people I need to see.'

'We're done for now. But will you be

remaining in Oxford in case I need to talk to you again?'

'I'll be here for another day or two.'

'Thank you, Mr Sadler. Please do let me know when you plan to leave.'

'Sure. Whatever.' He scraped back his chair and stood up, then walked away from the table, leaving Bridget to pay the bill.

CHAPTER 8

Bridget was halfway back to St Giles' when her phone rang. It wasn't a number she recognised. 'Detective Inspector Bridget Hart?'

A man's voice came over the line, deep but smooth and well-spoken. 'This is Ian Dunn, Diane's ex-husband. I understand from Annabel that you'd like to speak to me.'

'That's right,' said Bridget. 'Thank you for calling me, Mr Dunn.'

'No problem. I just wanted to let you know that our son, Daniel, has arrived from London. He's with me now, and we're both available to speak to you if it's a good time.'

Bridget thanked him and assured him that it was a perfect time. She noted down the address he gave her, and hurried back to her car.

St Andrew's Road was located in Old Headington, very convenient for the John Radcliffe hospital where, according to Annabel, Ian worked as a consultant. Bridget parked her Mini behind a silver Lexus Coupé and walked up the short garden path to a rather charming ivy-clad, three-storey Georgian house. Tulips, hyacinths and bluebells were in full bloom in the neatly tended borders of the front garden, and a magnificent magnolia took pride of place in the centre, its branches swathed in delicate pink-white flowers. It was the sort of place where you might expect to find the parson from a Jane Austen novel.

No parson opened the door however, but a tall man in his early sixties with a full head of silver-grey hair and a neatly groomed beard. His eyes were a striking blue. 'Ian Dunn.' His good looks were matched by his charming manner. He held out a hand and gave Bridget a gleaming smile. 'Thank you so much for making the time to come and see us, Inspector. It is Inspector Hart, isn't it?'

'Yes,' said Bridget, accepting the handshake. 'And it's no trouble at all. It's part of my job to speak to as many people as possible who were connected to the victim. It helps me to build up as broad a picture as I can. But first, may I offer my condolences. The news must have come as a rather nasty shock.'

'It did,' said Ian, stroking his beard with one hand. 'But of course we'll be more than happy to answer any questions you might have about Diane. Come on in. We're just through here.'

Bridget stepped over the threshold and followed Ian through a door to the right of the entrance hall. She found herself in a perfectly proportioned, high-ceilinged sitting room decorated in a sunny shade of yellow. The walls were hung with equally colourful oil paintings of Tuscan landscapes and Mediterranean hillside villages. A couple of armchairs and a brown leather sofa covered in scatter cushions were arranged around a centrepiece Persian rug in vivid shades of red and cream. The effect was warm and welcoming.

'Please let me introduce my son, Daniel.'

A dark-haired man of around thirty years of age stepped forward from where he'd been standing by the window. 'Daniel Dunn,' he said, shaking Bridget's hand.

'I'm sorry for your loss, Mr Dunn,' said Bridget.

The young man, who bore a striking resemblance to Diane, was wearing a smart, dark suit and looked as if he'd just stepped from the office. 'Thank you. And please call me Daniel. "Mr Dunn" sounds too much like my father.'

'Daniel, then,' agreed Bridget.

'Please do take a seat,' said Ian, gesturing to the leather chair nearest the window.

Bridget was about to sit down when a strikingly glamorous woman with tanned skin and glossy dark hair tumbling over her shoulders entered the room, carrying a tray loaded with a cafetière, china cups and saucers, a jug of cream, some sugar in a small bowl and a plate of biscuits. She set the tray down on an antique chest and rose again to greet Bridget.

'This is my wife, Louise,' explained Ian.

Standing in heels, Louise was at least as tall as

her husband, if not an inch or so taller. She was also perhaps twenty years younger than Diane Gilbert. 'Louise Morton,' she said, shaking Bridget's hand. 'I kept my own surname when I married Ian. For professional reasons, you understand.'

'Professional reasons?'

'I'm a paediatrician at the John Radcliffe. That's where Ian and I met.'

'I see.'

Ian began pouring cups of coffee. 'Annabel explained the circumstances of Diane's death when she phoned this morning,' he said. 'Needless to say, it's come as a terrible shock to all of us. Annabel is taking the death of her sister particularly hard. They were very close.'

'Of course,' said Bridget. She declined the offer of biscuits – mentally awarding herself a gold star for resisting temptation – but gratefully accepted a cup of coffee with real cream.

When everyone was settled, she began her questioning. 'Mr Dunn –'

'Ian, please.' He gave her an encouraging smile. No doubt smiling to put patients at their ease was a skill he'd had many years to master.

'Ian, then. If you don't mind, I'd like to start with some background on your relationship with the deceased.'

'Of course.'

'Let's go back to the beginning. How did you and Diane first meet?'

'I actually met Diane through her sister. I knew

Annabel from university – we were both involved in student politics, and of course Diane had very strong political interests too. She was always much more committed to the cause than either of us, I have to say. It's a very long time since I went on a protest march. But at the time it was a shared interest that helped to bring us together.'

'And how long were you married to Diane?'

'Twenty-five years. But we divorced ten years ago.'

'Do you mind if I ask why?' The question wasn't strictly necessary, but so far Ian hadn't shown any reluctance to talk about his personal life, and Bridget wanted to draw as much information out of him as possible.

'I don't mind at all,' he said. 'There was no big bust-up, no extra-marital affairs, no dramatic falling-out. We just drifted apart, without really noticing it. Diane had her career, I had mine. Suddenly our silver wedding anniversary was on the horizon and when our parents – who were all still alive at the time – suggested we should do something special to celebrate, we both realised that we had no desire to throw a lavish party or even to go out for a romantic dinner together. Diane always believed in brutal honesty, so when we sat down to talk about our relationship, we came to the conclusion that it was over and there was no point pretending otherwise. We hadn't made the time for each other and by then it was too late. Daniel had grown up and left home. He didn't need us anymore. So we agreed to separate and eventually got a divorce. There were no histrionics or recriminations, just an amicable parting of the ways.'

How civilised, thought Bridget, recalling her own acrimonious split from Ben. 'And you met your current wife at the hospital?'

Ian reached across the sofa and took Louise's hand in his. 'Louise is the best thing that's ever happened to me,' he said, 'except of course for my son, Daniel.'

Daniel, who was sitting rather sullenly, sunk into an armchair, elbows resting on the sides, his neck disappearing into his shoulders, acknowledged the compliment with the slightest nod of his head.

'And how long have you two been married?' asked Bridget, looking from Ian to his gorgeous new wife.

'Seven years,' said Louise, smiling.

'And we're very happy together,' said Ian, giving her hand a squeeze.

'Do you have any children of your own?' Bridget asked.

Louise shook her head, making her glossy chestnut hair bounce on her shoulders. 'No. But perhaps it's a blessing. I see so much suffering amongst young people in my work at the hospital. I couldn't bear it if a child of my own ever fell seriously ill.'

'I can understand that,' said Bridget. As a police officer, she was all too aware of the many and diverse ways that a teenage girl might become a victim of crime, and had been unable to stop herself picturing Chloe in each situation. From car crashes to kidnapping to murder, Bridget had lived each scenario a thousand times in her imagination. She had paid less attention to the possibility of serious or terminal illness. Perhaps that ought to feature more prominently on her list of parental concerns.

She turned back to Ian. 'After the divorce, how was your relationship with Diane? Oxford isn't such a big place. You must have bumped into one another from time to time.'

'We got on well enough,' said Ian. 'As I explained, there was no terrible break-up, just a parting of the ways. We still met up for coffee now and again. She told me about her book, and when I saw that she was appearing at the literary festival I thought about going to hear her talk, but I had another engagement that night. Now I rather wish I'd gone to the festival.'

'Did Diane have any other relationships since the divorce?'

'You mean a boyfriend?' said Ian. 'Not to my knowledge.'

Bridget turned to Louise. 'What about your relationship with Diane? It can't have been easy being Ian's second wife. Did Diane ever show any resentment towards you?'

Louise seemed amused by the suggestion. 'Not at all. Diane wasn't a jealous woman. I can't say that she was my best friend, but we certainly never exchanged any unpleasantries. And if you think I had any problem being Ian's second wife, you couldn't be further from the truth. It didn't bother me that I didn't get to him first, I was simply glad that he was available when I met him.' She held Ian's arm and leaned in towards him affectionately.

This was all very grown up. Bridget's mind conjured up an image of Tamsin, Ben's *fiancée*. No matter how many times she repeated the word, she still couldn't quite come to terms with the fact that her ex- was about to remarry. Bridget still hadn't met Tamsin, but her mental picture of her always resembled the beautiful but wicked stepmother from *Snow White*. Bridget couldn't imagine the soon-to-be Mrs Tamsin Hart being as magnanimous towards her as Louise was towards Diane. Of course, there was always the possibility that it was Bridget who was at fault, harbouring irrational and unpleasant jealousy towards her replacement. She shook her head, dismissing the absurd idea as quickly as it had arisen.

'What was your other engagement on the evening of Diane's talk?' Bridget asked Ian, getting back on track.

'A retirement party for one of the hospital consultants.' He stopped and gave her a questioning look. 'Are you asking me to provide you with an alibi? I can give you the details if you like.'

'Please.' Although Bridget had no reason to suspect Diane's ex-husband of foul play, no detective ever got results without being nosy.

'The party was at a restaurant in Thame. Louise and I went together and got a taxi back here afterwards.'

'What time did you arrive home?'

Ian looked to his wife for confirmation. 'Was it around midnight?'

'Just before,' said Louise. 'I remember because I turned the radio on in the kitchen whilst I was making myself a cocoa. It helps me unwind before going to bed.'

That reminded Bridget of something that she'd been meaning to ask Ian. 'Was Diane a heavy sleeper?'

'Diane?' Ian sounded surprised. 'Not a bit of it. She always slept lightly. And she tended to wake up early. She used to say that life was too short to spend it asleep.'

'One last thing – can you think of any reason why someone would have wanted to harm your ex-wife?'

Ian shook his head from side to side. 'Diane wasn't always the easiest person to get on with, but I can't think of anyone who would hate her enough to kill her.'

Bridget turned to the son who had so far sat in silence, drinking his coffee and eating the biscuits. Crumbs lay scattered over the trousers of his suit. 'It must have been a terrible shock to hear the news of your mother's death this morning.'

Daniel brushed the crumbs absently onto the

Persian rug where they disappeared into the intricate pattern. 'A shock, yes. But I can't say that I was terribly upset.'

'You didn't get along with your mother?' Bridget knew from personal experience that the parent-child relationship could be tricky. She lived in constant fear that she and Chloe would grow apart. Bridget's own parents had grown distant from herself and her sister Vanessa after the death of Bridget's younger sister, Abigail, and it was only during this most recent Christmas that the gulf that had separated them for so many years had finally been bridged and the family had come together again. But whatever rift had developed between Daniel and his mother could now never be healed. Would he spend the rest of his life regretting that? From his expression and body language, Bridget doubted it.

Daniel twisted awkwardly in his chair. 'How can I put this kindly? The maternal instinct didn't come naturally to my mother. She was always too focussed on her career and her politics. All she ever talked about was Israel, Palestine, and American imperialism. She didn't have time for me, and she didn't have time for Dad either.'

'Daniel, is that really fair?' asked Ian. 'Your mother loved you deeply.'

Daniel folded his arms across his chest. 'Well, she had a strange way of showing it. If she'd shown you a bit more love, perhaps you wouldn't have had to divorce her.'

Bridget intervened before a full-blown family row could erupt. 'You felt your mother neglected you?'

'In a word, yes. Dad was always there for me, despite having such a demanding career. And Aunt Annabel too. She's been more of a mother to me than my own mother ever was. I spent almost as much time in her house growing up as I did in my own.'

He smiled warmly at the memory, and Bridget could imagine Annabel's higgledy-piggledy cottage being a much more welcoming place for a young child than Diane's imposing house, where nothing was out of place. His kind-hearted aunt might well have provided Daniel with the affection he craved, and that his mother was unable to give him.

'And Louise has always been very kind to me as a stepmother,' Daniel added. 'It was only my mother who didn't care.'

Bridget stepped in quickly again, before Ian could say anything. 'Some women find it difficult to relate to small children. They get on better with their children once they've grown up.'

Daniel gave a short, unpleasant laugh. 'If anything, our relationship deteriorated once I grew up. As a child it was just a matter of maternal indifference on her part. But as I grew older, I became so sick of her left-wing politics that as soon as I had the vote, I rebelled by voting Conservative. I even joined the Conservative

Party. Imagine that! Who joins the Conservatives in order to rebel? Anyway, my mother was horrified, which was of course my intention. That was when we really started to argue. And then I dealt the final blow to her by becoming an accountant, working right in the heart of the capitalist system.'

Daniel's cheeks had become bright red during his tirade, and his chest was heaving. He leaned back in his chair, gripping the armrests tightly, and looked around the room as if daring his father or his stepmother to contradict him. Wisely, they declined to rise to the bait.

'So now you live in London,' prompted Bridget, seeking to steer the interview into less turbulent waters.

'I rent a place in Camberwell,' he said. 'Not particularly glamorous, but...' He trailed off.

'Daniel would like to buy a place with his girlfriend,' said Ian, 'but London property prices are sky-high, even with two salaries. Diane and I tried to help out financially, but...'

'I can imagine,' said Bridget. Even in Oxford, getting a first step onto the property ladder was a challenge. She knew that Jake, on his sergeant's salary, was still renting a small flat in East Oxford. And in London, even in somewhere like Camberwell, south of the river, prices were prohibitive for many people starting out on their careers.

The mention of property prices led her nicely onto another tricky question. 'On the subject of money, who stands to inherit Diane's estate?'

'Well,' said Ian, 'it's no great secret. Diane rewrote her will after our divorce was finalised, and she told us all what she'd done. Daniel will inherit everything. Diane may have struggled to express her love for Daniel in a direct way, but in truth she was devoted to him. Her will leaves everything to him.'

CHAPTER 9

A feeling of gloom settled heavily on Grant Sadler as his bus swung around the corner of the High Street and nudged into the congestion of St Aldate's, heading south. The wide road quickly narrowed as the bus proceeded slowly past Christ Church. Grant gazed forlornly out of the window as the great edifice of Tom Tower appeared briefly on his left and then was gone. The best part of Oxford was behind him now, and ahead lay only the river and the grim terraced houses of the Abingdon Road. Beyond that, the sprawling Park & Ride, the Travelodge and ultimately the ring road.

The edge of the world.

His phone rang in his jacket pocket making him jump. He dragged it out and eyed the screen nervously, fearful that the police wanted to speak to him again. It was a relief to see that it was just Diane's publisher calling.

'Hi, Jennifer. What can I do for you?' The bus bounced wildly over a bump in the road, and he pressed the phone to his ear.

'News of Diane's death is out.'

Grant lowered his voice, wishing he was somewhere less public. 'Yes, I've just been speaking to the police. That Inspector Hart who was at the talk last night.'

'Oh, her. What angle are the police taking?'

'What do you mean, what angle?'

'I mean, what questions did she ask you?'

'Mainly about Diane, and what I did last night.'

'They think you're a suspect?'

People on the bus were staring Grant's way now, and he turned his head to look out of the window. 'No. Why would they?'

'Don't be a fool, Grant,' said Jennifer. 'Of course you're a suspect. So be careful what you tell them. Anyway, listen, I've arranged for you to be interviewed by some of the TV networks. Sky News, the BBC and Channel 4. I'll be handling the radio interviews and newspaper journalists myself.'

Grant marvelled at Jennifer's insensitivity. 'Seriously? Diane's body is barely cold.'

'That's why we need to move right away. If we play this right, *A Deadly Race* will soon be flying off the shelves.'

'Isn't that rather mercenary?'

'I'm surprised you're taking that attitude, Grant. I thought you'd be keen to garner as much publicity as possible. After all, as I'm sure you don't need reminding, you'll be receiving fifteen per cent of earnings.'

'Fifteen percent,' said Grant. 'Hardly a life-changing percentage.'

'That depends on what it's fifteen percent of, doesn't it? Diane's book now has every ingredient necessary to make it into a bestseller. A death threat; claims of state collusion in arms sales to a repressive government; the murder of an Oxford academic. The conspiracy theorists will go wild.'

'I'd rather have a successful living author on my books than a dead one-hit wonder.'

'Would you really, Grant? Some of the biggest books in history have been one-hit wonders, as I'm sure you know. *Gone with The Wind* was the only book Margaret Mitchell ever published. It was so successful she spent the rest of her life doing nothing but responding to fan mail.'

'Well, this isn't *Gone with The Wind*. And Diane Gilbert won't be responding to any fan mail.'

'No, she won't. But what about you, Grant? How exactly do you plan to spend the rest of your life? Do you think you'll even be in business five years from now? Everyone knows that the world of publishing is changing, and it's no secret that you need the money. So I suggest you have a long, hard think about how you're going to continue to put butter on your bread, and then smarten yourself up and get down to the studio to do those interviews.'

The line went dead.

★

Since returning from the Blavatnik School of Government, Jake had spent his afternoon immersed in the dispiriting world of social media. It seemed that an outspoken writer on a controversial topic was destined to receive a torrent of abuse. It was shocking what some people were prepared to write when they believed themselves to be untraceable and unaccountable. There were a lot of haters out there, but none of their abhorrent outpourings went as far as the death threat Diane had received by post.

After several hours trawling through Twitter, Jake realised that he was in danger of becoming mired in defamation and loathing. There was only so much antagonism a guy could take, even when it was directed at someone else. He yawned, stretched, and switched off his computer. He'd put in a long shift the previous day too, watching Diane Gilbert give her talk at the Bodleian, and then he'd been called unexpectedly early that morning with the shocking news that she was dead.

He couldn't help feeling a little responsible for the writer's murder. They still didn't know how the killer had gained access to the property. Had the murderer secretly been hiding somewhere inside the house – perhaps even in one of the rooms that Jake had searched? He shuddered at the idea that his own negligence might have led to a woman's death. But, no. The intruder hadn't been lying in wait. They'd broken in through the back door during the night. If anyone was to blame, it was surely those two constables who'd been watching the house. Diane's murder had taken place right under their noses. As uncomfortable as he might feel about the situation, Jake was very glad he wasn't in their shoes.

On the other side of the incident room, Ffion snapped shut the big, hardback edition of Diane Gilbert's book that she'd been reading. She'd been totally absorbed in her task all day and hadn't noticed Jake surreptitiously watching her. At least he didn't think she had. Her green eyes had remained firmly on the book, flicking across the words at lightning speed, and the rate at which she turned pages was astonishing. How could she absorb so much information so quickly? These days Jake hardly ever read a book at all. The last proper book he remembered reading from cover to cover was John Steinbeck's *Of Mice and Men* which he'd had to study for his English GCSE. He'd done a play as well – *An Inspector Calls* – and had quite enjoyed it. It might even have been one of the reasons he'd decided to become a police officer. Righting the wrongs of the world, and all that. He hadn't got on so well with Shakespeare though – too many words that weren't proper English. Now he lived in a city where books outnumbered people a hundred-fold. Even Ryan, that dark horse, had lent him a thriller to read, but it was still sitting on his bedside cabinet, unopened. At nearly six hundred pages long, it was likely to stay there until Ryan asked for it back. At least *Of Mice and Men* had been short.

Ffion stood up, stretching her arms above her head, and Jake found his eyes drawn inexorably to her long, slender, catlike form. Green eyes. Leather trousers. Spiky blonde hair. He knew the details by heart, but still couldn't turn away.

'Good book?' he ventured, not wanting to be caught staring at her with his mouth open and nothing to say.

His working relationship with Ffion was back on a more even keel in recent months. Things had lurched briefly off course after a short-lived and ultimately disastrous romantic detour and for a while they had barely spoken. In fact he had seriously considered leaving Oxford entirely and moving back north to Yorkshire. He was still feeling his way tentatively through the minefield of their relationship, and any suggestion of anything more than friendship was strictly off limits, but for the most part he and Ffion could hold normal conversations again. Although with Ffion, no conversation was ever completely normal.

'Diane Gilbert argues her case well,' she said, lifting the heavy book off the table and brandishing it in Jake's direction, 'although she uses long words when shorter ones would do just as well, and her sentences are unnecessarily convoluted. That's why the book is so long. I think she could probably have said everything in half the number of pages.'

'You wouldn't recommend it as bedtime reading?'

'I prefer books where the author's personal biases aren't so evident.' Ffion rattled off a list of books that she'd read recently and that Jake had never heard of. The titles sounded heavy-going. 'What about you?'

'Me?'

'What do you like to read?'

Was she teasing him? She must have noticed during their brief time as a couple that his flat wasn't exactly stuffed with works of literature. Or books of any kind, in fact.

'I like, um...' he offered lamely. What did he like? He liked to watch a football match on the telly. 'Plenty of action,' he suggested. 'Something exciting with a good twist at the end.' Maybe he ought to try that thriller Ryan had recommended. He might surprise himself.

'I prefer non-fiction,' said Ffion. 'I like learning new things and challenging my preconceptions.' She started to pull on her green biker's jacket.

Jake rose from his seat. 'Off home? I was just leaving too.' He hesitated. Wisdom cautioned him not to say any more, but when had wisdom ever been any fun? 'Are you doing anything tonight? Do you fancy a drink? Just as friends, I mean. You could tell me what I should be reading.' He ventured a half-smile of encouragement.

'No, sorry,' said Ffion. 'I've got a date tonight.' She zipped up the leather jacket and grabbed her phone from her desk.

'Oh,' said Jake. This was certainly news. And not exactly welcome. Not that he entertained any designs on Ffion himself. Obviously he didn't. And he could hardly expect her to lead the life of a nun just because she was no longer going out with him. That would be totally unreasonable. 'Um...' he said, following her out of the office.

'What is it?'

Good question. What was his problem, exactly? 'So, um, who's the lucky guy?' he asked, although he really didn't want to know.

She turned and leaned against the doorframe. '*Her* name is Marion and *she's* a junior research fellow at the university.'

'Oh right, yeah, good,' said Jake, trying to wrap his brain around this latest piece of information. He had – of course – known that Ffion was bisexual. She had told him often enough. Yet somehow, until this moment, he'd never really taken onboard the reality of that fact. There was probably a word for blokes like him, but he didn't know what it was. He didn't think he wanted to. 'Well, have a nice evening.'

Ffion was already on the move again. 'You too,' she called over her shoulder.

Me too, right.

But what did Jake's evening hold in store for him? A takeaway curry, a couple of beers, and another night slumped alone in front of the football. *Plenty of action,* he thought miserably. *Something exciting with a good twist at the end.* He needed to be more careful what he wished for. This story had certainly sprung a surprising twist, and he wasn't at all sure that he liked it.

CHAPTER 10

'So you still have nothing,' concluded Grayson.

By the time Bridget had returned to Kidlington, everyone had gone home except for the Chief Superintendent, who had stayed behind to hear her report. She gave him a verbal summary of her meetings with the various members of Diane Gilbert's family, her literary agent, and the head of department at the Blavatnik, as well as itemising all the actions she had assigned to her team members.

Grayson seemed distinctly unimpressed.

'That's hardly fair, sir,' she countered. 'We've covered a lot of ground in one day.'

'Yet all you've really got to go on at the moment,' said Grayson, 'is the unusual method of killing, and the controversial nature of her book. Plus the death threat.'

'I'm still waiting for forensics to get back to me on that. And for the post-mortem to establish the cause and time of death. And for SOCO to work out how the murderer got into the property.'

Grayson lifted his pen from his desk, but thankfully there was no tapping this time. 'Let's hope we get all that soon. In the meantime, what's your gut feeling about this? Do you think this was a domestic matter?'

'Her son didn't like her, and has a clear financial motive in wanting her dead, but as far as I know he was in London yesterday. As for the other members of her family, they have no motive and seem to have got on perfectly well with her. Even her ex-husband had an amicable relationship with her by all accounts.'

'What about her work colleagues?'

'Her boss clearly held a strong dislike for her personally, and didn't approve of the direction of her academic research or her book, but that hardly seems like a strong enough motive for murder.'

'So what does?'

Bridget took a deep breath. 'Diane's agent suggested to me that her killing might be the work of the British security services.'

Grayson raised a steely eyebrow. 'Is that what you think?'

'In all honesty, I don't know, sir. The death threat... the way the murderer broke into Diane's house when it was under the watch of the police... the unusual method of her killing... and of course the nature of her book. They all support the theory that she might have been assassinated by a foreign government or some other powerful party. But of course that's just speculation,' she added hurriedly, unwilling to offer Grayson any reason to doubt her judgement.

To her surprise, Grayson didn't dismiss the idea out of hand. 'National security. It's a possibility that we have to consider. If that's the case, you're going to need some help.'

'Sir?'

'Leave it with me. I'll follow up via the official channels. See if I can find out anything.'

'Thank you, sir,' said Bridget. 'I appreciate that.'

He dismissed her with a grunt and a wave of his hand. Grayson, she realised, just didn't know how to handle gratitude. Perhaps that's why he was so bad at expressing any himself.

★

Bridget drove back to Wolvercote just as the sun was disappearing from view, turning the sky over Port Meadow a pink salmon, and casting deep shadows across the village green. Sounds of cheer and laughter escaped from the brightly-lit interior of the White Hart and drifted over to her, but when she let herself into her darkened cottage, a still silence met her like a wall. She had never imagined that such a small house could feel so empty, but with Chloe still away, the low ceilings seemed to be pressing down, and the cheerful disarray of the kitchen felt chaotic and cluttered.

She switched on all the downstairs lights and put *The Marriage of Figaro* on the CD player in an attempt to bolster her fragile mood.

Why was she feeling so low? It wasn't just Diane's murder and the pressure she was under from Grayson to solve the case. It wasn't even that she was missing her daughter. Something deeper was stirring, and she had a creeping sense that her life was about to be upended.

The root cause of that unease was her ex-husband.

Why should it matter so much to her that Ben and Tamsin were getting married? She had faced the pain and heartache of his infidelity many years ago, and long since moved on from the wreck of her marriage. She was proud of what she'd achieved with her life since leaving him. She'd brought up a daughter single-handedly, and built her own career. It shouldn't make any difference what Ben did with his life.

But it did, and Bridget knew why.

Despite her best efforts, despite everything she'd done to protect Chloe and to build a wall around the painful past, slowly but surely Ben had succeeded in worming his way back under her skin, reaching out for Chloe, and reclaiming his daughter for himself. Now she was with him in London, going out to expensive restaurants, trying on dresses, having fun with her future stepmother.

She is my daughter! Mine!

The Mozart played on, but its uplifting melody was out of tune with her own discordant thoughts.

I am getting this out of proportion.

She breathed deeply, seeking to bring her runaway emotions back under control. Whatever Ben was up to, Chloe was still her daughter, and there was no question that she would ever move to London to live with her father. Tamsin, the wicked stepmother, surely wouldn't want it. So Bridget just had to learn to share. Chloe was old enough to make her own decisions, and Bridget would have to trust her.

She paced the kitchen restlessly. It would be so much easier to face this if Jonathan was at her side. What time was it in New York? Bridget found that she didn't really care. She picked up her phone and dialled.

Soon Jonathan's reassuring voice was on the line, and Bridget felt her problems begin to melt away.

'Hi,' he said. 'How's it going?'

Terribly. 'Oh, you know. Missing you. How's New York?'

'Great. But it's exhausting. Galleries, exhibitions, auctions. I've only just got back to the hotel after dashing around all day.'

It sounds wonderful. 'I can imagine.'

'What about you? How's that writer you're looking after?'

Bridget groaned. 'Please don't ask.'

'Okay. Then tell me what you're doing right now. Where are you?'

'Home. Alone.'

'Don't worry. Chloe will be back soon. And so

will I.'

'Yes.' Just the thought of his return was giving her the strength to carry on. 'So what are your plans for tonight?'

'I've got a restaurant booked for eight. A couple of gallery owners offered to take me out to this great new Peruvian place in the East Village.'

'Sounds amazing.'

'What about you?' he asked brightly. 'Are you cooking tonight, or getting a takeaway?'

Bridget swung open the door of her fridge with one hand and took a quick look at its contents. Half a block of Cheddar cheese, some limp slices of ham, a pint of milk well past its use-by date, and a mouldy lettuce. She'd planned to go shopping after escorting Diane back from her radio interview.

'A takeaway, I think.'

'Good choice,' said Jonathan knowingly. 'Anyway, I have to go now. Take care. I'll call you tomorrow. Love you.'

'Love you.'

She hung up, already feeling better for hearing Jonathan's voice. And while she couldn't depend on him to solve all her problems, at least she now knew how to fix her most immediate concern. She dialled again and was soon placing an order for home-delivered pizza with garlic bread and a tub of pistachio ice-cream.

Life always looked better from the other side of an ice-cream tub.

CHAPTER 11

It was a Saturday morning but there was to be no time off while Diane Gilbert's killer was still at large. Bridget waited for her team to assemble in the incident room, eager to hear what each member had to say. Once the last of them had taken a seat, mug in hand, she rose to her feet and invited them to give their reports.

Andy and Harry had little to report from their door-to-door enquiries in St Margaret's Road and the nearby streets.

'Nothing doing, ma'am,' said Andy apologetically. 'We got the impression that most people in that road don't really know who their neighbours are. They certainly didn't know Diane. She seems to have kept herself to herself. And no one heard or saw a thing last night, not even the people next door.'

It was disappointing, but Bridget thanked them for their efforts and turned to Ryan. He had spent the previous day at the house trying to work out how the intruder had gained access to Diane's property.

'I took a bunch of constables with me up to the

house, ma'am. We carried out a fingertip search of the entire grounds – front garden, rear garden, garage and outbuildings.'

'What did you find?'

'Absolutely nothing. No dropped items. No footprints in the soil. No signs of a ladder being used to climb over the wall. The shed in the back was padlocked, and the garage was secure. The windows were all locked too. There was no forced entry, apart from the back door of the house itself.'

'So how did they get into the garden and out again under the nose of the constables?'

'Could someone have already been hiding inside the house when you dropped Diane off?' queried Andy.

Bridget noticed Jake squirm in his seat, and perhaps not surprisingly. He had been the one who had searched upstairs, while Bridget checked the downstairs rooms of the house. It was conceivable that an intruder had concealed themselves so well that they had escaped discovery, but the possibility simply raised more unanswerable questions. How had they gained entry to the house? And more pertinently, if they had already been inside, why would they have smashed the back door open? It didn't make any sense.

'No,' said Bridget. 'The house was clear. The killer broke in some time after we left Diane for the night.'

'That's what I figured,' said Ryan. 'But if they

didn't get in the back way, they must have come in from the front. The only scenario that makes any sense to me is if those two constables nodded off, or slipped away to grab a quick coffee. Diane's killer might have been watching them, and nipped in when he saw his chance.'

'That would also explain why they didn't hear the glass in the back door being smashed,' said Jake.

Bridget nodded reluctantly. She had believed the two officers' account, and hoped that her trust in them wasn't misplaced. 'It's a possibility. But it still doesn't explain why Diane herself didn't hear the glass break and wake up.'

'Heavy sleeper?' suggested Ryan.

'Her ex-husband said not.' Bridget gave a summary of her own investigations, recounting what the various family members had told her about Diane, and also telling them about the strong personal antipathy that her boss at the Blavatnik School had harboured towards her.

'Does that give him a sufficient motive for murder?' queried Ryan.

'Professional rivalry?' said Bridget. 'We'll need something more compelling than that before we consider Professor Al-Mutairi to be a suspect. Jake, did you check Ian Dunn's alibi?' An ex-husband was always an obvious suspect in any murder enquiry, even though on the face of it Ian Dunn had come across as quite charming.

Jake referred to his notes. 'I spoke to two of the guests who were at the party Ian attended in

Thame. They both confirmed that he and his wife didn't leave until after eleven o'clock.'

'Okay, good.' It was of course conceivable that Ian had attended the party with the express intention of creating an alibi for himself, and then committed the murder on his return to Oxford, but that required the meticulous planning and ruthless efficiency of a criminal mastermind. As far as Bridget could tell, the guy didn't even have a motive, having been amicably divorced from his ex-wife for many years, and not benefitting in any way from her will.

Bridget turned her attention next to Ffion. The young constable was sitting with Diane's book on her lap. 'I don't suppose there's any chance you managed to finish your reading assignment?' Bridget asked her.

Ffion gave the enormous book a pat. 'Cover to cover.'

'Very impressive. And what was your verdict?'

'On Diane's political viewpoint? I think she makes some good points, but she only considers one side of the argument.'

'I meant on whether it sheds any light on her murder.'

Ffion didn't blink before responding. 'The book's central thesis is that the British and American governments collude with the companies that manufacture and export weapons, in order to supply regimes that they know to be repressive. She claims they do this not just for commercial advantage, but also to further their own expansionist geopolitical agendas. On the basis of what I read in her book, various countries must have regarded her as a threat to their national security. In particular, the British, American and Saudi Arabian governments.'

This was the last thing Bridget had hoped to hear. But it confirmed what Grant Sadler had told her at the coffee shop. In particular he had pointed the finger at the British security services. She told the rest of her team what the literary agent had said.

'With all respect, ma'am,' said Ryan, 'surely you can't seriously believe that Diane Gilbert was assassinated by MI5? I think you've been reading too many John le Carré novels.'

Bridget's problem was that she never had enough time to read novels of any kind. But Ryan was right. It was far too soon to start pointing the finger at governments and security services.

'But, she's dead, isn't she?' retorted Ffion. 'So someone must have killed her, and national security is an obvious reason. The method of killing suggests a professional assassination. Don't forget about the death threat, either.'

'Where are we with that?' asked Bridget. 'Have forensics finished with the letter yet?'

'Their report came in late yesterday afternoon,' said Ryan, producing a short document. He paged through it, reading out the highlights. 'The letter was sent in an envelope postmarked central London. The type of paper used was cheap lined paper from a refill pad, and the envelope was of the white self-sealing kind, so there was no DNA from saliva. It was written with a fountain pen using blue ink from a Parker cartridge. Nothing particularly expensive, just the sort of item you can buy from WH Smith's. The handwriting itself is unremarkable. Obviously we have nothing to compare it with, but in the opinion of the handwriting expert, the writer didn't bother to disguise their writing style. She points out that the writing is fluid and shows no signs of pen lifts or words being restarted. So if we were able to obtain a sample of writing from a suspect, we'd probably have a good chance of matching it.'

'Any fingerprints?' asked Bridget, ever hopeful.

'Only the victim's own prints, and those of the literary agent and the publisher, who she showed it to. Presumably the writer wore gloves while writing and posting the letter. There were no hairs or fibres either.'

'So we have no fingerprints, no DNA, no footprints, no physical evidence of any kind.' Bridget had checked for emails from Vik on first arriving at work that morning, but the SOCO team had still not unearthed anything she could use. She would have liked to give Ffion the task of analysing the victim's mobile phone and laptop, but frustratingly those items were still with forensics.

Andy raised his hand to speak again. 'After Harry and I got back from the door-to-door, I had time to do a bit of background research on the victim.'

'Go on,' said Bridget.

'Well, it seems she was arrested a few times back in the early nineteen-eighties for protesting at Greenham Common.' He produced a black and white photograph from a newspaper and passed it over to Bridget, who pinned it to the board for everyone to see. The year of publication was 1982. The picture showed a much younger Diane Gilbert being forcibly dragged through the mud by a pair of helmeted bobbies.

News of Diane's past political activism didn't greatly surprise Bridget, given what she already knew about the academic. The Greenham Common Women's Peace Camp had become famous – or infamous – during the eighties because of the hundreds of women who camped outside the RAF base in Berkshire to protest at the decision of the British government to allow American cruise missiles to be deployed there. Margaret Thatcher had been in Number Ten at the time and the effects of free market capitalism were just beginning to make themselves felt in the economic boom in the City of London. Other parts of the country, with an industrial base rooted in the previous century, were faring less well. It had been a turbulent time in British history, and Diane Gilbert would have been a young woman, full of political conviction and self-righteous indignation. Greenham Common would have been her natural habitat.

'So it's very likely that MI5 have a file on her dating back a few decades,' concluded Andy. 'And given what we know about her recent activities, they may have continued to watch her.'

Bridget thanked Andy for his diligent research. Much as she disliked the idea, all the available evidence seemed to be pointing in the direction of a national security connection, and she couldn't afford to ignore it. 'The Chief Super is on the case, knocking on the doors of power to see what he can find out. In the meantime, let's work with what we've got. Jake, Ryan, I'd like you to go back to the Blavatnik School of Government and talk to the rest of Diane's colleagues. See what you can unearth, bearing in mind everything we've talked about this morning.'

'We're on it, ma'am,' said Jake.

'Andy, carry on with your background checks. I want to know everything there is to know about Diane and her political activities. Harry, start following up on her phone records.' She turned to Ffion. 'You can come with me. I think that after spending all of yesterday with your head in a book, you could probably use some fresh air.'

CHAPTER 12

The wall that bounded Diane Gilbert's back garden stood eight feet tall. Bridget looked up at it doubtfully. It would be impossible for her to climb, and Vik had assured her that there were no footprints or tell-tale marks in the soil beneath the wall that a ladder might have made. But whoever had gained entry to Diane's house had come and gone somehow.

'What do you reckon?' asked Bridget. She waited whilst Ffion eyed up the brick wall. At almost six feet in flat shoes, Ffion could just about reach the top if she stood on tiptoes.

'You want me to give it a go?'

'If you don't mind,' said Bridget.

Ffion accepted the unusual request without comment, appearing to relish the challenge. She bent forward and touched her toes, jogged on the spot for a moment, then took a running leap at the wall. She managed to grab hold of the top, but even with her long legs she struggled to gain a foothold on the vertical surface. She tried swinging her right leg up to the top of the wall, but it was simply too far. For a moment she hung there, suspended above the shrubbery, then let herself drop back down, landing with a feline grace. She returned to Bridget, rubbing mud and moss from her hands, looking obviously disappointed not to have made it over the top.

'Good try,' said Bridget. 'You proved the point.' She indicated the deep impressions that Ffion had left in the soil of the flowerbed. 'Even if someone had managed to climb over, they would have left clear marks behind. And Vik assured me that there were no marks.'

'So if they didn't come over the top, might they have come through that door?' asked Ffion, pointing to the solid wooden door in the wall.

'Not unless they had the key,' said Bridget. The door fitted flush to the wall, and was secured with a standard mortice lock. 'The key was found hanging in the kitchen. And since the intruder had to break the glass in the kitchen door to get into the house, it's unlikely they would have had a key to the garden door. In any case, it was locked when Vik's team examined it. Why would someone bother to lock the garden gate after smashing open the kitchen door? It doesn't make any sense.'

'No,' said Ffion, 'so we still have no idea how they got in?'

Bridget was reluctant to admit that the most obvious explanation was staring her in the face – that Sam and Scott had not been telling the truth about staying on guard all night. If it could be proved that they had lied to her, their careers might well be over before they had barely started. She felt a stab of pity, but also a fair amount of anger.

They walked round the rest of the garden, but there was no obvious way by which the intruder might have entered, if not through the front driveway. Bridget re-examined the garden shed, but it was firmly padlocked as before. An inspection of the garage revealed nothing new either. With a sigh, Bridget had to accept that they would be unable to solve this particular part of the mystery by further examination of the grounds.

'Let's take a look inside the house.'

The back entrance was sealed off with crime tape, and broken glass still littered the kitchen floor, so they circled round to the front of the house where a uniformed constable let them inside.

The broken pane of glass in the kitchen door was letting the damp April air inside, and the house had taken on a chill feel. Bridget kept her coat on as she and Ffion began their examination of the ground floor.

In the kitchen, everything seemed to be in order apart from the break-in itself, but the room offered few clues to Diane Gilbert the person.

'She had good taste,' said Ffion, inspecting the polished granite worktop, sleek chrome fittings, high-spec gadgets and multi-function hob.

'And the money to indulge it,' said Bridget. It was obvious that Diane had been able to afford the best quality on offer in the showroom. Presented to such a high standard, the massive Victorian house located in the highly sought-after area of North Oxford would command an eye-watering sum on the property market. Diane's son, Daniel, stood to inherit a small fortune. Not so small, in fact.

It was certainly a far cry from the Women's Peace Camp at Greenham Common where Diane had spent her protest years. Bridget pictured groups of women huddled around camping stoves, singing rousing songs and living off tins of baked beans. Clearly, it was possible to tire of such a lifestyle.

They moved on to the dining room, which backed onto the rear garden, commanding views over the long lawn all the way to the far wall. In summer, with a display of flowers outside, it would be a glorious vista. Even on this slightly overcast April morning, the purple and yellow cups of tulips helped lift the spirits.

Just like the kitchen, the room was designed to impress, with a modern crystal chandelier hanging from the central ceiling rose, and abstract works of art adorning the walls. The table seated eight people in its leather high-backed chairs. But once again, there was something soulless and untouched about the room that gave Bridget the feeling that it had never hosted the sort of large dinner party that it was clearly intended for. If she'd been hoping to find a clue to Diane's personal life from her home, perhaps the main takeaway was that Diane had no personal life. For the high-powered academic, work had meant everything.

They entered the lounge.

The south-facing bay window of the room overlooked the front garden, letting soft light flood into the high-ceilinged room. To either side of the marble fireplace, the alcoves accommodated shelves tightly packed with books. Bridget scanned the titles on the spines. The books were mostly about politics, in particular the geopolitics of the Middle East and international relations, but there was also quite a collection covering surveillance, the secret state, and code-breaking. There was little in the way of fiction. Bridget recognised a heavyweight American novel that had won the Pulitzer Prize a few years back. Vanessa had given her a copy that year for Christmas, and Bridget had gamely ploughed through the first hundred pages before admitting defeat and donating the book to a charity shop, where she hoped it might find a more dedicated reader.

The bottom shelf was taller and contained what appeared to be photograph albums. Perhaps this would finally reveal something about the real Diane Gilbert. A cream-coloured album caught Bridget's eye and she pulled it from the shelf. It was a wedding album.

Diane may have divorced her husband a decade earlier but here, preserved for eternity beneath thin layers of tissue, a snapshot of her and Ian's story was revealed.

The wedding had taken place at Oxford's registry office with a reception at some country house hotel, the bride wearing a floor-length dress in pure white silk, the groom in traditional morning suit with a silver waistcoat. An order of service tucked into a sleeve at the front of the album revealed that the date had been June 1983. In those days, just two years after the wedding of Princess Diana to Prince Charles, it had been almost impossible to find a bride clothed in anything but virgin white. It was clearly the height of summer because it was a gloriously sunny day and, apart from Diane herself, all the women had bare arms. The only other people Bridget recognised in the photographs were Diane's sister, Annabel, and Annabel's late husband, John, though whether the couple had been married back then, Bridget didn't know.

She recalled the black and white photo of Diane getting arrested at the Greenham Common protests, taken when she was just a year younger. It seemed that Diane had moved on from her anti-nuclear protesting relatively quickly, and settled down to embrace a more conventional married life. The change clearly hadn't done her any harm – in the photographs here she appeared to be radiantly happy. Bridget's own wedding day had been one of the happiest days of her life. Neither she, nor Diane – nor Princess Diana, for that matter – could have had any inkling that the marriage would one day end in divorce.

Ffion was sitting cross-legged on the floor turning rapidly through the pages of the other albums.

'Anything interesting?' asked Bridget.

'Lots of pictures of her son growing up,' said Ffion. She handed Bridget a couple of albums and she began to turn the pages. 'People would just share all this stuff online now,' continued Ffion, 'but I suppose back then you had to print the photos and stick them in an album.'

'Yes,' said Bridget, who still remembered taking rolls of film along to the local camera shop to be developed, and returning to collect the prints days later. Someone as young as Ffion probably couldn't even begin to imagine such a world.

It didn't take Bridget long to discover that while Diane and Ian had been the focus of attention in the wedding album, these other albums were all about their son. Bridget skimmed through picture after picture of Daniel growing up – from cute baby to chocolate-smeared toddler; from knock-kneed infant schoolboy to bashful teenager. According to Daniel, his mother was never there for him growing up, but the evidence contained in these pages didn't support that view. In fact they suggested that Diane had been far more of a doting parent than Daniel had given her credit for.

For the first time since their initial meeting, Bridget began to feel some sympathy towards the murdered academic. It was crystal clear now that Diane had loved her son very much, and yet in his eyes she had been a cold, indifferent mother – one that he had ultimately rejected. Perhaps that was why Diane cultivated such a hard, unfeeling exterior, and why she had never remarried – to protect herself from future heartbreak. Bridget thought once more of Chloe, and a cold fear filled her heart at the prospect of her own daughter ever turning her back on her. She would not allow that to happen. However hard Ben tried to infiltrate himself into their daughter's life, no matter how Chloe responded, Bridget resolved always to be there for her, and to support her in whatever choices she made. Alfie, Chloe's boyfriend, would be joining them all for lunch at Vanessa's on Sunday – proof no doubt of just how far the relationship had come – and Bridget was determined to be on her best behaviour and say nothing that would embarrass her daughter in his presence.

The final photograph in the album had been taken at Daniel's graduation ceremony at Durham. There, Diane and Ian stood either side of their son, but there was a distant look on their faces, as if the marriage was already showing signs of the fault lines that would result in their so-called amicable divorce. Despite Ian Dunn's assertion that the split had been without rancour, Bridget wasn't sure that any marriage could fail without recrimination and resentment. But maybe that was her own personal experience colouring her view, and other people were able to handle the matter more maturely.

Ffion handed her another album, this one red, and Bridget opened it, expecting to find yet more pictures of Daniel as a child, but this album was older than all the others. On the inside front cover someone had written *Italian tour, April 1983*. The same year as Diane and Ian's wedding. Bridget had a fondness for all things Italian – pasta, Chianti, opera, art, sun, piazzas, and, of course, gelato – and couldn't resist turning the pages for a sneak peek. The pictures told her that in the spring of that year, Diane, Ian, Annabel and John had embarked on a three-week road trip around Italy in a Fiat Panda. The two sisters and their respective boyfriends had started in Milan, detoured to Venice via Verona, then worked their way down the spine of the country, sampling the architectural and culinary delights of Bologna, Florence and Rome before arriving in Naples. In the shadow of Vesuvius, they had rented a palazzo-style villa of quite idyllic charm. A photograph that had presumably been taken by an obliging local showed both couples seated around an outside dining table laden with mouth-watering bowls of pasta and glasses of red wine.

It was a vision of yet another version of Diane, a carefree, young woman, with a taste for fun and the simple pleasures of life. Somehow that woman had vanished over the years, submerged beneath adult responsibilities of marriage, motherhood, and a demanding academic career. Diane had made many choices travelling along that road. One of them had – perhaps – led to her death. But the solution to that mystery wouldn't be found within these old photo albums.

'Ma'am?'

Bridget closed the album and dragged her thoughts away from sun-drenched Italy back to a damp and still chilly Oxford. 'Sorry, yes?'

'Should we move upstairs?'

'Yes,' she said, returning the album to the shelf, and wrapping her coat firmly around herself. 'I think we've done all we can here.'

Bridget had visited Diane's bedroom before, on the morning of the discovery of the body. This time, however, with the curtains drawn back, the body removed to the morgue, and the sense of urgency gone, she was able to take a proper look around. As expected, the room was furnished to the highest specification, with fitted walk-in wardrobes and an en-suite bathroom. But even here there was little sign of any personality. The bedside table held nothing but a reading light and a small glass jar of lip balm.

Ffion swept her gaze around the minimalist interior. 'Not a single book on display. I thought that writers were supposed to spend all their spare time reading.'

It was a little surprising, given that there were so many books downstairs.

Bridget made her way into the bathroom which, like the kitchen, was all gleaming surfaces and high-spec functionality.

The skincare products, displayed like works of art, were all brands that Bridget coveted but had never been able to convince herself that she was worth spending that amount of money on. But that wasn't what interested her most.

She pulled open the doors to the bathroom cabinet and rummaged inside. But amongst the prosaic packs of Paracetamol, Ibuprofen and indigestion tablets, there wasn't a single packet of sleeping pills. She was still no nearer to explaining how Diane, supposedly a light sleeper, had not been awoken by the sound of breaking glass in the middle of the night.

CHAPTER 13

Bridget returned to Kidlington with much on her mind: a dead woman, killed while under her responsibility; the seemingly unavoidable conclusion that matters of national security were to blame; not to mention the implied threat to Bridget's own career prospects if she screwed this up.

The circumstances of the murder itself were cloaked in mystery and Bridget's visit to Diane's house had done nothing to shine any light on them. And if all this wasn't enough, the undercurrent of resentment that Ben had aroused in her tugged heavily at her emotions, and the continued absence of Jonathan and Chloe was beginning to feel like a void in her own heart.

Ffion, too, seemed lost in thought, but Bridget took some solace in the sense that her constable's thoughts might be lighter and happier than her own.

On returning to the station, her luck began to change. After fetching a coffee from the machine, she made her way back to her desk and discovered an official-looking envelope waiting for her. She immediately recognised it as having been sent from the mortuary department of the John Radcliffe hospital. No doubt an email was waiting for her in her inbox, but Dr Roy Andrews still believed in the value of paper. She opened the envelope and found that just as she'd hoped, Roy had pulled out all the stops and completed the post-mortem that morning.

Whilst in person Roy could be accused of being overly fond of the sound of his own voice, on paper he was unfailingly concise. The report's conclusion was clear and to the point. The victim had died from cardiac arrest. The time of death was estimated to be anywhere between eleven o'clock at night and one in the morning. Although natural causes couldn't be completely ruled out, the pinprick on Diane's chest was, as Sarah had suggested, the surface mark from a hypodermic needle that had penetrated all the way to the left atrium of the heart. The post-mortem had been unable to determine the nature of any injected substance, but blood samples had been sent to toxicology and the results would come through in the next few days.

Bridget laid the report aside, marvelling both at the miracles of modern forensic science, and the frustrating delays associated with them. *A few days? Damn all weekends and holidays!* What was she to do while she waited for the toxicology report?

The surface of her desk was already littered

with unfiled reports and documents relating to this and other cases. One day she would work out a system, and her desk would be as clear and empty as Grayson's. But not today. Next to the discarded post-mortem report was a programme of events for the Oxford Literary Festival. She picked it up and flicked idly through the pages, stopping when she reached Diane's talk on Thursday evening. This was where it had all started. Just a few days ago, and all had been running smoothly. Then, the protection of a reluctant and ungrateful academic had seemed like an unnecessary waste of Bridget's time. Now, the artfully-shot photos of the Divinity School seemed to mock her. If she could rewind the clock and start that day again, what would she do differently? Other than remain at Diane's side throughout the night, it was hard to know.

Her eyes skipped over the text on the page and came to rest on the name of the man who had interviewed Diane that evening. Michael Dearlove, the journalist. Dearlove had been chosen because he was known for his work in the same topics that Diane had written about in *A Deadly Race*. If anyone could provide fresh insight into why Diane might have been murdered, it was surely him.

Bridget scanned the upcoming events and discovered that Dearlove was interviewing a writer of political biographies right that very minute and was due to finish in half an hour. The talk was taking place at the Oxford Martin

School, situated on the corner of Catte Street and Holywell Street, just opposite the Bodleian.

Leaving her cup of coffee untouched, she scooped up her keys and phone and rushed back out to her car.

★

By the time Bridget arrived at the Oxford Martin School, the talk was already over. A steady stream of people was coming down the stairs and she made her way in the opposite direction, ignoring the rude stares of the bibliophiles as she pushed past them. By the time she reached the lecture theatre only a few stragglers remained.

Housed within the old Indian Institute building, the Oxford Martin School was a modern addition to the university, founded with the stated goal to "find solutions to the world's most urgent challenges". There was nothing like setting yourself an ambitious target, thought Bridget, chastising herself once more over her inability to meet even her modest New Year's resolutions, though whether her problem was that she aimed too low or too high was anyone's guess.

The lecture theatre was a much smaller venue than the Divinity School, and clearly reflected the current writer's place in the pecking order. Nevertheless, the audience must have enjoyed themselves, because the young man from Blackwell's who Bridget recognised from

Diane's event looked a lot happier than he had done when she had last seen him, and appeared to have sold out all his books.

Bridget spotted Michael Dearlove at the front of the room gathering his notes together. She hurried to catch him before he left.

'Mr Dearlove?'

He looked up at her, a slight frown flitting across his forehead as he tried to place her. 'Yes?'

'I'm Detective Inspector Bridget Hart.'

His expression cleared. 'Ah, yes, I knew I recognised you from somewhere. You were Diane's bodyguard on the night she was murdered.'

Bridget winced at this reminder of her failure to prevent the writer's death, but judging from Dearlove's expression, he had intended no malice. He appeared sad, not angry. He put out a hand to shake Bridget's.

'Call me Mick. Or Michael, if you find Mick too informal.'

'Michael then, I was wondering if you could spare a few minutes to talk to me about Diane?'

He dropped his notes into a leather briefcase. 'I'd like nothing better. Diane's been on my mind constantly since her death. I still can't believe what happened. But what I want most of all right now is a cigarette. Do you mind?'

Bridget followed him down the stairs and back outside, where he immediately lit up. 'That's better,' he said, inhaling deeply and blowing out a stream of smoke through his nose. 'I'd given up, but Diane's death put paid to that. I've been smoking like the chimney of a nineteenth-century cotton mill ever since I heard the news. Absolutely shocking. I can't tell you how upset I've been.'

'You knew her well?'

Dearlove nodded and set off in the direction of Radcliffe Square. Bridget fell into step beside him, doing her best to keep up with him on her short legs.

'Diane and I knew each other since way back. God, I can't bear to think how many years that must be. Suffice to say, we were students together back in the day.'

'Here at Oxford?'

'Not likely. I would never have got in here' – he gestured at the Radcliffe Camera, the Bodleian Library and the other university buildings that surrounded them – 'and Diane wanted a university that was more in keeping with her socialist principles. We were at Manchester together. That was a wild place to be back in the seventies. We didn't just smoke tobacco then, I can tell you.'

They began to circle around the domed Radcliffe Camera, the towering spire of the University Church of St Mary the Virgin ahead of them, the ornate crenellations of All Souls College to their left.

'Do you mind me asking exactly how close you were?'

Dearlove chuckled grimly. 'Is it that obvious?

All right, we slept together a few times at university. God, it was the seventies. Everyone slept with everyone!' He tossed the stub of his cigarette aside, grinding it into the cobbles with the toe of his shoe. He hesitated, then reached into his pocket and lit up another one. 'That was before Diane met Ian, of course. We lost touch for a few years, as people do, but then our mutual interest in politics and current affairs drew us back together.'

'You wrote about similar topics.'

'Yes,' said Dearlove. 'That's why the publisher sent me an ARC of her book.'

'An ARC?'

'Sorry, that's publishing-world jargon. An advance reading copy or an advance review copy. It's what publishers send out to reviewers before the finished version of the book goes to the printing presses. They wanted me to read and review it so that I could give them a quote to put on the final cover.'

'*This book will make you rethink everything you know,*' recited Bridget, remembering what she had read on the cover of the book at the festival.

'You've read it?' asked Dearlove.

'Only the back-cover blurb,' she admitted. 'I've been a little preoccupied trying to find out who killed Diane Gilbert and why.'

Dearlove took a deep drag of his cigarette. 'What progress have you made in that direction?'

'That's really why I came to speak to you today,' she said. 'We're building up a profile of

Diane Gilbert, speaking to friends, family and colleagues.'

'Oh yes?' Dearlove inhaled deeply and blew out more smoke. He hadn't been exaggerating when he'd compared his smoking to a Victorian-era mill.

'But everything keeps pointing back to the same thing.'

Dearlove nodded crisply. 'A politically motivated assassination.'

'Exactly.' However much she had hoped to avoid that conclusion, Bridget couldn't ignore the evidence. 'So who do you think might have killed Diane?'

'On the basis of her political interests and research publications, I'd say that you're looking at MI5, the CIA, or even the General Intelligence Presidency.'

'Who?'

'The GIP is Saudi Arabia's primary intelligence agency, reporting directly to the king,' explained Dearlove. 'The Presidency has close ties to the *Mabahith*, the Saudi secret police, and also has links with the CIA. It's the outfit many people believe planned and carried out the murder of the journalist Jamal Khashoggi.'

'I see.' If Dearlove was right in his speculation, it was a daunting list of potential suspects. 'If what you say is true,' said Bridget, 'then doesn't that also make you a potential target? After all, you cover a lot of the same topics in your newspaper articles that Diane wrote about in her book. Have you received any death threats?'

Dearlove laughed mirthlessly, smoke billowing out through his nostrils. 'Death threats? Sure. I'm a journalist. There's always some nutcase on Twitter who wants to see me dead. But I'm just a cynical old hack and I don't pay any attention to that kind of thing. If some government agency really wanted me dead, they could stick a poisoned umbrella tip into me right now, and there's nothing that you or I could do to prevent them.'

Bridget glanced around. Fortunately, the only umbrella in sight belonged to a tour guide who was pointing the potentially lethal item skywards and corralling his flock to follow him towards the gates of All Souls.

Dearlove finished his second cigarette and threw it onto the cobbles in disgust, stamping it out in a splutter of embers. 'Can you tell me how she died? I keep thinking of her, all alone in that big empty house of hers, trying to picture her in her last moments. Was it a very violent death?'

Bridget was reluctant to reveal any details about the investigation to Dearlove, but given that he was also a potential target, she figured he had a right to know. 'We think that Diane may have been given a fatal injection.'

'Really?' He took a moment to digest the news. 'Well, that just confirms my suspicions. How many organisations would have the capability of carrying out that kind of murder, especially while the target was under police protection?'

'So what do you suggest I do?' Bridget knew she was getting out of her depth. So far Grayson's efforts to make progress through official channels had turned up nothing. She needed to find another way forward.

'Seriously? Forget it. Walk away. None of the groups I mentioned to you are ever going to admit anything. And the minute you start investigating the British security services, you'll be shut down. The Deep State won't allow you to get close.'

'If you don't mind me saying so, Michael, you're beginning to sound a little paranoid.'

He grinned. 'Mock me if you like, but don't say I didn't warn you.'

'What I was hoping,' said Bridget, 'was that you might be able to help me. What I really need is a way in.'

His eyes narrowed in suspicion. 'You want me to give you a contact?'

'Don't journalists have all the best sources?'

'We prefer to keep them to ourselves.'

'But if you want me to properly investigate Diane's death...' She let the sentence dangle, like a hook on a rod.

Dearlove studied her face, perhaps weighing up whether he could trust her. 'All right,' he said at last. 'Leave it with me. I'll get you a name. For Diane's sake.'

'Thank you,' said Bridget, giving him her card. They had completed a full circle of Radcliffe

Square and were now back on Catte Street, near the festival marquee. Booklovers were entering and leaving the tent in an almost constant flow.

Dearlove pocketed her card and waved farewell, before turning back. 'While I work on getting you a contact, perhaps you should begin by looking a little closer to home.'

'Meaning?'

'Diane's boss at the Blavatnik. Everyone knows that Al-Mutairi and Diane hated each other. He's in thrall to the Saudis and thinks that the British and Americans are the Middle East's best buddies. He has friends high up in the Saudi regime, and he'll know more than he's told you, you can count on that.'

And with that he strode away, leaving Bridget with the lingering scent of tobacco and a growing sense of unease.

CHAPTER 14

Bridget's phone rang as she was walking back to her car, and Ffion's name flashed up on the screen. She answered immediately, glad of a distraction from the world of international espionage and intelligence agencies.

As always, the Welsh detective wasted no time getting to the point. 'Good news, boss, forensics have finished with Diane's phone and laptop.'

'That is good news. So how soon can you get hold of them?'

'Already have.'

'And?'

'I've haven't been able to get into the laptop yet,' said Ffion, 'but I've got access to her phone. I'm working through all her emails and messages.'

'Find anything significant yet?'

'Not yet. There are thousands to look at. I just wanted to let you know before I finished for the day.'

'Okay.'

It was unlike Ffion to make a call unless she had something of real significance to report.

Bridget waited.

'There was one other thing.'

'Yes?'

'One of the apps she used most regularly on her phone, apart from messaging apps, was an e-reader.'

'You mean for reading books?'

'Exactly.'

Personally, Bridget hadn't yet made the leap from paper to digital. It wasn't just with books that she lagged behind the times. Despite Chloe's constant urging for her to ditch her old music collection and embrace the world of streaming she was still unwilling to move on from CDs. She was clinging to the past perhaps, or putting her faith in physical objects that she could hold in her hands. Perhaps because of all she had lost in her life – her sister, her husband – that was understandable.

'So what kind of books did you find?'

Bridget recalled the heavily laden bookshelves in Diane's house, stacked full of political and other non-fiction books, and sensed that Ffion was about to reveal something surprising.

'Hot romance. Hundreds of books, all with covers featuring half-naked men with ripped torsos. You know the kind of thing.'

'Right,' said Bridget, who didn't, and for whom "hot romance" meant *Jane Eyre*. 'So I guess this explains the lack of reading material on Diane's bedside locker. She was secretly reading this stuff on her phone.'

'Guilty pleasures,' said Ffion, sounding amused.

It was yet another insight into Diane Gilbert's secret world. On the outside, in full command of her emotions. Underneath, a lonely woman with an unsatisfied craving for love. Ian Dunn had said that there had been no romantic relationships in her life since their divorce. Bridget was almost starting to feel sorry for the woman.

'Diane Gilbert liked to present herself as a heavyweight intellectual,' said Ffion, 'but behind the façade she was human, like the rest of us.'

Ffion was certainly right about that. Everyone had guilty pleasures and Bridget didn't need to gaze very deeply into her soul to reveal her own. Chocolate. Red wine. And double cream.

★

It had been a long tiring week, especially after working all day Saturday, and Jake was more than ready to head home for a quiet evening by the telly. If there was nothing much on, he might even pick up that book Ryan had lent him. You never knew – maybe there was something to this world of books that everyone was suddenly talking about.

'Come off it, mate,' said Ryan when Jake revealed his plans to him. 'It's Saturday night. Time to grab a few beers and let off some steam. Why don't you join me and Andy down the

King's Head? Even young Harry's agreed to come along.'

Jake had doubts. While it would be good to have some company instead of another night stuck on his own, the King's Head could get quite rowdy on a weekend, and he wasn't sure how much steam Ryan intended to let off. But he figured that if Andy and Harry were going to be there, it would probably be okay.

'Well, all right,' he said. 'Is Ffion coming?'

Ryan shook his head. 'I asked her, but she's already meeting someone. Some girl, apparently.'

'Marion, I expect,' said Jake, recalling the name of Ffion's new date.

Ryan cocked his head to one side. 'You know more than me. So forget about Ffion, it's a boys' night out for you. No escape.'

By the time Jake had packed away his gear and headed over to the pub, Ryan was already on his second beer. Jake bought himself a pint and a packet of crisps and joined him and the other guys at a corner table. Soon he was listening to a steady stream of Ryan's banter and ribald jokes, and beginning to relax. He sipped his pint and wondered where Ffion was, and what she was doing right now. If this Marion was a researcher at the university, she was probably just Ffion's type. Jake pictured a tall, slim blonde with a penetrating stare and a talent for turning men into blocks of ice. Another version of Ffion, in fact.

'Another round, lads?' asked Ryan, breaking into his thoughts.

'Not for me,' said Andy, finishing his drink. 'I need to get back to the wife and kids.'

'Me, neither,' said Harry, who was a teetotaller and had been drinking lime and soda. 'I want to fit in a session down the gym.'

Jake tore open the packet of salt and vinegar crisps, admiring Harry's self-discipline. It was no wonder that the young detective constable was so lean and trim. Yet all that fitness sounded like way too much hard work.

Ryan stared at Harry incredulously. 'You're going to the gym on a Saturday night?'

'Yes,' said Harry. 'I've got a slot booked for seven thirty. It's a popular time. Maybe you should give it a try yourself. You're putting on a bit of flab.'

Ryan examined himself, prodding at his belly in curiosity. 'This is not flab. I've just banked a few extra pounds ready for a rainy day.'

'Well, just saying,' said Harry, standing up to leave. 'Maybe you should try pumping iron now and again.'

'Nah, you're all right,' said Ryan. 'I'll stick to lifting pints.' He looked to Andy. 'Just another half?' he asked hopefully.

'Sorry. I don't want to be late back. Sally's got a home-cooked lasagne in the oven, and I don't want to miss that.'

'Right, lucky you,' said Ryan. 'If someone was cooking me a lasagne, I'd probably be rushing off too. If I want a lasagne, I have to microwave one from the supermarket. It's not the same.'

'You could learn to cook,' said Andy.

Ryan looked as if Andy had just suggested he take up the flying trapeze. 'Geez, what is it with all the advice all of a sudden?' He waved farewell to Andy and Harry, and went to the bar to get more pints in.

Jake didn't refuse. He might as well hang out with Ryan for a bit. It wasn't as if he had anything better to do.

Ryan returned to the table with a pint in each hand. 'So, to business,' he said, sitting down and passing one of the beers across to Jake. 'We need to sort out your love life.'

'What?' said Jake, coughing as he mis-swallowed a mouthful of beer.

'Romance,' said Ryan. 'That's what's missing from your life, and it's time we got it sorted. You've had more than enough time to get over your break-up with Ffion, and in any case my detective instincts tells me that she's already moved on. That ship has sailed, mate, so let's get you fixed up with someone new.'

'Who did you have in mind?' asked Jake warily. He glanced around the pub, wondering if Ryan had already fixed him up with a blind date. If he'd known that Ryan was planning this, he'd never have agreed to come out to the pub.

'Not who,' said Ryan, 'but how.' He pulled out his mobile phone. 'Internet dating.'

'You have got to be joking.'

'Me? Joking?' said Ryan. 'When does that ever happen? Seriously, mate, don't judge it till you've tried it.'

Jake took another swig of his beer, making sure that this went down the right way. 'And you're an expert, I guess?' Ryan might not like receiving advice, but he wasn't shy when it came to dishing it out.

'As it happens, I've had some considerable success in that area,' said Ryan. 'And I hate to see you being left on the shelf. Stay there too long, and you'll be past your sell-by date before you know it.'

'I'm not anywhere near my sell-by date,' said Jake. 'People don't even have sell-by dates. And anyway, if you've had such amazing success with internet dating, why are you in the pub with me instead of in the arms of some gorgeous woman?'

'An act of selfless charity on my part,' said Ryan. 'I am sacrificing the pleasures of my own Saturday night in order to get you some. Now, come on, get your phone out.'

Jake pulled his phone out of his pocket with a sigh. Ryan obviously wasn't going to let the matter drop, so he might as well play along. Anyway, maybe Ryan was right for once. Maybe this was the best way for him to meet someone. Had Ffion met Marion on an internet dating site? He'd never considered it before.

'This is the best app I've found,' said Ryan, showing Jake his phone.

Jake typed in the name of the app and his

screen was soon displaying pictures of happy, smiling couples, assurances of trust and safety, and the offer of thousands of potential partners. He was only looking for one.

'You just give them a few details about yourself,' said Ryan, 'and then sit back and wait for the matches to come flooding in.'

To be honest, it didn't look too hard. Jake selected "male" looking for a "female", gave his date of birth and said he lived in Oxford. He needed to submit a photograph of himself but he didn't have any recent ones on his phone.

'Give it here. I'll take a picture of you.' Ryan snapped a few shots, selected the best one and handed the phone back to Jake.

'How should I describe myself?' asked Jake.

'Normally, I'd say add an inch or two to your height, but in your case' – Ryan looked up – 'I don't think there's any need. Just say you've got a great sense of humour. Girls always go for that. Whatever you do, don't mention your musical tastes.'

'What's wrong with my taste in music?' Jake was quite proud of his taste in indie rock. Although, he recalled, Ffion had hated it.

'Trust me, mate,' said Ryan. 'Just don't go there.'

'Should I say that I work for the police?'

'I'd leave it out. You can always own up to it later if the relationship starts to get serious.'

'Own up to it?' said Jake. 'It's nothing to be ashamed of, and it's a big part of my life. Isn't it important to be completely honest from the start?'

'Blimey, if everybody's description was a hundred per cent accurate, we'd all still be single. Listen, think of this more like a marketing pitch than the bare truth. The trick is not to give too much away. It's better to be enigmatic.'

Jake had his doubts, but he followed Ryan's advice and within minutes his online profile was surfing the internet, in search of true love.

★

Marion Badeaux was in many ways different to Ffion. Where Ffion's hair was short, blonde, and clipped strictly into shape, Marion wore hers long in a heavy untamed mass of chestnut curls. Ffion's skin was pale in hue, whereas Marion's face and arms carried with them the sun-drenched heat of Southern France. Ffion's slender build also contrasted markedly with Marion's generous curves, and while Ffion liked to run long-distance and practise Taekwondo, Marion had a Gallic contempt for all forms of exercise. But while there were obvious differences, the two women shared many similarities too. They were both outsiders, for one thing.

Ffion had earned her outcast status while growing up bisexual in a small Welsh mining community, while Marion had been born into a conservative Catholic family in Toulouse, resulting in bitter rejection by her parents when she had come out as gay. They had both found Oxford to be a much more welcoming city than the places they had been born.

Unlike Ffion, who had dated both women and men – most recently, Jake – Marion had only ever been interested in girls. She'd known from a very young age that she never wanted to be with a man. And while Ffion had enjoyed only a very small number of tentative, short-lived relationships, Marion had been out with many girls, enjoying wild, ardent romances both in France and in England.

All this Ffion had learned on her very first date with Marion.

Marion, it had to be said, was very free with her opinions and her confidences. It was one of the things that Ffion loved most about her. When they were together there was none of the stilted conversation and awkwardness that had dogged her relationship with Jake. Words flowed effortlessly between them, and there were so many things that didn't even need to be said. They understood each other, wordlessly, and she could simply relax and be happy.

Dating a guy, by contrast, was a minefield of complications and difficulties. Ffion recalled her first tortuous exchanges with Jake, dancing around each other, uncertain who might make the first move, if either of them. It had taken her ages simply to admit to him that she was bisexual. Marion hadn't been at all surprised when she had told her about their messy break-up. 'This Jake sounds to me like every other man. They are all the same. Devils. Snakes. Men cannot be trusted. All women know this, so why do they deceive themselves?'

Ffion smiled to herself. Marion's views on men were unduly harsh perhaps, but it was hard to disagree with her when she spoke so passionately, and with such a colourful French accent. Her voice was sultry and seductive, and Ffion could happily listen to it all day. She thought of Jake's downbeat northern vowels, and of the deep rumbling gravel of his voice. Sometimes his thick Yorkshire accent had been like a foreign language.

'So, what are we eating?' asked Marion. Ffion had brought her to one of her favourite restaurants in Oxford, the Al-Shami in Walton Crescent, famous for its Lebanese cuisine.

'The vegetarian specials are good,' said Ffion. She was particularly fond of the artichokes and vegetables served in a delicious sauce.

Marion tossed back her long hair. 'For me, I am too hungry. I need meat. A mixed grill, I think. Kafta, kebab, chicken and lamb.'

Some things hadn't changed so much. Jake liked his meat too. But he was less adventurous than Marion. Curries were his favourite, and fish and chips, and of course his mother's Yorkshire puddings, which he had once described to Ffion in great detail. Vegetables had been more of a challenge for him, unless they were clearly identifiable as peas or carrots. Her thoughts lingered on Jake a little longer, and she recalled his great height, his ginger hair and full beard, his broad shoulders and strong hands. They had shared some good times together, as well as some awkward moments. Ffion was glad that they had patched up their differences after the break-up and were back on friendly terms. Jake was a nice guy and she hoped that he would soon find someone as nice as Marion.

They placed their orders with the waiter, then Marion reached her hands across the table to enclose Ffion's. 'This was a good place to come. Thank you for bringing me here tonight.'

'I'm glad you like it,' said Ffion. It was good to be sharing the places that she loved with the new love of her life. Marion wasn't into everything that Ffion liked – motorbikes, for instance, or running, or herbal tea – but there was plenty of time to win her over. For now, it was enough that they could talk so easily and that they could be themselves in each other's company.

'What shall we do later? Dancing? A nightclub? It's Saturday night.'

Ffion laughed at Marion's enthusiasm. 'We haven't even eaten yet.'

'You are right,' said Marion. 'But I want us to make the most of every moment together. Time is precious. Let's not waste any.'

'Of course,' said Ffion. 'But we've got a lifetime of moments ahead of us, haven't we?'

'Sure, naturally,' said Marion. 'A lifetime, of

course. But for now, let us live in the present. Who knows what the future might bring?'

CHAPTER 15

The next morning was Sunday, a day of rest. *As if*, thought Bridget, but she permitted herself a half-hour lie-in and a leisurely breakfast (although it wasn't the same without Jonathan's trademark scrambled eggs) before driving to the short-stay car park at Oxford station to await the arrival of Chloe's train from London. Her daughter had been away for three full days, and Bridget was missing her dreadfully. She had spoken to Jonathan again the previous evening, and he had helped to soothe her fraying nerves, but almost as soon as she'd finished the call, her problems had begun to close in on her again. When she was alone in the house, they had a habit of crowding in to fill the void, especially in the darkest hours of the night. She would be very glad to have Chloe back home, causing all her usual noise and disruption to the smooth running of the house, and generally helping Bridget to put her troubles into perspective.

The train came in on time and a minute later Chloe appeared, sauntering across the car park with a wide-brimmed hat on her head, laden with shopping bags, and dragging a suitcase on wheels behind her. Bridget jumped out of the car to greet her.

'Hi Mum!'

'Hi.' Bridget wrapped her arms around her in a big hug, or at least as far as she could with Chloe being so encumbered with shopping. 'Is everything all right?'

'Of course!' Chloe was breathless with excitement. 'I had the most amazing time.'

'It looks like you've been shopping.'

'Well, sure, Mum, that was the whole point of the trip.'

'Let's get everything into the car and you can tell me all about it. Just put everything on the back seat for now.' Bridget opened the car door and stood aside to allow Chloe to shove all her gear into the back.

As soon as they were moving, Chloe reached behind her and pulled out a bag featuring the logo of an expensive footwear brand. She lifted the lid off the box and extracted a pair of patent red leather stilettos with heels like skyscrapers. 'Look at these, Mum! Aren't they amazing!'

Bridget stole a quick glance at the shoes, then slammed on the brakes to avoid a double-decker bus that was lumbering round the drop-off zone outside the station entrance. 'Can you walk in them?' she asked.

'Of course I can. At least I'll be able to with a bit of practice. Tamsin showed me how to do it. They're just perfect for my dress.'

'Are they really?' asked Bridget, as she turned out of the station and into the flowing traffic on Frideswide Square. 'So what's the dress like?'

It was obvious that Chloe was bursting to tell her. 'Oh my God, it's just so amazing. It's in red silk, cut on the bias so it's really clingy, and it's cut away at the back in a plunging V, so obviously I won't be able to wear a bra with it, but it's designed with hidden support at the front which gives my figure a real boost.'

'It sounds...' Bridget was lost for words. If she was honest, it didn't sound at all suitable for a fifteen-year-old girl. 'Will it be warm enough?' she asked lamely.

'Oh, Mum, don't be such a frump. Who cares about being warm? Anyway, the wedding's in the summer. It'll be perfect. Have you chosen your outfit yet?'

'Not yet,' said Bridget. 'I'm a little tied up at work right now.' Oh God, what was she going to wear? There was no point trying to compete with Chloe in her figure-hugging, bare-backed silk gown. She might as well cover herself from head to toe in some shapeless garment that would hide the extra inches she'd added to her girth since Christmas. With luck, no one would recognise her. But that was foolish thinking. The last thing she wanted was Tamsin taking one look at her and thinking no wonder Ben had left her. She would have to make an effort, for her own sense of dignity. Maybe Chloe would be able to offer her some good advice.

She cast a sideways glance at her daughter. There was another thing – make-up. Subtly and expertly applied, but clearly visible nonetheless. It made Chloe look much older than her fifteen years. That was presumably another of Tamsin's influences. Bridget felt her own influence slipping further and further away.

They dropped the bags off in Wolvercote and then drove round to Sunderland Avenue to pick up Chloe's boyfriend, Alfie. After weeks of cajoling and dropping not-so-subtle hints, Bridget had finally persuaded Chloe to bring him back to the house a fortnight earlier so that she and Jonathan could meet him.

Bridget had been just as nervous as the young couple themselves, wondering what she'd do if Alfie turned out to be the unsuitable boyfriend that she had convinced herself he was. But she had been pleasantly surprised. Alfie turned out to be a delightful young man, if a little on the skinny side, with wavy dark hair that reached almost to his shoulders. He stood about a head taller than Bridget. 'Pleased to meet you, Mrs Hart,' he'd said, holding out his hand to her, and Bridget had been quite charmed. 'Call me Bridget,' she'd replied, beaming at him.

Afterwards, she'd had second thoughts. And third thoughts. Was he too polite? Had his politeness been nothing more than a cynical act? And, most worrisome of all, was the reason she'd found him so alluring because of his striking resemblance to her ex-husband, Ben? But

Jonathan, as usual, had dismissed her concerns. 'He makes Chloe happy,' he told her. And that was certainly hard to deny.

Today, for the first time, Alfie would be joining them at Vanessa's house for Sunday lunch. It felt like a big step, welcoming Alfie into the wider family, and Bridget was pleased that he had accepted the invitation. Knowing Vanessa, she'd have gone to extra trouble to cook something special for the occasion. Although, come to think of it, Vanessa always went to extra trouble. Bridget wasn't complaining. It would be the first decent meal she'd had all week.

She pulled up outside Alfie's parents' house in Sunderland Avenue – a white, detached 1930s house on the northern edge of Oxford – and waited in the car while Chloe went to fetch him. Bridget had met Alfie's parents briefly after dropping Alfie back home after his visit to Wolvercote. They were a little older than Bridget, but seemed nice. Alfie's father, Jasper, ran his own dental practice on the Banbury Road. His mother, Autumn, was a wildlife photographer who always seemed to be away in search of endangered species. Their demanding careers and laissez-faire attitude to child-rearing meant that Alfie had grown up with a lot of freedom. Too much, in Bridget's opinion. They were lucky that their son had turned out so well.

Chloe and Alfie emerged from the house after a short while, hand in hand. Vanessa, Bridget knew, would take one look at Alfie's skinny arms and torso and immediately serve him double helpings. She hoped he had a good appetite. Most teenage boys did.

'Morning, Bridget,' said Alfie as he and Chloe clambered into the Mini. He grinned cheerfully at her from the back seat.

'Good morning, Alfie.' Bridget could hardly complain about Alfie being over-familiar by using her first name. It was she who had invited him to do so. In any case, it was impossible to be cross with a boy who smiled so nicely.

Bridget drove the short distance to Vanessa's house in Charlbury Road, and parked on the drive behind Vanessa's Range Rover.

'Nice house,' said Alfie appreciatively, admiring the large, detached property that dwarfed Bridget's own modest abode. The house was even bigger and grander than Diane Gilbert's house on St Margaret's Road a short distance away. Vanessa's husband, James, ran his own highly successful, cutting-edge computer business, leaving Vanessa free to concentrate on raising the children, cooking the perfect roast and tending the garden. It was a lifestyle that Bridget envied from time to time, before reminding herself that she was hopeless in the kitchen and would hate to be cooped up at home all day.

'Just wait till you've tasted Aunt Vanessa's cooking,' said Chloe. 'She's the best.'

It was a fair comment, and Bridget was glad that Chloe was still happy to join her and

Vanessa for lunch every Sunday. The weekly occasion was a family tradition that Bridget hoped would continue for years to come. She just wished that Jonathan could be there too. Indeed, it was at a Sunday lunch at Vanessa's that Bridget had first met Jonathan – no chance meeting, but a result of Vanessa's matchmaking. Bridget had to admit that Vanessa had chosen well. Thankfully, Jonathan would be flying back the following day.

Once all the introductions had been made, Chloe took Alfie outside to look at the back garden, leaving Bridget alone with Vanessa and James.

'So, what's up with you?' asked James. 'How has Jonathan been getting on in New York?'

'It sounds like he's having a fabulous time.'

'And you?'

'So, so. To be honest, I've been feeling very alone with him and Chloe away.'

'You should have called me,' said Vanessa. 'That's what sisters are for.'

'Yes, I suppose so.'

'Is there something in particular on your mind?' asked Vanessa

Bridget knew she shouldn't discuss her work with her sister and brother-in-law, but it would be good to get her problems off her chest. She still hadn't had a chance to talk to Jonathan properly. She took a deep breath and plunged in. 'It's work. A new case. A writer was killed in Oxford after appearing at the Oxford Literary

Festival and it's my fault.'

'I heard about that on the news,' said Vanessa. 'But how can it possibly be your fault?'

'No doubt you've heard about the death threat? I was supposed to be protecting her.'

'Oh, I see. That is awkward.'

'It's more than awkward. It could be the end of my career.' Bridget felt tears welling up in her eyes, but she refused to let Vanessa see her cry. She wiped them quickly away. 'I know that you've never approved of my career choice, but you know how important it is to me. I spent years in the slow lane, working reduced hours while I looked after Chloe. I can't afford anything to go wrong now.'

'It wouldn't be the end of the world, would it?'

'I'm nearly forty, Vanessa. What else would I do with my life?'

'Well,' said James, before Vanessa could make any suggestions, 'the answer seems quite straightforward to me.'

'Really? What?'

'Get on with it. Solve the case.'

Bridget laughed dismissively at his matter-of-fact solution. 'It's not that easy. There are all kinds of complications involving national security. I'm treading on eggshells and I feel completely out of my depth.'

'You've solved difficult cases in the past,' said James. 'Just hang in there. I'm sure you'll make a breakthrough sooner or later.'

Her brother-in-law's faith in her was

endearing. Bridget just wished she shared it.

'Can Alfie and I take Rufus for a walk?' asked Chloe, returning from the garden. Rufus, the family's Golden Labrador, wagged his tail enthusiastically at the mention of his name and the word "walk". 'We'll be back in time for lunch.'

'Of course,' said Vanessa. 'Let me fetch his lead.'

'They just want to spend a bit of time on their own,' said Bridget, once Chloe and Alfie had been dragged out of the house by Rufus.

'Ah, young love,' said Vanessa. 'But I'm glad they've gone out for a short while. I wanted to talk to you on your own too.'

'What about?' Whenever Vanessa had something to discuss, it usually involved telling Bridget off, or offering her some unsolicited advice about how to run her life.

'Come into the kitchen. You can stir the gravy while I tell you.'

Bridget followed her in with some trepidation. She had never before been trusted with such an important job in Vanessa's kitchen. She accepted a wooden spoon and began to stir the aromatic brown sauce on the hob while Vanessa donned a pair of Cath Kidston oven gloves and checked the progress of the Yorkshire puddings. Satisfied that they were rising nicely and that Bridget wasn't about to ruin the sauce, Vanessa leaned back against her Smallbone cupboards and began to speak. 'It's Mum and Dad. I'm worried

163

about them.'

'Why? Has something happened?'

After a rift lasting many years, the barriers that had separated Bridget and Vanessa from their parents had finally been broken down during a family reunion at Christmas. Now Bridget was enjoying regular phone calls with her mum and dad and, although their weekly conversations were not long, she felt closer to them than at any time since they'd moved away from Oxford to retire to Dorset. Her father always said that everything was going well and then asked her about her work. Her mother would give a brief update on her state of health – new pills from the doctor, a check-up at the hospital – and then ask after Chloe and Jonathan. Bridget felt that she was pretty well informed about the state of things in Lyme Regis. But had they been hiding things from her? Was it possible that everything wasn't quite as rosy as her father claimed?

'Mum's health is not at all good,' said Vanessa.

'Well, yes,' said Bridget. 'I know that.'

Just before Christmas, their mother had fallen and sprained her wrist. She had become quite doddery and was no longer able to manage the stairs. And yet she was only in her seventies. How frail could she be?

'They gloss over the facts, but I've been doing my own research with the help of Dr Google. Her eyesight's going, you know. She has glaucoma and it's starting to affect her peripheral vision. That's why she keeps bumping into things and falling over.'

'I had no idea,' said Bridget. 'But can't that be treated?'

'Damage to the optic nerve is irreversible. She's taking eye drops now, which will hopefully stop it getting worse, but it's already too late to restore her lost vision.'

'I see,' said Bridget, then immediately chided herself over the tactless expression. Vanessa gave her a dirty look and Bridget immediately resumed her stirring of the gravy, which had lapsed momentarily.

'And she's on blood pressure tablets too. She's at risk of having a stroke or a heart attack. She's really not well at all. Dad pretends he's coping with everything, but it's getting too much for him down there. Lyme Regis is far too hilly for people of their age.'

Now Vanessa was sounding ridiculous. 'But lots of old people retire to Lyme Regis,' protested Bridget. The gravy was starting to bubble and thicken and she stirred it more vigorously to prevent any lumps from forming. She was beginning to suspect that Vanessa had assigned her the task so that she could be blamed when it went wrong.

She was wondering how she could extricate herself, both from Vanessa's hypochondria by proxy and also the burden of responsibility for the gravy, when her phone buzzed with an incoming message. 'I have to check this,' she said. 'It might be important.'

'Yes, of course,' sighed Vanessa, taking over the stirring of the gravy. 'It always is.'

Bridget studied her phone and found a text message from Michael Dearlove. After the previous day's conversation walking around Radcliffe Square, the journalist had fixed up a meeting for her with his contact at the Saudi Embassy in London. That was quick work. She was still waiting for Grayson to sort out something with MI5. Dearlove didn't give the name of his contact, but the meeting was scheduled for tomorrow at ten o'clock.

Bridget slipped the phone back into her bag with a smile. What had James advised her? To get on and solve the case? It looked like she might just be about to do that.

Vanessa handed her the tureen of gravy. 'You can carry this through to the dining room.'

'Did it turn out all right?'

'Yes,' admitted Vanessa grudgingly. 'Not bad.'

Perhaps there was hope for Bridget in the kitchen too.

CHAPTER 16

It seemed that every time one of Bridget's problems was solved, another appeared in its place. Chloe might be safely home from London, but Vanessa had planted fresh worries about their mum's state of health. Even so, Bridget couldn't allow herself to dwell on that now. She barely had enough time for a quick team meeting before she would need to dash off to catch her morning train to London. In the briefing room, she asked everyone to give a quick update on what they'd discovered so far.

'Jake, Ryan, you can go first.'

'We managed to speak to most of Diane's colleagues at the Blavatnik,' said Jake.

'It was the weekend, so some of them took a bit of work to get hold of,' added Ryan.

'A few of them reported hearing raised voices coming from the Head of Department's office a couple of days before Diane was killed. But no one thought anything of it at the time.'

'Really?' said Bridget. 'Why not?'

'Apparently, heated arguments between Professor Al-Mutairi and Dr Gilbert weren't that uncommon.'

'Did anyone say what the argument was about?'

'No one knows for sure,' said Ryan. 'It took place behind closed doors, and people were reluctant to listen in. But one person thinks he heard the professor threaten to fire Diane if she carried on the way she was. Everyone stressed how much Al-Mutairi is concerned about reputation. He doesn't want the institute to become associated with controversial viewpoints. Whereas Diane Gilbert seemed to go out of her way to embrace radical politics.'

'What about Professor Al-Mutairi himself? Did you ask him about the argument?'

'We would have, but he was away from Oxford for a meeting.'

'How convenient for him,' said Bridget. She turned to Ffion. 'How are you getting on with the phone and laptop?'

'Still working on the phone,' said Ffion. 'There's a lot to go through. But hopefully I'll move onto the laptop later today.'

'Good. Where are we with the toxicology report?' Bridget was met with blank stares. 'Okay, Ryan, I'd like you to get onto the lab and chase it up. Go over there in person if you have to, and make sure they're dealing with it as top priority. We need to know exactly what it was that killed her.'

'Righto, ma'am,' said Ryan.

'And Jake, could you check out Diane's bank

accounts and phone records?'

'Sure.'

'Andy, have a dig around and find out all you can about Diane's political affiliations. Was she involved with any groups, formally or informally? Who were her connections? I'm particularly interested in radical organisations, the kind of people who want to overthrow the status quo.'

Andy made a note in his notebook and Bridget checked her watch. It was time to be off if she was going to catch her train.

'What about me, ma'am?' asked Harry.

'Just help out with anyone who needs it,' said Bridget, wishing she had something more definite for the eager young DC to get stuck into. 'I'm going to London now,' she told her team. 'I'm following up a lead from Michael Dearlove, the journalist who interviewed Diane Gilbert at the literary festival.'

They looked at her expectantly, obviously curious about what she would be doing in the capital.

'It's a long shot, but I'm going to speak to someone at the Saudi Embassy.'

Ryan whistled. 'Are you sure they allow women in there?'

Bridget wasn't sure if this was a serious question, or Ryan's idea of a joke. She hoped she wasn't about to cause a diplomatic incident. 'Well, I've got an appointment, so they better had.'

'Good luck, ma'am,' said Jake.

'Thank you.' She had a feeling she was going to need it. 'And if anyone makes any progress, text me.'

She supposed that she really ought to let Grayson know where she was going. This was presumably just the kind of thing he'd meant when he'd asked to be kept informed, but when she peered through the glass walls of his office, he was on the phone, and she really didn't have time to hang around.

Twenty minutes later, as she hurried across the footbridge that led from the long-stay car park to the station entrance, she was suddenly filled with a sense of alarm. What if someone from the Saudi Embassy really had killed Diane Gilbert? She would be walking straight into the wolf's lair. Dearlove hadn't revealed to her the identity of his mysterious contact, but if the man she was about to meet knew enough to be of any use, he was almost certainly involved in the plot himself. Jake's solidly reassuring presence came into her mind, and she wished that she'd had the sense to bring him with her. But it was far too late for that now. Her train would be leaving Oxford in five minutes.

CHAPTER 17

The Royal Embassy of Saudi Arabia was located on Charles Street in the heart of Mayfair. The grand, Palladian-style building with its perfect proportions and symmetrical design ranged over three floors with huge Venetian windows and a double-layered pillared portico that looked out onto formal flower beds and immaculate lawns. Bridget couldn't help but be reminded of a tiered wedding cake. The impending marriage of Ben and Tamsin was still obviously playing on her mind. In front of the white-painted building, the green flag of Saudi Arabia fluttered gently from a flag pole, but the wind wasn't strong enough to lift it high.

Bridget had arrived just in time for her appointment, having taken a taxi across town from Paddington station. She was slightly surprised to discover two uniformed British police officers on duty outside the gates to the embassy. The officers were wearing black bulletproof vests and were armed very visibly with automatic rifles. Bridget approached them and showed her warrant card. 'Any trouble here?' she enquired.

'Just routine, ma'am,' said the senior officer, a sergeant. 'Part of our normal protection duties here in the capital. Nothing to be concerned about.'

Bridget nodded, hoping that was true. She wondered if the officers' presence had anything to do with Diane Gilbert's death, but decided that it was probably just normal. London was permanently on heightened alert for terrorist incidents these days. It was reassuring to know that friendly forces were stationed immediately outside the embassy, although she knew they had no legal power to enter the grounds or the building, even to prevent a crime taking place. Once inside, Bridget would be entirely on her own, and at the mercy of a foreign power.

Taking a deep breath, she stepped through the metal gates that led from the street and made her way to the grand entrance.

While the exterior of the building was classically refined, the reception hall of the embassy was – in Bridget's opinion at least – excessively ornate, with polished marble floors, an ornamental ceiling formed from scrolling and curving plasterwork, and gilded touches applied to any surface that may have felt left out of the general opulence. A young woman wearing a dark jacket, her hair covered with a scarf, sat behind the mahogany desk, and two men in black suits stood on guard beside the front door. There was no doubt in Bridget's mind that these men were armed.

'Welcome.' A tall, olive-skinned man dressed in a well-cut suit strode across the marble floor to greet her. His hair was black and glossy, and he sported a neatly-trimmed beard. 'Ms Hart, I presume? How good of you to come.'

'It's Detective Inspector Hart.'

'Of course, forgive me.' The man's manner was gracious, almost servile, but when he requested, in the politest possible tone, that she switch off her mobile phone and hand it over "for her security and comfort", there was a steel in his voice that made it clear he would not be argued with.

Bridget complied with his request. Then, divested of her only means of contact with the outside world, she followed the man – who had not given his name – past marble pillars, crystal chandeliers, and yet more gold leaf, to a room where two high-backed chairs upholstered in silk brocade were arranged either side of an octagonal table whose dark wood was inlaid with geometric patterns. The effect was exquisite.

Bridget felt that an appreciative comment might be in order. 'What a beautiful table,' she said, picking out the one detail in order to avoid being totally overwhelmed by her palatial surroundings.

'Yes,' said her host. 'It is made from ebony inlaid with mother-of-pearl and tortoiseshell, and dates from the Ottoman Empire. Please do take a seat.' He gestured to one of the chairs and

Bridget sat down, crossing her feet at the ankles and tucking her legs under the chair. Was this how prime ministers felt at their weekly audiences with the Queen? 'I have ordered tea to be served,' said her host.

As if on cue, a young man dressed in a traditional Arabic tunic and headwear appeared bearing a silver tray on which stood a tall silver teapot and two gold-leaf-trimmed glasses with handles. He set the tray down on the table, bowed, and withdrew without saying a word. Bridget's host filled the two glasses with deep amber tea and offered one of them to her. She accepted it and took a sip. The drink was hot, strong and very sweet, just what she needed.

'Thank you for agreeing to meet me,' she said.

He regarded her with eyes like deep, dark pools. 'Not at all. We are honoured to be able to help our British friends.' His lips expressed gratification, but the eyes did not change. 'I understand that you have questions regarding the death of the academic and writer, Diane Gilbert.'

'Yes, that's right.'

Her host's lips twisted down in obvious displeasure. 'Diane Gilbert was not a friend to Saudi Arabia. Nor to your own country. She was, in fact, an enemy of the state.' The smile returned. 'Of course, she is not the only person in the world to voice criticism of the close relationship between our two governments, and in any case, that is no reason to wish her dead.

We were deeply sorry to learn of her death.'

'You were?' asked Bridget.

'Of course. Death is always a tragedy, but one that is natural and unavoidable.'

'In this case, we believe that Dr Gilbert's death may not have been natural.'

'Indeed? What reason do you have to be suspicious?'

The man was clearly fishing for information, but Bridget wasn't going to reveal how much – or how little – she knew. 'It is the job of the police to investigate all such deaths.'

The man's smile broadened. 'Of course.'

'Are you aware that Dr Gilbert received a death threat shortly before her death?'

Her host's dark eyebrows rose, expressing surprise. 'How could I possibly be aware of such a fact?'

Bridget held his gaze. 'The threat made reference to Dr Gilbert's new book, which as you know revealed information about the supply of arms to your country.'

'A legitimate trade, sanctioned by your own government.'

'You know nothing about who killed her?'

Her host's smile dimmed, and a look of disappointment took its place on his face. 'I believe that you do me a great injustice by asking such a question, Detective Inspector. Whatever you may have heard, my country is not in the business of making threats to foreign citizens, much less acting on them.' He sipped his tea then returned his glass to the tray and steepled his long fingers beneath his chin. 'Inspector Hart,' he continued in a more conciliatory tone, 'I do understand why you felt it necessary to come here today, but I can assure you that the Kingdom of Saudi Arabia had nothing whatsoever to do with the unfortunate death of Diane Gilbert. Even supposing, hypothetically, that we had wanted to kill her, why would we have sent her a death threat? Would it not have been more efficient simply to carry out the killing without warning?'

That was, Bridget was forced to concede, a more logical way to act.

The man smiled again. 'Perhaps the threat was made by someone who intended merely to frighten Dr Gilbert. It might not have been sent by the actual murderer. Have you considered that?'

Bridget gave no answer. There seemed little more for her to say now that her host had so categorically denied that his country had any involvement in Diane Gilbert's murder. She finished her tea, thanked him once again for his time, and was escorted from the premises, collecting her mobile phone on the way.

Once the gates of the embassy clanged shut behind her, she paused and breathed a sigh of relief. She might not have learned anything very new from her visit, but she was glad to be outside again in a London street. It was possible that she had been fobbed off, but she was confident of two facts. First, that she had no desire to step foot inside the embassy building again. And secondly, that this was the only meeting she was ever going to be granted.

CHAPTER 18

Ffion wasn't in the habit of getting distracted at work, but it was hard to put thoughts of Marion aside. Their night out on Saturday had been great, and they had spent Sunday morning together too, walking through the University Parks and exploring its Genetic Garden, planted with all kinds of interesting species and hybrids. It had been a thoroughly beautiful weekend.

But Diane Gilbert's phone and laptop weren't going to give up their secrets unless Ffion knuckled down to some hard work and gave the task her full attention. She went to the kitchen to fetch herself a mug of her new favourite tea. *Yerba maté* was brewed from the leaves of a South American variety of holly tree. It had a smoky flavour similar to lapsang souchong, and gave a sustained energy boost, said to aid focus and concentration.

She carried it back to her desk and returned to the task of sifting through Diane's emails. She had divided the messages on Diane's phone into two categories: personal and work-related. The personal correspondence was mostly with her son, Daniel, her sister, Annabel, and her ex-husband, Ian.

The messages to her son were of most interest and seemed to reveal an imbalance in their relationship. On a number of occasions Diane had messaged Daniel to say that she would be in London for one reason or another, and did he want to meet up for lunch or afternoon tea? Her tone was always light and friendly, not expecting too much, just making the offer. But in every instance, Daniel had offered some excuse for not being able to see her – he had a meeting; he was snowed under at work; he was visiting a client in Essex. If he'd declined just one or two invitations, Ffion wouldn't have thought anything of it. But to turn down every invitation? The pattern suggested that he was deliberately avoiding her. Yet Diane had persisted with her efforts to meet up with him. Her behaviour suggested a powerful desire to win her son back, whatever the reason for his antipathy. Ffion made a note of her observation and moved on to the message thread with Annabel.

From these conversations, Ffion learned that Diane had enjoyed a much closer relationship with her sister than she had with her son. She and Annabel had met up frequently in Oxford for a coffee and occasionally for lunch, and had been regular visitors to each other's homes.

Despite the *yerba maté*, Ffion found her thoughts drifting to her own sister, Siân. She and Siân had never enjoyed a relationship as warm as

Diane and Annabel's, but they had kept in touch over the years, and Siân had been instrumental in bringing about the family reunion and reconciliation that had occurred this Christmas. Now Ffion had begun to talk more regularly with her sister, and hoped to visit her and her family again soon.

She shook her head, forcing herself to return once again to the task in hand. This new habit of losing focus was becoming a nuisance, and she was going to have to discipline herself better.

She moved on to the conversations between Diane and Ian. She was surprised to discover that they had met up now and again for coffee or lunch. Ffion couldn't imagine being on such friendly terms with an ex-partner. What could they have talked about? Daniel, possibly? But it wasn't as if he was a child and they had to discuss his schooling or childcare arrangements. More to the point, what did Louise, Ian's new wife, make of these meet-ups between her husband and Diane? There was no indication that Louise had been included. Ffion jotted down a couple of thoughts before turning to Diane's work-related messages and correspondences.

Diane's discussions with her colleagues were often esoteric and highly academic in nature and mostly beyond Ffion's understanding. But a string of emails from her boss at the Blavatnik stood out. Professor Al-Mutairi, it seemed, had been in the habit of raising concerns about Diane's papers and publications. His sustained attacks might even be described as a vendetta. In one particularly virulent message he had warned her that her new book was likely to create a political storm and urged her to withdraw it from publication. In a final message from Diane to her boss, which she had sent shortly after the argument that her colleagues had overheard at the institute, Diane threatened to expose the professor if he tried to take any kind of action against her. Ffion made a note.

Having reached the last of the messages, she put the phone aside and moved on to the laptop. This was where she expected to find out about the real Diane Gilbert. Text messages and emails might reveal someone's outward-facing persona, but it was the private contents of a computer that gave a glimpse into their soul. Ffion was buzzing with excitement at the thought of extracting the documents from the hard drive.

She powered up the laptop and waited for the login screen to appear. As expected, it was password protected. Ffion had a few goes at guessing the password, before reaching for her trusty alternative. A USB cloning device. She plugged the pocket-sized gadget into one of the laptop's spare ports and waited for the machine to boot up. Her handy device would bypass the laptop's operating system and make a copy of all its data so that she could examine it on her own computer. The process didn't take long. By the time she had refreshed her mug of tea, a cloned copy of Diane's data was waiting for her and she sat down to peruse it at her leisure.

Within seconds her hopes were dashed. The data on the laptop was encrypted. Without knowing the password, there was nothing she could do to access the files on the drive. From beyond the grave, Diane Gilbert had slammed the door in her face and bolted it firmly shut.

CHAPTER 19

As Bridget headed along Charles Street in search of a taxi or an underground station to take her back to Paddington, she switched her phone back on, hoping to see some updates from her team. But there was nothing from Ffion, Jake, Ryan or Andy.

What she did see was a message from Chief Superintendent Grayson.

Her heart skipped a beat. Was he angry at discovering that she had dashed off to London without informing him first? If so, she was ready with her defence. If she'd hung around at Kidlington waiting to speak to him, she'd have missed her train, and she didn't think her contact at the Saudi Embassy would have looked kindly on her arriving late. But whether Grayson would see it that way was another matter. She paused on the street corner to read what he had written.

To her surprise, the terse message was neither a reprimand nor a summons to return immediately to Kidlington. Instead, Grayson had made good on his promise to fix her up with a meeting at MI5. He had secured an appointment for her to speak to someone in – she checked her watch – precisely twenty minutes. Oh God, how was she going to get from Mayfair to Westminster in such a short amount of time?

She turned into Curzon Street and was amazed to find that luck was with her. A black cab was just about to move off after dropping a passenger outside the Curzon Arthouse Cinema. She ran into the road and flagged it down before it could drive off.

'MI5, Millbank, please,' she called. 'As quickly as you can.'

The driver's jaw dropped open. 'I've been waiting my whole life for someone to say that to me. Hop in, darling.'

Bridget clambered breathlessly into the back, ignoring the sexist endearment. Now was not the time. The cab was on the move before she had even strapped her seat belt on.

'Grosvenor Place is blocked right up with roadworks,' said the cabbie. 'So we'll have to take the tourist route. But don't worry, I know these streets like the back of my own hand.'

There was no point arguing. London cabbies were a law unto themselves. Although technically, Bridget supposed, she was the law. But she would just have to trust that the driver knew where he was going. She tried to relax as the taxi flew down Constitution Hill and circled around Buckingham Palace. The Royal Standard was fluttering in the breeze from the top of the flag pole, indicating that the monarch was in residence.

Bridget studied the map on her phone to see how far away they were from the MI5 offices at Millbank. It shouldn't take too long if they turned down Buckingham Gate, but to Bridget's frustration, the driver was heading up The Mall towards Trafalgar Square, a distance twice what she had expected. She rapped on the glass window that separated her from the front of the cab. 'Where are you going?'

'Trust me, love. This is the quickest route.'

Bridget had little choice in the matter, so she sat back and tried to focus on the meeting ahead. Grayson's message had contained scant information about who exactly she was supposed to be meeting, or what they might be able to tell her.

Soon they were passing beneath one of the three great archways of Admiralty Arch, circling the roundabout at the southern end of Trafalgar Square and heading down Whitehall, past Big Ben and the Palace of Westminster. The cabbie hadn't been lying when he'd said they'd take the tourist route. From the Foreign & Commonwealth Office, past Downing Street to the Houses of Parliament, here was the heart of the British government set out in all its power and glory. The "deep state" according to Michael Dearlove. The very institutions that Diane Gilbert had railed against for all of her adult life. Was it the British state – or its security service – that sanctioned her untimely death?

Bridget shivered at the thought as the taxi finally pulled up outside an imposing stone building on the bank of the Thames.

She paid the driver and tipped him generously. Despite the many detours, he had succeeded in delivering her to the doors of MI5 – or the Security Service to give the organisation its proper name – just in the nick of time. She smoothed down her hair, took a deep breath, and looked up at the huge, square building in front of her.

Thames House was vast and imposing, like one of the great edifices that lined Red Square in Moscow. But being in London, there was no room for a grand open space to offset the building's bulk. Rather, the office block was positioned on a main road running right along the side of the Thames. The river glinted pewter in the spring sunshine, and one of London's many river buses chugged past, ploughing furrows in the water as it carried passengers downstream towards Canary Wharf and Greenwich.

Bridget located the main entrance to the building and hurried inside. For the second time that day, she was obliged to switch off her mobile phone. This time, however, she was issued with a key to a wall-mounted storage locker where she was able to secure it for the duration of her visit. A security guard then directed her towards a security capsule. She stepped inside and the capsule doors closed behind her. When she emerged on the other side, a man and a woman were waiting for her.

'Inspector Hart,' said the man, stepping forwards to shake her hand. 'Welcome to Thames House.'

The woman nodded at her, but remained silent. They were both dressed in anonymous, dark suits, and could have been accountants or bank managers. Or paid assassins.

'Who do I have the pleasure of meeting?' asked Bridget.

The man smiled. 'John.'

'Jane,' said the woman.

'I see,' said Bridget. 'Do you have business cards?'

'This way, please,' said "John", ignoring her question.

They took her up in a lift to the seventh floor then led her along a faceless corridor marked with door after closed door, before finally ushering her into a meeting room. The room housed a long table marked with circular stains from coffee mugs, a dozen chairs, and little else. It was very different from the Saudi Embassy. But it did offer a splendid view of the river, the glass and steel developments rising up on the opposite bank and, nestling amongst the trees just beyond Lambeth Bridge, Lambeth Palace, the official London residence of the Archbishop of Canterbury. Bridget suspected she was going to need some divine intervention if she was going to get anywhere with these people.

Once they were seated, "Jane" spoke for the first time. 'I would like you to understand that this meeting is strictly off the record. Nothing you hear from us today will be admissible as evidence in court, and if pressed we shall issue a denial of anything you claim. We are able to discuss the circumstances of the murder of Dr Diane Gilbert, but we will not be able to comment on any other matters. Is that clear?'

Bridget responded in her politest, most detached tone. 'Entirely clear.'

'As you no doubt already know,' continued the woman, 'the remit of the Security Service is domestic counter-intelligence and international counter-terrorism where it threatens the security of the UK.'

'You mean spying on our enemies,' said Bridget.

Jane stared back at her impassively. The man glanced at his watch.

Bridget tried a less antagonistic approach. 'Is it possible that Diane Gilbert may have been considered a threat to national security?'

This time John answered. 'Dr Gilbert was a person of interest to us. Somebody with her background and activities would always attract our attention.'

'What can you tell me about her activities?'

'What do you already know?'

God, it was hard work talking to these people. Like playing poker, and Bridget had never been any good at card games. They clearly had more practice than her at this particular game, and Bridget had no option other than to lay her cards on the table. 'As a young woman, Diane Gilbert was arrested at Greenham Common for repeated breaches of the peace. In later life she conducted research into areas of policy relating to British and American arms exports to the Middle East. Shortly before her death she wrote a book which, to put it mildly, doesn't portray the British government in a favourable light and puts at risk contracts worth billions of pounds.'

'She was also an active member of CND, the Campaign for Nuclear Disarmament,' volunteered Jane.

Bridget felt as if she'd been thrown a crumb. The news was hardly surprising given Diane Gilbert's political views. Probably all the women at Greenham Common were members of CND. That was the point. She waited to see if any further information would be offered, but John and Jane had nothing to add. Bridget was damned if she had come all this way just to learn something she had already worked out for herself. 'Given Diane's political background, her research interests and the fact that she had written a deliberately contentious book,' she said, 'not to mention the fact that she had received a death threat, I have to consider the possibility that her death was a politically motivated assassination.'

She waited to see what effect that would produce.

'What did your contact at the Saudi Embassy have to say to that theory?' asked John.

Bridget tried to hide her surprise. She had said nothing about her visit to the embassy. No one knew about it apart from her own team – and Dearlove. 'How did you know about that?' she demanded.

'It's our job to know.' Was that amusement playing on John's lips?

The woman remained as sour-faced as ever.

'The Saudis denied any involvement,' said Bridget.

'What did you expect them to say?' asked John, giving her a patronising smile.

'Not much,' admitted Bridget. 'But so far you've told me even less than they did. I came here hoping for some assistance. May I remind you that a British citizen has been murdered. How does the murder of a civilian rate as a threat to domestic security?'

She could tell that her accusation had finally hit the mark. John opened his mouth to speak, but Jane raised her hand to stop him. 'We are doing our best to assist you, Inspector Hart. But perhaps you aren't asking the right questions.'

'What question should I be asking?'

But that only resulted in a shake of the head.

Bridget tried again. 'Is it your belief that the Saudi security services played any part in Diane's murder?'

'If we had any evidence to suggest that possibility, we would be conducting our own investigation.'

'And are you?'

'I can't answer that question.'

'Then,' said Bridget, 'is it possible that the British Security Service had any involvement in her death?'

Jane was ready with her answer. 'Contrary to popular belief' – she cast a disdainful look in Bridget's direction – 'our officers are strictly prohibited from breaking the law. So it would be an impossibility for us to have carried out a murder or to have engaged in any kind of illegal activity.'

'I see,' said Bridget. The answer was the clearest and most definitive response she had been given this entire day, and she guessed that it was the best she could hope for. It was just as she had expected all along – an outright denial of any involvement by the Security Services in an extra-judiciary killing. Effectively a brick wall placed in her path.

'On the other hand,' added John, 'sometimes our informants take matters into their own hands.'

'Your informants?'

'Sometimes known as agents. Members of the public acting informally on our behalf as intelligence gatherers. They engage in covert activities and report back to us on an *ad hoc* basis.'

'And do you have an informant in Oxford?'

'I'm afraid that we couldn't possibly

comment. To do so would compromise our operations and endanger our agent. If there was one.'

Jane rose to her feet, scraping back her chair loudly. 'I think we're done here.'

John also stood up, and Bridget was obliged to follow suit. Game over. She wasn't sure how well she'd played, but the odds had been stacked against her from the beginning. 'If I have any further questions, can I contact you again?' she asked as they descended to the ground floor.

'No, I'm afraid that would not be possible,' said John. 'But it was very nice to make your acquaintance.' He shook her hand as he led her to the security gate. As before, Jane made no attempt to do the same.

★

'Any luck yet, mate?'

Jake looked up from his computer where he'd been entering his notes into the HOLMES database. 'Huh?'

'Got any dates lined up?' said Ryan, seating himself on the edge of Jake's desk and dislodging some papers onto the floor.

Jake reached down in irritation to pick them up. 'Careful where you park your fat arse. And keep your voice down, will you?' He glanced in Ffion's direction, but she was away from her desk for the moment. 'I thought you were asking if I'd solved the case.'

'Nah, I'm asking about the important stuff.'

Jake logged out of the database and shut down his computer. It was obvious that he wasn't going to get any more work done today. 'Believe it or not, I've had a few responses already.'

'You sound surprised.'

'Well...' Actually Jake was quite amazed by how quickly his profile had attracted attention. He'd hoped that maybe one or two girls might get in touch, but to have garnered several replies from attractive women so quickly... well, it was good for a guy's self-confidence, wasn't it?

'I told you it worked,' said Ryan smugly. 'So, have you fixed up any dates?'

'Not yet. I need to consider them all carefully before I make my decision.'

Ryan let out a sigh, and Jake could tell that more advice was coming his way. 'No, no, you've got it all wrong. You don't want to spend ages thinking about it or they'll assume you're not interested. There's no need to make any decisions. Just reply to all of them.'

'All of them?'

'Yeah, start with a bit of chat, then hit them up with an invitation to go out. These girls get a ton of attention. If you're too slow, you'll miss your chance.'

'But how can I invite them all out? What if they all say yes?'

'Try a different one each night. That way you'll soon find out who's right for you.'

Ryan leaned back casually, knocking some

more papers off the desk. He looked like a man who knew what he was talking about. But Jake wasn't so sure. Was this why Ryan had never settled down with anyone despite claiming to have loads of dates?

'Here, pass your phone over, let me have a look.'

Reluctantly, Jake handed over his phone. Ryan opened up the app and started scrolling through the results. 'What about her?'

The first woman who'd responded was a raven-haired, pale-skinned girl whose eyes were loaded with heavy black mascara and eyeliner. She claimed that her name was Winter.

'She looks pretty scary.'

Ryan resumed his scrolling, flicking lazily down the list with his thumb. 'What about this one? She says she likes a guy with a great sense of humour. Sounds like fun. She looks nice too.'

'Show me,' said Jake.

The photo showed a woman with blonde, wavy hair that reached to her shoulders. Her full lips were curved into a generous smile.

'Her name's Tilly,' said Ryan.

'That can't be a real name, can it?' asked Jake.

'It's probably short for something. Matilda, Natalie, Tallulah… why don't you fix up a date with her and you can ask her yourself?'

'I don't know…'

'You've got nothing to lose.'

Jake glanced over at Ffion's desk again. It was still empty. As was his social diary. Ryan was right – he literally had nothing to lose. 'Oh, go on then,' he said. 'I'll send her a message. See if she wants to meet up for a drink.'

He took his phone back and dashed off a message before his courage failed him. It was easier than asking a girl out in person, but his fingers still trembled as he tapped out the words. The idea that she might reject him was suddenly terrifying – almost as terrifying as the prospect that she might accept. How long would he have to wait for an answer?

Her reply came before he even had time to put his coat on. She would love to meet him tonight. Five minutes later, a time and a location had been agreed – a pub on the Cowley Road not far from Jake's flat. There was just enough time for him to go home, have a shower, and get changed.

★

Normally Bridget would have liked nothing better than a day out in London, enjoying the hustle and bustle of the capital and passing an hour or two at a gallery or museum before calling in at a restaurant to round off the day. But this was a work day, and there had been no galleries or restaurants – no time for even a quick stop at a sandwich bar – and the hustle and bustle of the big city was simply exhausting. Her visits to the Saudi embassy and MI5 hadn't got her very far, but perhaps her expectations had been too high. What had she been hoping for? A signed confession? She should perhaps be glad that she'd managed to get in and out without anything terrible happening to her. She turned to look behind her, half expecting to see a shadowy figure dressed in a raincoat and trilby hat lurking down the street, but there was no one sinister, just the usual assortment of people you encountered in London.

She was stressed, tired and hungry, and needed to get home to Oxford.

She walked a little further, as far as the Tate and was wondering whether ten minutes spent browsing the Pre-Raphaelite collection might put her in a better mood, when her phone buzzed with an incoming message. She was delighted to find a text from Jonathan. He'd landed at Heathrow and was on the Heathrow Express to Paddington, from where he would catch a train to Oxford.

Bridget called him back straight away. 'Hi, it's me. Don't catch a train. I'm in London too. I'll meet you at Paddington.'

'See you by the clock?' said Jonathan.

'I'll be there,' said Bridget.

She made her way to the nearest underground station at Pimlico, and twenty minutes later she was standing under the famous three-sided clock on platform one as hassled commuters hurried towards the trains. Only the bronze statue of Paddington Bear, sitting astride his battered leather suitcase beneath the clock seemed at rest in the busy station.

When Jonathan emerged from the crowds, wheeling a small black suitcase, Bridget ran into his arms.

'Well, this is romantic,' he laughed. 'We just need a steam train and some orchestral music.'

'I've missed you.'

'I've missed you too. Next time you'll have to take time off and come with me. Are you hungry?'

'I'm starving.'

'Come on then,' said Jonathan, taking her hand. 'I know the perfect Italian restaurant in Soho. Their tagliatelle with truffle cream sauce is to die for.'

CHAPTER 20

'Before I go into details about my trip to London yesterday,' said Bridget, 'does anyone have any updates for me?'

She was still feeling full after the previous night's dinner in Soho. The restaurant had been tucked away in the maze of streets off Shaftesbury Avenue. Over delicious bowls of pasta, rich chocolate dessert and a bottle of the house red, Jonathan had told her about his time in New York and she had told him about the Saudi Embassy and MI5, without of course going into the details of the case. She had listened contentedly while he talked about the Metropolitan Museum of Art, the Guggenheim and the Frick Collection, and all the colourful characters he had met during his trip. They had finally caught a late train back to Oxford and Bridget had fallen asleep almost as soon as her head hit the pillow.

Now she was acutely aware that she had spent an entire day away from the office, and was keen to hear what progress everyone had made in her absence.

Ryan was first to deliver his news. 'We got the toxicology report back,' he said, waving a sheaf of papers in the air. 'Definitely no Novichok so we can rule out the Russians.' It was a bit too early in the morning for one of Ryan's witticisms and his remark was met with little more than a polite chuckle. 'However,' he said, pressing on undaunted, 'she was definitely poisoned. They found unusually high concentrations of phosphorous, magnesium and potassium in her blood. The guys in the lab were quite excited about it.'

Bridget raised a querying eyebrow.

'Yeah,' said Ryan. 'They'd never seen that particular combination before. Magnesium poisoning is extremely rare because the kidneys normally remove it from the bloodstream, but in very high quantities it can cause cardiac arrest. Potassium can also lead to heart failure in very high blood serum concentrations, so a combination of magnesium and potassium injected directly into the heart... well, that would be very nasty.'

'And phosphorus too, you said?'

'Yeah. They weren't too sure about the effects of that. But they were confident that the three substances mixed together would make a deadly cocktail, with almost instantaneous results.'

'Which helps to explain why Diane was still in her bed when we found her,' said Bridget. 'She didn't have time to move, or even to scream for help.' It was yet another indication that the attacker had known exactly what they were doing. 'Jake, how about you?'

Jake was sitting at the back of the room, his hands wrapped around his Leeds United coffee mug. He had a distracted air about him, but looked up when his name was mentioned. 'Yes. I got hold of her phone records. There were no calls on the night of her death, but in the preceding twenty-four hours she made and received calls to her agent, her publisher, some of her work colleagues at the Blavatnik, and family. Oh, and also the journalist, Michael Dearlove.'

'I expect that was about the interview at the literary festival,' said Bridget. 'What about her bank accounts?'

'Ah, now that's where things get more interesting. Diane had one bank account, and I've worked through all her statements for the past year. She spent a lot of money. As well as regular restaurant bills, clothes, and so on, she's had a lot of refurbishment done to her house in the past twelve months. And it's not what you'd call cut-price work.'

Bridget recalled the high-spec décor of the house and her impression that it was showroom-new. 'Had she come into money recently?'

'Well, there was a payment from her publisher a month ago.'

'I suppose that would have been the advance for her book,' said Bridget. 'Enough to pay for all the work she had done on the house?'

'Not by a long way. She also gets a monthly salary from the university. I checked and it's in line with what you'd expect for a lecturer of her years of experience. Similar to a detective inspector's salary in fact, ma'am.'

'Enough to pay the bills, and put a little aside.' Bridget managed well enough on her income, but it certainly didn't allow her to splash out on expensive refurbishments of her house in Wolvercote.

'But there's something else,' said Jake.

'Yes?'

'She also received monthly payments from a company called Per Sempre Holdings. These payments vary from month to month, but they are way in excess of what she earned from the university or her publisher.'

'Do you have the bank statements?' asked Bridget.

Jake passed them to her. He had highlighted the mysterious payments in orange marker pen. Bridget's eyes widened at the sums of money. No wonder Diane Gilbert had been able to fill her kitchen with high-end appliances.

'I checked out her tax return too,' said Jake. 'These payments have been going on for several years, getting steadily larger. She declared them on her tax return as company dividends.'

Bridget looked again at the bank statements. 'What do we know about this Per Sempre Holdings?'

'The company's registered in the Cayman

Islands, so it's not entirely straightforward to get the details. I've put in a request for disclosure, but it's still pending.'

'*Per sempre* is Italian for "forever",' said Ffion.

'Italian?' Ryan's interest picked up. 'Do you reckon it's a mafia outfit?'

'Could these payments be a bribe?' asked Andy.

'Or was Diane Gilbert blackmailing someone?' suggested Harry.

'Let's keep an open mind on that, shall we?' said Bridget. 'At least until Jake's found out a bit more about this company.'

She turned next to Ffion, who had so far said nothing about her own progress. 'What's the news with the phone and laptop?'

'Not much,' said Ffion. 'Her phone is full of personal and work messages, as well as those steamy romance books I mentioned before.'

At the back of the room, Ryan sniggered and nudged Jake in the ribs. Jake immediately turned pink.

Ffion continued, taking no notice of the men's behaviour. 'Her emails and messages were mostly with family members and work colleagues.'

'Anything of particular interest?'

'Maybe. Maybe not. Diane made frequent attempts to reach out to her son, Daniel, but he always had an excuse for avoiding her. She doesn't appear to have had many friends, but she met up with her sister regularly, and her ex-husband too, which I have to say I find a bit odd. As for work, the exchanges between her and her boss at the Blavatnik confirm what we already knew – that there was a fair bit of hostility between the two of them.'

'And the laptop?'

Ffion's face fell. 'It's encrypted. That means I can't read any of the data on the hard drive unless I can work out the password.'

'Okay,' said Bridget. 'Well, keep trying.'

She sensed they were all waiting to hear about her trip to London, so she gave them a summary, relating everything that her anonymous and pseudonymous contacts had told her. Which, now she recounted it, was tantalisingly little.

'So they both deny any involvement,' concluded Jake.

'Well, they would say that, wouldn't they?' said Ryan.

'So does that get us anywhere?' asked Andy.

Bridget had been giving a great deal of thought to that same question. 'My contact at the embassy suggested that the death threat might not have been serious, but simply intended to frighten Diane.'

'So the person who sent her the letter may not have been the same person who murdered her?' said Ffion.

'It's a possibility,' conceded Bridget. 'Or it might just be a way of putting us off the trail. Another possibility is what MI5 hinted at. That a rogue agent might be operating in Oxford, and took it upon themselves to kill Diane.'

'They didn't admit to having an informant?' asked Andy.

'No, but I don't think they would have suggested it if an informant didn't exist.'

'So they were nudging you in the right direction without actually confirming the existence of an agent.'

'Yes. Or else nudging me in the wrong direction.' Bridget's introduction to espionage and counter-espionage had proven to be an extremely frustrating one. In that murky world, friends and foes were indistinguishable, and equally unhelpful. At least her contact at the Saudi embassy had been courteous. MI5 hadn't even offered her a cup of tea.

'So all we have to do is find the MI5 informant and we've solved the case?' said Andy.

'Professor Al-Mutairi at the Blavatnik,' suggested Ffion. 'He fits the profile. Well-placed, with lots of contacts. Sympathetic to the British government's policy in the Middle East. Directly opposed to Diane Gilbert's activities, and believed that she was bringing the Blavatnik into disrepute. After the argument when he threatened to fire her, she sent him an email to say that if he did that, she would expose him.'

'Expose him for what?'

'The message didn't say.'

'Well, he's certainly the most obvious candidate,' agreed Bridget. 'Al-Mutairi might have sent Diane a death threat to try to stop her from publishing her book, or he might simply have had personal reasons to want her dead. But if he is an MI5 agent, he's not likely to admit it, and neither will MI5.'

'What should we do then?' asked Jake.

Bridget smiled. 'Let's go and rattle his cage and see how he reacts.'

CHAPTER 21

'Inspector Hart, this is a surprise.'

This time, Bridget had arrived at the Blavatnik School without an appointment, aiming to wrongfoot Professor Al-Mutairi by not giving him advance warning of her visit. But if she had hoped to find him engaged in sending encoded messages to his MI5 handler, she was disappointed. Instead he was busy giving the yellow-flowering plants in his office their fortnightly feed using a tiny watering can with a long, thin spout. She had already forgotten the Latin name of the plants. Al-Arfaj, he had called them. They certainly weren't going to get too much water the way he was dribbling tiny amounts into their pots.

Bridget studied him closely. Was he a little less relaxed than last time? Was his charming manner a little more forced? 'I have some more questions to ask you regarding the murder of Diane Gilbert,' she said.

He replaced the watering can on the windowsill next to a bottle of plant food and gestured for her to take a seat. 'I assumed this wasn't a social call.' He kept his voice light, although he was unable to conceal an underlying trace of anxiety. He took his seat opposite hers and leaned back, interlocking his long fingers.

Bridget didn't allow him any time to get comfortable. 'Where were you on Thursday night? The night that Diane was killed.'

'Am I a suspect all of a sudden?'

'If you could just answer the question, please.'

'Of course. I worked late that evening. There was a paper I wanted to finish before the weekend.'

'What time did you leave your office?'

'I would say around ten-thirty. And then I walked back to my home on Walton Street.'

'Can anyone confirm that?'

'I'm afraid not. I live alone.'

'What about your neighbours? Might they have seen you returning home?'

'I doubt it. Student houses either side, you see. They're either out late or listening to loud music.'

'And no one saw you leave work?'

'I believe I was the last person to leave the building.'

So, no alibi. And yet the professor didn't seem overly concerned by the fact. He seemed to be relaxing as the interview went on. Bridget needed to pierce Al-Mutairi's polished exterior and find out what lay beneath. She had briefly glimpsed his anger during her previous visit. Now she tried to stoke it.

'A number of your members of staff have reported hearing you arguing with Diane in the days before her death.'

He nodded. 'That may be true. We often disagreed.'

'And yet you were her boss. Was shouting at her the appropriate way of dealing with a disagreement?'

Al-Mutairi refused to rise to the bait. 'If I raised my voice, I regret doing so. But Diane did just as much shouting as I did – more in fact. She was a very difficult woman to manage. She refused to see reason.'

'Did you threaten her?'

'I am not prone to making threats.'

'A witness says that they overheard you say that you would fire her.'

'They may have misheard. Or misunderstood. I would certainly not make such a threat.'

Bridget persisted. 'Following that meeting – or should we describe it as a "row"? – Diane sent you an email. In it she wrote that if you tried to fire her she would expose you. Do you recall receiving such a message?'

Al-Mutairi's face betrayed nothing. 'I seem to remember that I did. But I have no idea what she may have been alluding to. As I recall she didn't spell out what she intended to expose me for.' There was a glint of amusement in his eyes now.

Bridget changed tack. 'You've made it very clear that you didn't see eye to eye with Diane's political views. Do you think that she was a threat to national security?'

'Since you ask, yes. I think that Diane and her ilk are potentially harmful to the stability of western democracy.'

'Harmful enough that it's worth silencing them once and for all?'

'Now you're putting words into my mouth,' said Al-Mutairi, becoming nettled for the first time in the interview.

'How about sending a death threat as a means of frightening her off? Making her think twice about the line she was pursuing?'

'Knowing Diane as well as I do, I would say that for someone of her convictions and temperament, a death threat would most likely spur her on to take an even stronger line.'

'Are you sure about that? She was persuaded to accept police protection, so she must have been worried, even if she didn't like to admit it.'

Al-Mutairi shrugged. 'I don't know what she really thought about the death threat. But whatever she thought, I can assure you that it didn't come from me.' He looked at his watch. 'Now is there anything else? I'm meeting one of my doctoral students in five minutes.'

How convenient. But perhaps this was an unsubtle sign that he wanted her out of his office. Bridget remained in her seat. 'That still gives us five minutes. Now, it would help us with our enquiries immensely if you could provide me with a sample of your handwriting.'

His eyes narrowed, but he didn't query her

request. 'Very well.' He opened his desk drawer and reached inside, drawing out a pad of lined writing paper. 'What should I write?'

'Anything you like.'

'In English or in Arabic?'

'English, please.'

He picked up a silver fountain pen and wrote a few lines of flowing text in blue ink. When he had finished he slid it across the desktop towards her. 'Will this do?'

Bridget scanned the sheet of paper. It contained several lines of beautifully handwritten prose. She placed it into a protective folder and rose to her feet. 'Thank you for your cooperation, Professor Al-Mutairi. I'll see myself out.'

Outside his office she paused to read what he had written.

Out of suffering have emerged the strongest souls; the most massive characters are seared with scars. Khalil Gibran.

CHAPTER 22

Bridget dropped off the note that Professor Al-Mutairi had written, asking Jake to get it across to forensics as quickly as possible. No doubt she would have to wait until the following day before they could tell her whether Al-Mutairi's handwriting matched that of the death threat, and Bridget was tired of waiting for answers. The financial authorities in the Cayman Islands may be dragging their feet over disclosing details of the mysterious Per Sempre Holdings, but perhaps there was an easier and quicker way to unearth the source of Diane Gilbert's money. Bridget tapped the number of Diane's publisher into her phone and waited patiently for the call to connect. It was answered on the second ring.

'Jennifer Eagleston speaking, who is this?' In the background Bridget could hear traffic and the sound of pedestrians.

'Detective Inspector Bridget Hart. I was wondering if you'd be available for a chat? I have some questions to ask you about Diane Gilbert in regard to the murder investigation.'

'Sure. I'm still in Oxford as it happens. I've

been attending events at the literary festival. Actually, I was just on my way to grab some lunch. Would you like to join me?'

In her time as a police detective, Bridget had learned never to refuse an offer of lunch. 'Where are you planning to eat?'

'The Eagle and Child on St Giles'. Do you know it?'

'Of course,' said Bridget. 'I'll be there in fifteen minutes.'

The Eagle and Child, sometimes known locally by its affectionate nickname, *The Bird and Baby*, was one of Oxford's most famous and historic pubs. Dating back to the seventeenth century, its dark wood panelling and exposed beams exuded the comforting air of a bygone age. The narrow building was always packed, and in the days before smoking was banned in English pubs, a thick pall of smoke had been permanently suspended beneath the low, sloping ceiling. Nowadays it was the cosy fug of conversation that filled the pub's cramped interior.

Bridget found Jennifer seated at a table by the window, partially secluded from the rest of the bar by a decorative wood screen.

'I always make a point of coming here when I'm in Oxford,' said the publisher as Bridget sat down to join her. 'I love the atmosphere, and of course the literary connection is so fascinating.'

'J.R.R. Tolkien and C.S. Lewis,' said Bridget.

The pub was famous for having been the

watering hole of *The Inklings*, an Oxford writers' group which had included the creators of the fantastical lands of *Middle Earth* and *Narnia*.

'Precisely,' said Jennifer, beaming her approval. 'I can just imagine them sitting around a table, smoking their pipes, talking about elves and witches and good and evil. What wouldn't I give to go back in time and be a fly on the wall during one of their lunchtime gatherings? People like to think of writers as lonesome individuals slaving away over their manuscripts, but as a publisher I can tell you that writing is more of a collaborative process than people think.'

'I'm sure it is,' said Bridget, who couldn't imagine writing a whole book on her own. How long would such a mammoth project take? Months? Years? A lifetime?

They ordered food from the day's specials chalked on a blackboard behind the bar – fish pie for Bridget and Lancashire hot pot for Jennifer – then took their drinks back to the table.

'So, do you have other authors promoting books at the festival?' asked Bridget.

Jennifer glanced around the pub in an exaggerated cloak-and-dagger fashion. 'Keep this to yourself,' she whispered, 'but I'm hoping to poach a few names from rival houses. The festival brings lots of big name authors, agents and publishers together. It may look dignified to the public, but behind the scenes it can be a feeding frenzy.' Her phone buzzed and she checked it quickly before slipping it back inside in her voluminous tote bag. 'Sorry, that was just the sales department updating me on the latest figures for *A Deadly Race*.'

'Oh?' said Bridget, curious to find out what effect the news coverage of Diane's death might be having on book sales.

Jennifer didn't need much encouragement to divulge her trade secrets. 'I have to say that volumes are way ahead of what we expected. The publicity for the book has been fabulous. We've already ordered a second print run, which is almost unheard of for a book of this type by a new author.' She bent down and pulled out a copy of the *Times Literary Supplement* to show to Bridget. '*A Deadly Race* has made the front page of the *TLS* and it's going to be featured in the *New York Review of Books*. It should easily make the *Sunday Times* top ten, possibly even the *New York Times* and *USA Today* bestseller lists. It has a bestseller tag on *Amazon* for its category too.'

Jennifer's obvious glee at the book's sales figures seemed a little callous. 'I see,' said Bridget. 'And you put the book's success down to the fortuitous murder of its author?'

'Oh, don't look at me like that, Inspector,' said Jennifer. 'Publishing is a tough business. You might hear about debut writers receiving huge advances for their books, but those people represent a miniscule proportion of the whole. Most of the books we publish from new authors are loss-making. We rely on windfalls like this to keep the industry going.'

'I'm not sure that everyone would describe a murder as a "windfall". And don't you think it's a shame that Diane won't be able to write a sequel?'

'Well, even that isn't necessarily a problem,' said Jennifer breezily. 'With the help of a ghostwriter we could probably turn some of her research papers into a follow-up book. If there's demand, we can always find a way to meet it.'

The barman brought their food to the table, and they paused their conversation to tuck in. The fish pie was deliciously creamy and topped with the perfect mashed potato.

'Speaking of money,' said Bridget once her hunger was at least partially assuaged, 'we've been working through Diane's bank accounts and found a payment of five thousand pounds from your firm, paid last month.'

'That would have been the final instalment of the advance,' said Jennifer, demolishing her Lancashire hot pot. 'For non-fiction works, we pay one third when we sign the contract, the next third on delivery of the manuscript and the final instalment on publication.'

'So the total advance was fifteen thousand pounds?'

'That's correct.'

'And how long did the book take her to write?'

Jennifer frowned. 'By the time you factor in all the research, planning, writing, re-writing and final polishing, around three years, I should say.'

'So Diane earned fifteen thousand pounds for

three years of work?' Even without doing the mental arithmetic, Bridget was pretty sure that worked out at less than the minimum wage.

'Less her agent's fee,' said Jennifer. 'You think we should pay our authors more?'

'It's not for me to say,' said Bridget.

Jennifer smiled grimly. 'Like I told you, most first books by new authors make a loss for us. We take a big risk by making an upfront payment to the author, on top of the costs of printing the book. A lot of the time the book flops and we never see a profit, but if it succeeds then the author will earn royalties once they've earned out the advance.'

'And how long would that normally take?'

Jennifer put down her knife and fork and picked up her glass of sparkling mineral water. 'Sometimes authors never earn out their advance – and the publisher probably won't take any further books by that writer. That's why publishers are more and more reluctant to pay large advances for debut books. In the case of a book like *A Deadly Race*, under normal circumstances it might have earned out its advance in a year or two, but by then it would be at the end of its life. Bookshops don't want to hold onto old stock, they want to fill their shelves with the latest releases. So when last year's titles become too difficult to sell, any unsold stock gets returned to us to be pulped.'

Bridget winced at the thought of all those unwanted books being turned into pulp. Years of work and millions of words all gone in a sudden thrashing of blades.

'So most authors don't receive anything beyond their advance?'

'That's right.'

The world of publishing sounded far more cut-throat than Bridget had realised and she would never again be able to look at the literary festivals and bestseller lists without imagining the spinning blades of the threshing machines, and the disappointed authors whose careers had been consigned to the dustbin of history.

'Was there something specific you wanted to talk to me about?' asked Jennifer. 'I have another event starting soon.'

'Actually, yes,' said Bridget, setting down her cutlery and taking a drink of her lime and soda. 'As well as Diane's university salary and the payments from your company, her bank statements also showed payments from a company called Per Sempre Holdings.'

Jennifer looked at her blankly. 'What's Per Sempre Holdings?'

'I was hoping you'd be able to tell me that,' said Bridget.

'Sorry, I've never heard of it. Are these payments significant?'

'They're monthly payments of five figures,' said Bridget.

The publisher's eyes widened to huge circles. 'Five figures? You mean, in excess of ten thousand pounds each month?'

'That's correct,' said Bridget.

'I don't know what to say,' said Jennifer, shaking her head. 'I wish I could help you, I really do, but I've no idea what these payments relate to. They're certainly not from sales of her book.'

CHAPTER 23

'So how did it go, mate?'

Jake looked up from his plate of food to see Ryan sitting down opposite and unloading his tray. 'You mean my date?'

Ryan tore open a sachet of tomato ketchup and squeezed the blood-red contents over his chips. 'Of course I mean your date. Come on, tell me all about it.'

Jake put down his knife and fork with a clatter. He'd spent the morning immersed in work, trying to blot out the epic fail of the night before. He didn't need to be reminded of it over his lunch. The canteen was serving one of his all-time favourites – roast chicken, chips and beans. It was the meal his mum used to cook for him every Friday evening after football practice. He just wanted to be left alone to enjoy it in peace. 'Let's just say that it wasn't a great success.'

Ryan began shovelling food down his gullet as if it might be taken away from him if he was too slow. 'Why not? Tilly looked pretty damn hot in her photo. Was that her real name after all?'

'Short for Matilda.' Tilly's name had turned

out to be just about the only thing about her that was real.

'So, what was the problem?' asked Ryan, reaching for the salt and vinegar and dousing his food in them. 'Spill the beans.' He scooped up a forkful of baked beans and stuffed them in his mouth.

'The problem was that her photo was a little bit out of date. And when I say a little, I mean by about two decades.' When Jake had walked into the pub, nervous but hopeful, he'd wondered if he'd come to the right place. There was no one there who looked remotely like the fresh-faced young woman he was expecting to meet. The real Tilly had been closer to forty, and it was fair to assume that she hadn't spent the past twenty years on a strict diet. In fact her love of fun didn't seem to have done her appearance any good at all. 'She was twenty years older than I expected, and twenty pounds heavier.'

Ryan chortled and slapped Jake on the shoulder. 'Sometimes people aren't entirely truthful in their online profiles. But that's just to be expected. Everyone wants to present themselves in the best possible light.'

'So you can't trust what you read online?' He shouldn't have been surprised by this revelation, especially after the long session he'd spent trawling through Diane Gilbert's social media accounts.

'You just have to be more open to surprises, that's all I'm saying. Don't expect everything to be exactly as it says on the tin. Anyway, there's nothing wrong with older women. Experience can be a good thing. Was she as much fun as she sounded?'

'Oh, she was fun, all right,' said Jake, chasing his baked beans half-heartedly around the plate with his fork. 'She put away a whole bottle of wine, and hardly stopped laughing the whole night.' He cringed as he recalled the vivid details of his train wreck evening.

'So, what happened in the end?' enquired Ryan. 'Did you take her home?'

'Are you joking? I called a taxi for her and wished her goodnight.'

Ryan shook his head in disappointment. 'Mate, you could at least have walked her home and gone in for a coffee.'

Jake glared at him, his arms folded across his chest. 'She just wasn't the kind of woman I was looking for.'

'Well, never mind. That's the way it goes sometimes. At least now you know how online dating works, so you can try another one.'

'Another one? You're not serious?'

Ryan munched on his ketchup-and-vinegar-sodden chicken. 'You know what your trouble is? You're far too choosy. And if you don't mind me saying, someone in your position can hardly afford to be.'

'Is that right?'

'It is. So, here's what you need to do. Pick yourself up, dust yourself off, and keep trying until you get lucky.' Ryan jabbed his fork in the direction of Jake's plate. 'And if you're not going to eat those chips, I'll have them.'

★

Lunch at the Eagle and Child had been a pleasant way to pass an hour, but other than a rather hard lesson in the precarious economics of the publishing industry, Bridget couldn't say that she had learned a lot. There was no doubt that Jennifer's publishing house would benefit immeasurably from increased sales of *A Deadly Race*. But did that make Jennifer herself into a suspect? Bridget made a mental note to get Andy to check out the financial status of the publishing house.

She returned to Kidlington to see if there was any progress on the handwriting analysis or any of the many other outstanding tasks, but before she could quiz her team on progress she was intercepted in the corridor by Chief Superintendent Grayson. She tried to slip past him unnoticed, but a clearing of Grayson's throat told her that she was about to be subjected to another grilling.

'DI Hart. My office, please.'

She followed him into his lair and waited while he lowered himself into his leather chair. He didn't invite her to take a seat. 'So, outline your current thinking,' he said.

Bridget knew that she needed to tell a good

story, regardless of her own distinct lack of confidence in her ability to identify Diane's killer. 'At this point, sir, we're following a number of clear leads.' She summarised her visit to London and her hope that analysis of Al-Mutairi's handwriting might identify him as the author of the death threat. She also filled him in on the mysterious payments into Diane's account.

Grayson's pen was treated to a workout as she went over the various points, but the Chief Super's eyebrows remained resolutely in a straight line, even when she revealed the total amount that Diane had received from the company in the Cayman Islands. 'So, you still have no idea what the source of this money might be,' said Grayson, 'and so far only one suspect.'

The criticism felt rather unfair to Bridget. 'A strong suspect, sir.'

'Maybe. What about the toxin that was used to kill the victim?'

Bridget nodded, glad to be able to answer at least one of the Chief's questions unambiguously. 'A mixture of phosphorous, magnesium and potassium. The injection into the heart led to instant cardiac arrest.'

'Do we know where it came from?'

'No, sir.'

'Well, you need to find out.'

'Yes, sir.'

'Time's running out, DI Hart. If you don't make real progress soon, I promise you, I'll bring in Baxter to take over.'

★

After escaping from Grayson, Bridget made her way to the incident room. There, everyone was busy, but had little to report. 'Find out what's happening with that handwriting analysis,' Bridget told Jake. 'That's our strongest lead.'

'Yes, ma'am.'

She realised that she had raised her voice at him and immediately regretted it. Just because Grayson was piling the pressure on her, there was no excuse for her to pass it on to her team. One look around the office told her that they were all working as hard as they could, and the best thing she could do would be to get out of their way and leave them to it. She turned around and left the office, wondering how she could best use the remaining hours in the day.

The top priority in her mind, after confirming whether Al-Mutairi had penned the death threat, was to find out the source of the Cayman Islands money. Since Jennifer Eagleston had been unable to help, it made sense to ask the one person who might be in a position to shed light on the matter. Ian Dunn, Diane's ex-husband. After all, the academic had made no attempt to conceal her unexplained income, declaring it on her tax returns – hardly the action of someone embroiled in illegal activities. Perhaps there was a completely innocent explanation for the money. If so, they could forget about the issue and focus the investigation elsewhere.

When she arrived at the house in Headington, the silver Lexus Coupé belonging to the hospital consultant was parked outside, and a black Volkswagen Golf was pulling up behind it. Bridget parked on the opposite side of the road and watched as Daniel Dunn got out of the car, carrying a zipped, black document folder.

She opened her door and crossed the road. 'Good afternoon. I was hoping for a quick word with your father, but if you're here too, all the better.'

He regarded her warily, but nodded. 'All right. You'd better come in.'

He seemed rather flustered by her appearance. Tucking the leather folder under one arm, he inserted the key into the lock and grappled with the door handle. The folder slipped from his grasp and fell to the ground. Bridget picked it up and handed it back to him. He snatched it from her without a word.

Ian must have heard their arrival, because he appeared immediately in the hallway, removing a pair of reading glasses from his nose. 'Daniel, and Inspector Hart too. Any news?'

'Just more questions, I'm afraid,' said Bridget.

'In that case, let's go into the sitting room. Would you like a drink? I can put the coffee machine on if you like.'

Bridget gratefully accepted the offer and Ian disappeared into the kitchen.

Daniel sat on the sofa and Bridget took a seat opposite. He regarded her inscrutably, the leather folder balanced on his knees, his hands crossed protectively over it. 'So, no progress on my mother's death?' he asked.

'We're following up several leads,' said Bridget.

'Oh?'

'Perhaps we could wait until your father returns.'

'Oh, yes, sure.' He lapsed back into sullen silence.

'You've been out?' asked Bridget.

'To the solicitors. To see about the will.'

'Ah, yes.' So that's what his precious folder contained.

Ian entered the room with three coffees on a tray. He had gone to the trouble of arranging the cups on saucers and laying out a plate of Amaretti biscuits. 'Oh, I really shouldn't,' said Bridget, eyeing the golden, almond-scented domes that always reminded her so much of Italy. 'But I'm sure that one won't do any harm.'

'I'm sure it won't,' said Ian indulgently. He turned to Daniel. 'So, how did you get on with the solicitors?'

Daniel gave Bridget an irritated glance before replying. No doubt he would have preferred to discuss his business in private. Well, too bad. 'It was a useful first meeting. But they can't do anything about the will until after the inquest. Everything is going to be delayed because of the murder enquiry.'

'It's normal for a coroner's inquest to be held in the case of a suspicious death,' said Bridget. 'But the purpose of the inquest is simply to determine the cause of death, not to assign blame. The murder enquiry shouldn't delay matters.'

'Yes, well,' said Daniel. 'It's all very stressful.'

'Of course it is,' said Ian soothingly. 'But you're doing a good job. Mum would have been proud of you.'

Daniel shrugged indifferently.

'But the will is all in order?' asked Ian.

'Yes. The will is exactly as Mum said it would be.'

'So you inherit everything?' pressed Ian.

'Yes.'

'Nothing at all for Aunt Annabel?'

'No.'

'I thought that Diane was very close to her sister,' said Bridget who had been watching this exchange between father and son as avidly as she would a Wimbledon final.

'They were,' said Ian. 'But Annabel has everything she needs, financially.'

'Whereas I'm the one struggling to get onto the housing ladder,' said Daniel petulantly.

Not for much longer, thought Bridget. 'The house must be worth, what…?'

'Several million,' said Daniel, making a rocking motion with his hand as if to suggest that one million here or there was of no great import.

'I've asked a couple of agents to give me a valuation. Of course, they can't look inside until your lot have finished doing whatever it is you do.'

'What about the royalties from her book?' asked Bridget, ignoring Daniel's implied criticism of police procedures. 'Who will receive those?'

'Me,' said Daniel. 'But I don't think it will be a significant sum. Who wants to read about my mother's ridiculous conspiracy theories?' He dunked his Amaretto into his coffee, but it slipped from his hand. 'Ow,' he said, scalding his fingers as he attempted to retrieve the floating biscuit. In annoyance, he levered it out with his teaspoon and deposited it on the saucer, where it sat sodden and dripping over the edge. 'She'd have been better off writing some potboiler novel. That would have made her more money.'

'I don't think your mother wrote for the money, Daniel,' said Ian.

'No, of course not. She had higher ideals. Earning money was for the rest of us.' He leaned back in the sofa, sulking like a man who had just lost a great deal of money rather than one who was about to inherit several million pounds.

'I think you might find,' said Bridget, 'that the royalties from sales of her book will amount to rather more than you expect. According to her publisher, the book's flying off the shelves.'

Daniel's interest was immediately aroused. 'Really? That is good news.'

Bridget turned her attention to the main reason for her visit. 'Ian, on the subject of money, we've been going through Diane's bank account and there was something I was hoping you might be able to explain.'

'Well,' said Ian, 'I'll help you if I can, but Diane hasn't shared any information about her finances with me since our divorce.'

'There's not any kind of problem with her account, is there?' asked Daniel, frowning.

'No, nothing like that,' said Bridget. 'But in addition to her university salary she was receiving a substantial sum each month from an off-shore company by the name of Per Sempre Holdings. On her tax returns she declared it as dividend payments.'

Daniel leaned forward with renewed interest. 'When you say "substantial", what sort of amounts are we talking about?'

'Well in excess of her salary as a senior lecturer,' said Bridget.

'And where did you say these payments were coming from?'

'A company called Per Sempre Holdings. It's registered in the Cayman Islands. Do either of you know anything about it?'

Father and son looked at each other and the surprise on their faces appeared genuine.

'I've never heard of this company,' said Ian, 'but as I say we've been divorced for around ten years now. When was the company registered?'

'We're still looking into all the details,' said

Bridget. 'As I said, it's an off-shore company so it's taking a little time to get to the bottom of it. I just thought that one of you might be able to give me an answer more quickly.'

'I'm sorry, I can't help you there,' said Ian.

Daniel shook his head. 'No, Mum never mentioned this company either.' But the prospect of yet more money coming his way seemed to have raised his spirits considerably.

Bridget finished her coffee and biscuit and put the cup and saucer back on the tray. 'Before I go, just one more quick question. I don't suppose either of you know the password to Diane's laptop?'

'No, sorry,' said Daniel.

'Me neither,' said Ian. 'Diane tended to be rather secretive about such matters.'

Bridget nodded. She was beginning to suspect that Diane had been secretive about a number of matters.

'You know,' said Ian, 'Diane had a strong interest in secret codes, the kind that spies used. She used to invent her own codes when she was a teenager, and she collected books on espionage, cryptography, and so on. She loved all sorts of puzzles, cryptic crosswords, secret languages and suchlike. So I imagine her password isn't going to be easy to guess.'

'Right,' said Bridget, standing up. It seemed that nothing Ian or his son told her today was going to be helpful.

'Before you go,' said Ian, 'I have a question for

you. We were wondering when it will be possible for the family to have access to Diane's house. There are documents that will be needed to complete all the formalities of her death, and although Daniel will inherit everything of value, there are personal items like photographs and other mementoes that should go to certain family members.'

'Yes, of course,' said Bridget. 'I don't see any reason why the house needs to remain off limits beyond the end of this week. I'll give you a call as soon as we've finished with it. I assume you have a key?'

'I have one,' said Daniel. 'And Aunt Annabel does too.'

'Actually,' said Ian, 'Annabel has lost hers.'

'Lost it?' queried Bridget. 'Do you mean somebody took it?'

'Oh no, nothing like that. I think she probably just misplaced it. She's been so upset, you know. I'm sure it will turn up.'

Bridget thanked the father and son for their time and rose from her seat. Ian showed her to the front door. He lingered, and she sensed there was something on his mind. 'Listen, please don't think badly about my son,' he said. 'I know that sometimes he appears to be mercenary and ungrateful, but he's not really. It's just that he and Diane didn't have an easy relationship.'

'So everyone keeps saying.' It was hard for Bridget to reconcile Daniel's resentful attitude towards his mother with the photograph albums that Bridget had seen in Diane's house, filled with photograph after photograph of her only son. It was obvious from those photographs that she had thought the world of him, and she had left everything to him in her will. Yet he clearly hated her.

Ian sighed. 'I suppose the truth is that Diane was a product of her time. Back in the eighties, women were being told that they could have it all. Even the woman Diane loathed most in the world, Margaret Thatcher, had it all – she ran the country and looked after her family at the same time. So Diane felt that in her own way she had to do the same. I suppose that she may have treated Daniel the same way that she treated her career – a project, with goals, targets and a timetable. It wasn't really what a young boy needed from his mother.'

'But Daniel enjoyed a good relationship with you?'

'Oh, yes, absolutely,' said Ian. 'You know, I would have liked to have had more children, but Diane was adamant that one was enough. She had already put a tick in that box with Daniel's birth, and she didn't have time for more. If I'm being completely honest, that was probably the main reason we drifted apart.'

'I see,' said Bridget. 'I'm sorry.'

So now the truth of the failed relationship was emerging. The "amicable parting of the ways" that Ian had described to her at their first meeting was little more than a fiction intended to conceal the usual bitterness and recriminations of a broken marriage. Well, Bridget couldn't blame Ian for that. No one wanted to dwell on love turned sour. Better to paper over the cracks, fix a smile to your face and soldier on. It looked as if Ian had found happiness with his second wife whilst maintaining a good relationship with his son from his first marriage. Not a bad outcome in Bridget's book.

CHAPTER 24

Ffion drummed her long fingers on the keyboard, her green-painted nails tapping at the keys idly, unconsciously beating out the four-to-the-floor rhythm of the techno music that she loved. But no matter what combination of letters and numbers she tried, none matched the password of Diane's laptop.

Ffion had cracked plenty of passwords in her time. Obvious passwords like birthdays and pet's names. Trickier ones that involved a combination of a date and a name. Even more obscure ones that required some kind of external key to crack them. But nothing she had tried here was working, and she was out of ideas.

If only the filesystem wasn't encrypted. Then her USB cloning device would have let her bypass the laptop's security and read the data with ease. But with encryption in place, there was only one way in, and that was with the password.

Why on earth had the academic gone to the trouble of encrypting her data? What had she wanted to hide? Ffion had asked some of Diane's colleagues at the Blavatnik School, wondering if this was official policy, but she'd been met with puzzlement. None of the other academics even knew how to encrypt a computer. Diane had clearly been determined to conceal something. And Ffion was equally determined to find out what.

Encrypting a filesystem wasn't an easy feat to pull off. It suggested a high degree of computer literacy, well beyond what most people were capable of, as well as a knowledge of encryption methods. Where did that knowledge come from?

Ffion's fingers stopped abruptly. A connection was forming in her mind. Encryption technology... surveillance techniques... the secret state. Diane's book collection back at her house in North Oxford contained a section on codebreaking and cryptography. Maybe it was worth going back to the house and taking a closer look.

Bridget was still out of the office but Ffion didn't think her boss would object to her looking through Diane Gilbert's book collection again. Not if it meant she was able to get into the laptop at last. On her Kawasaki, she could be there and back in half an hour. If nothing else it would be a welcome change of scene. Pulling on her motorcycle leathers and grabbing her crash helmet, she headed out of the station.

★

235

It was pleasantly warm in the spring sunshine, and the hanging baskets on the nearby pub were filled to abundance with spring flowers. Bridget turned her face to the sun as she walked the short distance from Ian Dunn's house back to her car. But the flood of pleasure was fleeting. Grayson's stern voice rang again in her mind like an echo that refused to die away. *Time's running out, DI Hart. I promise you, I'll bring in Baxter to take over.*

She was painfully aware of how little progress she had made that day. Time seemed to be slipping through her fingers with little to show for its passing. Her phone rang, and hoping that it was Jake or Ffion with an update, she answered without first checking the caller ID.

Mistake. It was Vanessa. 'Oh, Bridget, I'm so glad I caught you.'

'Actually, I'm working. Is it something important?'

Vanessa's voice was full of reproach. 'Well, yes, actually, it is. So if you can give me five minutes of your *precious* time.'

A car drove past noisily and Bridget returned to her own car. Inside, with the door closed, the background noise was much reduced. 'What is it?'

'It's Mum.' Vanessa sounded upset.

'What's happened?'

'She's had a fall.'

'Another one?' Bridget thought back to the sprained wrist their mother had suffered when she fell just before Christmas. 'Is she all right?'

'What do you mean, is she all right? Didn't you hear what I said? She's had a fall.'

'But, I mean, how serious is it... is she in hospital?'

'Dad took her in to be looked at, but they're back home now. She's broken her arm and has a black eye.'

'Have you spoken to her?' asked Bridget.

'Only briefly. I spoke to Dad mainly.'

'And how is he coping?'

'Well, you know him. He says he's managing perfectly well, but...'

'But?'

'Clearly he's not.'

Bridget took a deep breath. Arguing with Vanessa was always a mistake, but... 'If Dad says he's managing, then maybe he is.'

A pause greeted her suggestion, and Bridget recognised the signs of Vanessa gearing up for a lengthy oration. 'Bridget, our father is not managing at all. He hasn't been managing for the past year. I already explained to you how frail Mum has become. And Dad has health problems of his own. Even under normal conditions they barely muddle through. So now with Mum's arm in plaster and badly shaken-up –'

Vanessa was difficult to interrupt when she was in full flow, but Bridget needed to cut through the tirade. 'What do you think we should do?'

'I would have thought that was obvious. You and I need to go down there right away and make sure that they're all right. What Dad needs is a good rest while we take care of Mum. James has agreed to work from home for the next few days and look after the children, and I'm sure Chloe will be fine on her own, but she can always stay at our place if she doesn't want to fend for herself –'

'Vanessa, I can't just drop everything and go down to Lyme Regis. I'm in the middle of a murder enquiry.'

'You're *always* in the middle of something,' said Vanessa. 'Doesn't Thames Valley Police have any other detectives? Haven't you got a team you can delegate to? You're always making excuses.'

Vanessa's accusation stung, and Bridget knew that it contained a kernel of truth. Her life was a constant balancing act between competing pressures of work and family – one that she could never seem to get right. There simply wasn't enough of her to go around. But this time her career was on the line. 'Listen, I'll call Dad tonight and have a chat with him. If I think the situation is as bad as you make out, then I'll see what I can do about taking some time off. But I can't promise anything.'

'Well, suit yourself,' said Vanessa stiffly. 'I'm driving down to Lyme Regis tomorrow. Someone needs to step up, and it looks like it will have to be me. If you think you can spare the time to join me, call me back. If not, don't bother.'

'Ffion, love, how're you doing?'

Ffion had just been about to wrap up for the day when her phone rang. It was her older sister, Siân. She wasn't supposed to take personal calls while at work, but then again, it was already an hour past the time she was supposed to have finished. A pile of Diane Gilbert's books now stood teetering on her desk – books on codemaking, codebreaking, ciphers, cryptographs and cryptograms. She had begun to work her way through the collection, but it was too late in the day to be starting a new project. Anyway, since no one else was around, it wouldn't matter if she took the call. She picked up and was immediately cheered by her sister's friendly voice. Siân's enthusiasm was always infectious.

'I'm good,' she replied. 'How are you? And the kids?'

'Oh, you know. Arwen will be trying two days a week at pre-school next term, just for a trial run before starting properly in the autumn. That'll give me more time to spend with Owain. You know what a handful he can be. Always getting into trouble. Not anything bad, mind you. He's just a bit of a scamp.'

Ffion grinned to herself. Owain was only one year old. How much trouble could a one-year-old get into? Siân should try dealing with the criminals Ffion came up against in her job. On the other hand, she'd probably get them sorted out after a good talking to. There was no messing with Siân. When she set her mind to something, she got her way.

It was Siân who had engineered the reconciliation that had taken place after Christmas between Ffion and her parents. Ffion's mam had never approved of her daughter's sexuality, and the rift had driven Ffion away from home, away from Wales, and all the way to Oxford. There was no question of her ever moving back to live in Wales, but at least she was on speaking terms with her parents again, and was planning to visit them as soon as she could get a few days off work.

'So what's up?' asked Siân.

'Does anything have to be up?'

'No. But I'm hoping you've done something interesting since last time we spoke.'

Ffion laughed. 'As a matter of fact, I do have some news.' She proceeded to tell Siân all about Marion and the fun they were having together.

'She does sound nice,' said Siân. 'So when are you planning to bring her here?'

The question brought Ffion up short. 'You mean to Wales?'

'Sure. I'd love to meet her.'

'I hadn't thought about it.'

Ffion had spent years doing her best to keep her family away from the rest of her life. They'd never come to visit her in Oxford. She'd barely been back to Wales in seven years. But maybe it was time for that to change. Now that she was reconciled with her mam, perhaps there was no longer anything to fear. Perhaps the natural reluctance she felt at Siân's suggestion was nothing more than an old habit that needed to be unlearned. Well, what better way to start than to ask Marion if she'd like to spend a weekend in Wales? Could she do that? Take a girlfriend to meet her parents? To hang out in the village that had once felt so alienating, and yet held a natural beauty with its backdrop of mountains, its still lakes nestled between green peaks, and its small, close-knit community of two-up-two-down cottages? She knew that she could.

Although she hadn't been with Marion for long, the relationship was affecting a change in her. She was much more comfortable in her own skin these days, more confident in her sexuality, and perfectly relaxed in Marion's company.

She couldn't help noticing how different this relationship was to her time with Jake, when she had stressed over his unhealthy diet, the mess in his flat, his awful taste in music. Sometimes she wondered what she'd ever seen in him. Well, that was a little unfair. He was kind and steady and easy-going and he did have a great sense of humour. If only he could have learned to do the washing-up and put his dirty underwear in the laundry bag. But that was men for you. Like Marion said, men were different, and not just in the most obvious ways.

'I'd love to,' she told Siân. 'And I'm sure that

Marion would love to meet you too.'

The more she thought about it, the more the idea took hold. She was sure that Marion and Siân would hit it off immediately, and what better way to show her mam and dad how happy she could be in another woman's company? As soon as they saw her together with Marion, they would be bound to welcome her into their home.

Besides, if there was a chance that she might spend the rest of her life with Marion, then it would be best to make a start right away. What was it that Marion had said?

Time is precious. Let's not waste any.

CHAPTER 25

Bridget arrived at work the next morning conflicted with guilt. Was she doing the right thing coming into the station? Should she have requested leave and accompanied her sister to Lyme Regis to help look after their parents? It occurred to her that Grayson wouldn't have denied any such request, might even have been glad of an excuse to bring in DI Baxter without formally removing her from the case. She suspected her guilt was based, in part, on not wanting to give Grayson such an easy way out, which only made her feel even worse about herself.

On the drive from Wolvercote she told herself repeatedly that her decision to stay in Oxford and work on the case was a logical one based on the conversation she'd had with her father the night before. She'd phoned her parents at half past six, judging that they would have had their tea by then but probably wouldn't yet be watching any favourite TV shows that couldn't be interrupted. Her parents still tended to watch programmes at the time they were broadcast rather than on-demand. She'd thought her father had sounded tired when he answered the phone, but he perked up considerably when he realised it was Bridget calling. It was true, he admitted when asked, that her mother had had a fall and had broken her wrist and (he had lowered his voice) was a 'bit shaken up', but he insisted that they were managing just fine.

'I don't expect you to drop everything in the middle of the week and drive all the way down here,' he'd said when Bridget had mentioned Vanessa's plans. 'You've got a busy career. And a daughter to look after.'

'There are other detectives at Thames Valley Police,' she'd felt obliged to point out. 'And I have a team I could delegate to.' She almost wished her father would just admit defeat and then the decision would be made for her.

In the end they'd agreed to 'wait and see how things are in a few days.' It was a very British response, Bridget thought. Wait and see. Don't make any rash decisions. Stay calm and carry on. Vanessa, of course, took a different opinion. When Bridget had informed her – not without a certain trepidation – of her decision to stay in Oxford for now, Vanessa had made it abundantly clear that it was a good thing that at least one of them was willing to drop all her commitments and fly down to Lyme Regis on a mercy mission. *Vanessa the martyr*, Bridget had thought indignantly after they'd ended their less than harmonious phone call. Now she wondered if

Vanessa wasn't actually a saint, and she, Bridget, just a selfish person.

Well, she'd made her decision – she could always change her mind at the weekend – and for now the only thing to do was to get on with work. She clicked on her email and immediately discovered the first bad news of the day.

An email from forensics informed her that the Head of Department at the Blavatnik was not the author of the death threat. Or, at the very least, there was no evidence to link the letter that had been sent to Diane with the sample of handwriting that Professor Al-Mutairi had provided. But if Al-Mutairi hadn't written the letter, who had?

It was not a propitious start to the day. It seemed to Bridget as if every possible lead on this case was squashed almost as soon as it was suggested. Her meetings at the Saudi Embassy and with MI5 had come to nothing. There was still no ID on the sender of the death threat. Still no clear picture of how the intruder had entered Diane's property. And still the mystery of the payments into Diane's bank account. Despite her team's hard work, Bridget felt like she was no further forward now than she had been at the beginning of the enquiry.

What had Michael Dearlove told her? *Forget it. Walk away.* And yet she could not. It wasn't just a murder investigation that hung in the balance, it was her own career. If Grayson carried out his threat to bring in Baxter, she would never have a chance to vindicate herself. She thought too of PC Sam Roberts and PC Scott Wallis. The two young constables were already suspended from duty, and Bridget owed it to them to uncover exactly what had happened that fateful night. She hoped that the other members of her team would have something more positive to report.

'Who wants to go first?' she asked, scanning the room for volunteers once they were all assembled.

After a moment Jake stepped forward. 'I've had a reply from the authorities in the Cayman Islands.'

At last. Bridget felt her hopes rise. Was this the breakthrough she had been waiting for so desperately?

'So,' said Jake. 'The company register shows that Diane was the sole shareholder of Per Sempre Holdings, and she was also listed as its director. The registered address isn't a proper street address, just a mailbox with a forwarding service. So it seems to be just a shell company, with no actual office or employees.'

'So what is this outfit?' asked Ryan. 'Some kind of money laundering operation?'

'Not necessarily,' said Jake. 'Not all shell companies are a front for illegal activities. There are legitimate reasons for setting up a company in that way. Maybe for tax reasons. Companies registered in the Cayman Islands pay no business taxes, and there's no inheritance tax to pay on the death of a shareholder.'

'Still sounds dodgy to me,' said Ryan.

'But where was the company's money coming from?' asked Bridget.

'I was coming to that,' said Jake. 'We still don't know. The company register only tells us the officially registered information. It doesn't reveal anything about the business's operations. So now I've submitted another request to access the company's bank details. Once I have that, we'll be able to see the source of the income.'

'How long will that take?' It was hard for Bridget to keep the frustration out of her voice.

'I'm not sure, ma'am. It's been difficult working with the Cayman Islands because of the time difference. They won't be up for hours yet, and they don't seem to have much sense of urgency.'

'Okay, well keep trying.' She turned to Ffion. 'Any progress on the laptop?'

'Not yet, but I have some ideas. I went back to Diane's house yesterday and picked up a selection of books. I started reading through them last night. Diane seems to have been very interested in cryptography, and in steganography in particular.'

'Too many long words for this time in the morning,' quipped Ryan, stifling a yawn.

Ffion gave him a withering look. 'Steganography means "concealed writing". It's from the Greek.'

'Of course it is,' said Ryan. 'Silly me.'

'It's the technique of concealing one message

within another. For example, hiding secret text within plain text, or an image within another image, or a video within a video.'

'How does this relate to Diane's laptop?' asked Bridget.

'I'm going to see if I can use the method to work out her password.'

'All right, good.' Bridget decided to trust Ffion's judgment and leave her to it. It wasn't like she had any better ideas herself. 'What about the cocktail of chemicals that was used to kill Diane? Phosphorous, magnesium and potassium. Where did they come from? Who could have got hold of them? Are we any further forward?'

Ryan shrugged and even Ffion looked blank.

Harry raised a tentative hand. 'Ma'am, you find them in multivitamins. They're important for bone health.'

'Bone health,' repeated Bridget, making Harry look embarrassed. 'Well, it's a start, I suppose,' she added encouragingly. It was certainly more than anyone else in the team had managed. 'Ryan, why don't you see if you can find out any more? We have a world-class university in this city. There must be someone who can help us out.'

'I'll see what I can do,' said Ryan, but he didn't sound too hopeful.

'Andy, I'd like you to look into the finances of the publishing company that published Diane's book. Find out if it has any problems.'

'Will do.'

'And Harry' – Bridget's gaze came to rest on the most junior member of her team – 'help out with anyone who needs you.'

'Yes, ma'am.'

'In the meantime,' she said, 'I'm going to see Diane's agent, Grant Sadler again. He was one of the people who advised Diane to take the death threat seriously. I want to see if he can shed any more light on the matter.'

★

A Deadly Race might be on its way to becoming an international bestseller, but Grant Sadler had apparently resisted any temptation to upgrade his accommodation from the splendours of the Travelodge on the Abingdon Road. When Bridget phoned him, he was just leaving the hotel's reception. 'I'm about to catch the bus into the centre of Oxford,' he told her. 'I want to call in at Blackwell's to stock up on some books before heading back to London.'

'No problem,' said Bridget. 'I can meet you there.'

Located on Broad Street between the White Horse pub and the Weston Library, and directly opposite the Sheldonian Theatre, Blackwell's was Oxford's academic bookshop. The rather quaint exterior of the old, four-storey town houses that comprised the shop – shuttered, box-sash windows and dormers in the attic – belied its expansive interior. Bridget had spent countless hours there as a student, browsing the shelves of the history and literature sections and wishing that there was more time in the world to read all the books that vied for her attention.

When she arrived, she found the ground floor bustling with the usual mix of booklovers and tourists. This was where the bookshop pandered to popular taste and did its best to extract as much cash as possible from Oxford's large number of visitors. Books shortlisted for literary prizes competed with the latest thrillers from household names. Being Oxford, there were tables piled high with anything with a local connection. Books by Tolkien, C.S Lewis, Lewis Carroll and Colin Dexter were in abundance. A table near the front of the store was stacked with copies of Diane Gilbert's latest book, a newcomer to the ranks of bestsellers, attributable, as Bridget knew, as much to the circumstances of her death as to its readability.

Grant Sadler had told her that she would find him in the Norrington Room, and so Bridget steered a path past stacks of *Alice in Wonderland* and *Harry Potter*, and headed towards the stairs that led to the lower levels. Most tourists never made it this far, but they didn't know what they were missing. Never mind *Alice in Wonderland*, the basement of Blackwell's, named after Sir Arthur Norrington, one-time President of Trinity College, was simply a wonderland of books. The vast underground chamber, arranged on multiple levels, always made Bridget's spine tingle with excitement, as if she were entering a cathedral of words.

She descended a flight of stairs, following the black and white subject signs that hung from wires in the ceiling, searching for Grant Sadler amongst the book shelves. After passing through a corridor whose walls were towering bookcases she turned a corner and spotted him in the lowest part of the room and took a second staircase down to meet him.

Up close, his appearance was even worse than the previous time Bridget had encountered him. His hair stood on end, his face was unshaven, and his eyes were enclosed by dark rings. He looked as if he'd had no sleep and had tumbled straight out of bed.

'Mr Sadler?'

He was engrossed in a book and hadn't noticed her approaching. He jumped at the sound of his name and a slip of paper fluttered to the floor near Bridget's feet. She stooped to pick it up. The paper held a shopping list of book titles. His arms were already full of books.

She was about to hand the paper to him, but something held her back. She stopped to study the list of titles. There was nothing remarkable about the titles themselves, but that wasn't what had caught her attention. It was the handwriting. She studied it closely to make sure she wasn't mistaken. But no, there was that distinctive curling of the capital "C", the rightward slope of the cursive script as it hurried across the page, and the final flourish on the end of letters like "g" and "y" that looped below the line. There was no need to be a forensic handwriting expert. The likeness was plain enough for anyone to see.

Grant Sadler was the author of the death threat. He hadn't even bothered to disguise his handwriting.

He looked at her expectantly, a nervous smile twitching his lips. 'Does there seem to be a problem?'

'Grant Sadler,' she said. 'I am arresting you on suspicion of the murder of Diane Gilbert.'

CHAPTER 26

Grant Sadler sat across the table from Bridget, a quivering mass of nerves. His fingers trembled and his hands moved repeatedly to scratch at his face or push back his hair. Beneath the table, his knee bounced up and down so violently she could hear it knocking against the wood. His head turned at the slightest sound from the corridor outside the interview room.

Bridget felt no sympathy.

His lawyer sat at his side, his hair neatly combed, his hands folded in front of him, a model of stillness and neatness in contrast with Grant's manic display of untidiness.

'So,' said Bridget, pushing a pair of clear plastic evidence bags across the tabletop. 'Here we have two handwritten documents. The first, a list of books that you were planning to buy from Blackwell's bookshop this morning. The second, a letter that was sent to Diane Gilbert, threatening to kill her if she proceeded with the publication of her book. According to our expert the handwriting is consistent in the two cases. Even to a casual observer they look the same.

The letter was sent with a London postmark, and I'm sure I don't have to remind you that you live and work in London.'

Grant said nothing, but if anything his hands began to shake even more. He withdrew them from view and hid them in his lap.

His lawyer leaned forward to study the evidence, a pair of reading glasses perched on his long nose. The expression on his face didn't bode well for Grant's chances.

At Bridget's side, Jake cleared his throat and Grant jumped as if he'd been struck. 'Mr Sadler, would you agree that these two documents were written by the same person?'

'Yes,' said Grant, refusing to make eye contact.

'And can you tell us who wrote them?'

A pause. 'I did.'

'So you admit that you wrote and sent the death threat to Diane Gilbert?'

'Yes.' He looked up, his face holding a desperate appeal for Bridget's compassion. 'But I didn't kill her. You have to believe me!'

Bridget wasn't moved by his plea. 'Why should we believe you? All the evidence points to you.'

'You don't understand. I never wanted to harm Diane. I certainly didn't want her to die. She was my client! I had nothing to gain from her death.'

'Except for fifteen percent of all the revenues from her book sales. Which looks to be a considerable amount of money now that the book is becoming a bestseller.'

'I know!' cried Grant in anguish. 'I know how it looks. But it was never meant to happen like this.'

'You didn't want the book to become a bestseller?'

'Of course I did! That's why I sent her the death threat, but you have to believe me, I didn't murder Diane. I never had any intention of harming her.'

Jake leaned across the table. 'I think you'd better explain.'

Grant ran both hands through his hair, lifting the unkempt tufts to new heights. 'All right, this is how it was.' He breathed deeply, calming himself down. When he had himself back under control, he began to speak. 'Diane and I cooked up the death threat plan between us. It was my idea, but when I suggested it to her, she was enthusiastic. I wrote the letter and sent it to her, and when she received it, she showed it to her sister and to Jennifer, her publisher.'

'Are you saying that they were in on this plot too?'

He shook his head. 'No. They both thought the death threat was genuine.'

Bridget frowned. 'According to Annabel and Jennifer, Diane was dismissive of the letter. Initially she didn't even want to report it to the police.'

'Yes, but don't you see? That was all part of the act. Diane had to respond to the letter just as she would have done if it had been genuine. In other words, with her usual contempt. She needed to convince Annabel and Jennifer that it was real. That would make it more credible when she did eventually agree to take it to the police.'

He was starting to look embarrassed, as if he'd pulled a schoolboy prank that had gone too far.

'And what precisely was the purpose of this hoax threat?' demanded Bridget. 'A publicity stunt?'

'Exactly. It's a cut-throat business, the world of publishing. And the truth is that I've been finding it hard-going these past few years. I've had a string of bad luck, you might say. Authors that showed promise, but whose careers came to nothing.'

Bridget looked at the dishevelled man across the table from her. She pictured the budget hotel where he was staying at the far end of the Abingdon Road, the bus journeys he was having to make in and out of town each day, and the way that he had dodged paying for his coffee at the coffee shop. That his financial situation was dire – here was a fact she could believe.

'So,' he continued, 'I came to see Diane in Oxford to discuss plans for the book launch, and we were chatting about how to get more sales. She was saying that her appearance at the Oxford Literary Festival was a waste of time. I told her that was nonsense. It was an honour to appear at the festival, but she said there would only be a small audience for her talk at the Divinity School

– it wasn't as if they'd offered her the Sheldonian – and she wasn't particularly keen on meeting readers anyway. She said she would hate answering their stupid questions and signing books for them.' He raised his eyes to the ceiling. 'You know what Diane was like.'

Bridget nodded. That was exactly the kind of remark she could imagine Diane making.

'Anyway,' continued Grant, 'I said that if she wanted more publicity, then we needed to make the most of the controversial nature of her book. Half-jokingly, I suggested the idea of the death threat. I told her that if word got out that she had been threatened, we could use the story to generate more publicity for the launch. To my surprise, she thought it was a great idea, and so we agreed to do it. You know, I didn't really think it would work, but when the police took the letter seriously and offered to provide round-the-clock protection for Diane, I knew that we'd struck gold. It was going to make a great story.'

Bridget was furious. 'So you used the police simply to generate hype for a book?' If Grant was telling the truth, not only had she wasted her time accompanying Diane to the literary festival, but he had completely muddied the waters of the investigation and squandered yet more valuable time. And if he was still lying to her... 'How can you prove that what you say is true?'

Grant's lawyer glanced sideways at his client, perhaps wondering the same thing. But the nervous energy that had animated the agent throughout the telling of his tale suddenly drained away and his face seemed to crumple. He stared back forlornly across the table. 'How can I? The only witness who could corroborate my story is Diane, and she's dead. You just have to believe my account.'

'But why should we? Even if what you say about Diane being party to a publicity stunt is true, you might still only be telling us half the story.'

'What do you mean?'

'Maybe it was all going so well that you decided to go the extra mile. Let's say for the moment that you hadn't originally intended to kill her. But once you saw that you had the potential for a bestseller on your hands, you decided to take it to the next level.'

'No,' gasped Grant.

'A hoax death threat might have gained you a few column inches in the literary press, but by proceeding with the murder, you ensured that every newspaper and news channel in the country would give prime coverage to Diane and her book.'

'No!'

Bridget sat up straight in her chair, lending added conviction to her accusation. 'You were in Oxford on the night of Diane's death, you had a clear motive for killing her, and you've admitted to sending her a death threat. Unless you can come up with a more convincing account, it's very likely that we will be charging you with her murder.'

Bridget left the interview fuming. She couldn't be certain whether Grant Sadler was telling the truth, or if he was lying desperately to save his skin. At the very least, she was going to charge him with intent to cause harassment, alarm or distress. Not to mention making threats to kill. Both were serious offences. But if the death threat really was a hoax as Grant claimed, then she was no closer to finding the identity of the murderer. In fact, the new information threw everything they had been working on into doubt.

'What do you make of him?' she asked Jake. 'Do you believe him?'

'It's hard to believe a word he says.'

'Agreed. But if he is telling the truth…' She left the sentence unfinished, and stormed into the incident room, needing to put some space between herself and her suspect before she fully lost her temper with him.

In the office, all was calm, and everyone seemed to be busy with their tasks. Ffion was at her desk, her head buried in a book. In fact books were spread chaotically all over her normally tidy desk.

Bridget peered curiously over the young detective's shoulder. The books appeared to be the works on cryptography from Diane's house that Ffion had mentioned earlier. The page that

Ffion was currently reading was incomprehensible to Bridget, full of complex diagrams and strange symbols. She leaned in closer and saw the word "steganography" highlighted in yellow marker. Bridget quickly moved on, leaving Ffion to her task.

Andy looked up from his computer screen as she approached, a spark of excitement animating his normally bland features. 'There's been a development, ma'am.'

'What is it?'

'It's the CCTV from the Travelodge where Grant Sadler has been staying. We requested it last week, but hadn't had time to look at it properly. It didn't seem like a top priority. Besides, they have so much of it. Cameras in reception, cameras by the lifts, more in the car park –'

Bridget didn't really care where the hotel placed its cameras. 'Have you found something?' she asked.

'Well, yes. I've been working through it while you were conducting the interview, and the results are pretty interesting. On the night of Diane's murder, Grant Sadler didn't stay in his room watching TV like he claimed. The footage clearly shows that he didn't get back to the hotel until a few minutes before midnight.'

Bridget felt her anger beginning to rise once more. Was there no limit to the number of lies the unscrupulous literary agent had told her?

She spun on her heels and marched straight

back into the interview.

CHAPTER 27

Bridget took her seat across from Grant and studied his ashen face. Were his crumpled features an acceptance of his guilt at last, or simply a blind fear of his prospects? She waited to see how he would respond to her return.

He leaned towards her with a pleading look in his eyes. 'Please don't charge me with Diane's murder.'

'Give me one good reason why I shouldn't.'

'Because I've told you everything I know. You simply have to believe me.'

'Is that the best you can offer? Because I now have fresh evidence that I would like to put to you.'

If it was possible for a man who looked like he had lost everything to take on an even more deflated appearance, Grant Sadler did just that.

'When I spoke to you the day after Diane's death,' said Bridget, 'you told me that after leaving the literary festival, you stopped for a quick pint at the White Horse and then went back to your hotel.'

Grant shifted nervously in his chair. Beside

him, his lawyer sighed, clearly aware that more bad news was coming.

'CCTV from the Travelodge now shows that you didn't return there until just before midnight.' Bridget referred to a copy of the post-mortem report that she had brought into the interview. 'The pathologist who carried out Diane's post-mortem stated that the time of death was between eleven o'clock and one in the morning. That gave you plenty of time to kill her and then return to your hotel. So unless you can account for your whereabouts that night, I'm going to recommend that you are charged with her murder.'

Grant lowered his forehead to the table in a gesture of defeat. Finally the knee that had been bouncing almost continuously beneath the table came to a halt. Bridget wondered if he had simply given up on life.

He lifted his head from the table as if it were a solid lead weight, and stared at her with a look of abject hopelessness. 'The truth is, I lied,' he said. 'Or at least I didn't tell you the whole truth. I did go to the White Horse, but I stayed there longer than I may have implied. I should have told you this earlier, but I didn't think it was important.'

Bridget pursed her lips, waiting.

'You see, I was meeting someone there.'

'Who?'

'Jennifer Eagleston and Michael Dearlove.'

Bridget frowned at this latest claim. 'But Michael Dearlove said that he was driving straight home to London after the talk. When Diane asked him if he wanted to go out for a drink, he told her that he had to get away.'

'Yes,' said Grant, 'but that's because we were keeping the meeting a secret.'

'Why?'

Grant rubbed at his blackened eyes, as if all he wanted to do was fall asleep forever. 'Michael has a book he wants to write, but his current agent hasn't been able to find a publisher for him. So after my success at getting Diane's book published, he asked me if I would put him in touch with Jennifer.'

'Why did that have to be kept secret?'

'Because of Michael's contract. He has an agent already, so he was breaking his exclusivity terms by speaking to me. The whole situation is very delicate.'

'Not as delicate as your current predicament,' said Bridget.

'Quite. So that's why I'm telling you everything now.'

'You claim that you met Jennifer and Michael in the White Horse after Diane's talk finished? We can easily verify that, you know.'

'Yes. As long as they're willing to admit to it.'

'Let's hope for your sake that they are. How long did this meeting last?'

'Until eleven? Perhaps not quite as long as that. Let's say a quarter to eleven.'

'So why did it take you more than an hour to return to your hotel? Don't tell me that you missed your bus.'

'No, although the buses aren't very frequent at that time of night. The plain truth is that I just fancied a walk. After a whole evening sitting down, and a long meeting in a crowded pub, I needed to clear my head. So I walked.'

Bridget did a quick calculation. The distance from the pub to the hotel was a little over two miles. Grant's claim that he had spent an hour walking just about held up.

He leaned forward again as if keen to press home his case. 'Look, I'm not proud of how I've behaved. I've done some terrible things. The death threat hoax. Going behind people's backs. Lying to you. But my business has been in desperate trouble. I'm right on the brink of going bust. I had to do *something*.'

Bridget eyed him suspiciously across the table. 'Do you know anything about payments that Diane received from a company called Per Sempre Holdings?'

He seemed alarmed by the sudden shift in questioning. 'Per Sempre Holdings? I've never heard of it. What is it?'

'It's a Cayman Islands company. Diane appears to have been its sole director and shareholder. Might she have been doing secret book deals that you were unaware of, just like the one you were trying to arrange with Michael Dearlove?'

'Impossible,' said Grant. 'The agreement between an author and their agent is a legally binding contract. You must understand that my discussions with Michael and Jennifer were just informal talks. If Jennifer gives us the go-ahead to proceed, Michael will need to terminate his contract with his current agent and appoint me to manage his negotiations. He can't just do it himself. Publishers aren't interested in receiving manuscripts directly from authors. They rely on trusted agents to filter out the dross.'

'So Diane couldn't have gone behind your back?'

'Certainly not. Anyway, why would she? I negotiated her a good deal for her book. Jennifer wanted to pay her far less, but I got her to up the advance by twenty percent. I'm good at what I do.'

'That may be so,' said Bridget, although Grant's dire financial predicament tended to suggest otherwise. 'Yet Diane was earning a sizeable sum each month from this company of hers. Far more than she's likely to make from sales of *A Deadly Race*.'

★

It was of little surprise to Bridget to discover that Jennifer Eagleston was still hanging around Oxford, attending talks and schmoozing with writers and their agents. In the light of what Grant had said about shady deals conducted over pints of beer in dimly-lit corners of pubs, Jennifer's comment about poaching writers from

266

other publishers had taken on more sinister implications. If Grant was to be believed, Jennifer wasn't above breaking the law to get what she wanted.

'DI Hart?' she said breezily as she answered her phone. 'How nice to hear from you again, but I'm a little busy to do lunch today, I'm afraid.'

'I wasn't going to suggest lunch,' said Bridget. 'This time it would be more convenient if you came to speak to me at the station.'

A stony silence greeted her words. A background buzz of conversation filled the void. Bridget heard a voice saying, 'Jennifer, can I get you another drink?'

'Is there a problem, Inspector?' asked Jennifer after a moment.

'I'm sure there won't be,' said Bridget pleasantly. 'I'll send a car to pick you up right away.'

The publisher arrived at Kidlington half an hour later, looking flustered. But as always, her armour of red lipstick and scarlet nail varnish were firmly in place. She clutched her enormous tote bag in front of her like a shield.

'This way, please,' said Bridget, ushering her into the interview room so recently vacated by Grant Sadler.

Jennifer took a seat, glancing nervously around the spartanly furnished room. She folded her hands neatly in front of her. Bridget had never seen the woman looking so meek. 'What is it you'd like to know?' she asked.

'I would like to know,' said Bridget, 'exactly what you did after leaving Diane's talk at the Divinity School on the night of her death.'

'Ah,' said Jennifer. 'You've been talking to someone. Might I ask who?'

'Please could you just answer my question, Miss Eagleston.'

'Well, I wasn't doing anything wrong,' said Jennifer. 'I had a meeting with Grant Sadler and Michael Dearlove.'

'A *secret* meeting,' said Bridget.

Jennifer snorted. 'If you don't mind me saying, that's a very melodramatic way of putting it. It was an informal conversation, that's all.'

'And what was the purpose of this conversation?'

'We were just talking about a book Michael wants to write. There's nothing wrong with that, is there?'

'Except that Michael has an agent who represents him, and so Grant should never have introduced him to you.'

'Well, these contractual terms can be rather vague,' said Jennifer. 'Like I said, we were just a few friends having a chat over a drink.'

'Can you confirm where this meeting took place, and at what time you left?'

'It was at the White Horse. Do you know it? It's a charming little pub on Broad Street. And I guess we must have finished, oh, I'm not sure when. Time flies when you're in good company, don't you think?'

'What is your best estimate of the time?' asked Bridget through gritted teeth.

Jennifer frowned. 'Elevenish. Maybe a little earlier, maybe a little later.'

The time tallied roughly with Grant's own account. Not that Jennifer Eagleston could be counted as a very reliable witness.

'And what did you do after the meeting?'

'I walked back to my hotel.'

'And the other two? Grant and Michael?'

'Michael needed to drive back to London, and I assume that Grant went straight back to his hotel.'

Bridget gazed at her across the table. 'What would you say if I told you that it was Grant Sadler who wrote the death threat that was sent to Diane?'

Jennifer's eyes opened wide in shock. She opened her mouth to speak, but for once, no words came out.

★

Three people had met in secret immediately before Diane's death, and it didn't take Bridget long to track down the third participant in that meeting. A quick search on the Oxford Literary Festival's website revealed that Michael Dearlove was currently hosting an informal question and answer session at Blackwell's marquee next to the Bodleian. Bridget got into her car and set off for central Oxford.

By the time she arrived, the session was finishing, and the audience members were drifting off to browse the tables of books on display beneath the large canopy of the marquee. Michael Dearlove was chatting politely to an old lady but gave the impression that he was keen to get away. Perhaps he had somewhere else to go, or more likely he was simply gasping for another cigarette. Bridget decided to rescue him.

'Ah, Inspector Hart,' he exclaimed as she approached. 'I was just about to leave.'

'Perhaps you could spare me a little of your time before you dash away.'

'Of course. Anything I can do to assist the police with their enquiries.'

The old lady took the hint and allowed Bridget to guide the journalist away. Once outside he immediately lit up, inhaling deeply as if his life depended on it. 'My God,' he said, 'that's better. I'd forgotten how quickly this stuff gets a grip on you.'

Bridget waved the smoke away with one hand. She was quickly losing patience with Michael Dearlove and his cigarettes. 'I have some more questions to ask you.'

'Fire away,' said Dearlove. 'You don't mind if we take a stroll, do you?' He set off along the same path they had walked last time she'd spoken to him, in the direction of Radcliffe Square. 'So, what is this about?'

'It's about your meeting with Grant Sadler and

Jennifer Eagleston.'

'Oh, right. That meeting. It's hardly a police matter, is it?'

'I'm interested in establishing the facts, since it took place on the night of the murder.'

Dearlove stopped and faced her. 'You can't think that one of us had anything to do with her death, do you? That's ridiculous! I've already told you what I think.'

'You did. In fact, you were very quick to point the finger at the security services. If I recall, you also advised me that I would have no hope of getting anyone associated with the security services to talk to me.'

He puffed at his cigarette. 'Well, did they talk?'

'They talked. Although obviously they denied any involvement.'

'Obviously.'

'So now I'm exploring an alternative line of enquiry.'

'Are you suggesting that I might have killed Diane?' A genuine anger animated him now. He seemed affronted by the idea.

'I'm not suggesting anything,' said Bridget. 'But I'd like to hear your account of the meeting that took place that night.'

They turned into Radcliffe Square, and Dearlove took a moment to stare up at the golden pillars and arches of the Camera, crowned by the green-grey leaden dome of its roof. 'God, it's beautiful, isn't it? It's almost enough to make you want to throw in your principles and join the elite.'

'It didn't take much for you to throw in your principles, did it, Mr Dearlove?'

He cast a look of annoyance in her direction. 'Look, this meeting, it's not such a big deal. The fact is that I've been trying to land a publishing contract for a while now. It shouldn't be so hard. I'm a well-known journalist with a solid track record. But my agent just can't seem to find an opening with any of the big publishing houses. She's been trying for almost a year with no success. Frankly, it's been galling to watch Diane bringing her book to publication while I twiddle my thumbs on the sidelines. So I decided to have a quiet word with Grant before Diane's talk, and he suggested that I meet Jennifer. In fact, it was a very productive meeting. We're already moving forward with some ideas.'

'And where and when did this meeting take place?'

'At the White Horse, just after Diane's talk.' He looked abashed. 'I had to tell Diane that I was driving straight back to London. I feel bad about that now. It was the very last thing I said to her, and it was an untruth.'

'And what time did the meeting finish?'

'We left the pub at about five to eleven. I remember checking the time, because I wanted to estimate when I could expect to get home. I called my wife just as I was setting off to let her know that I wouldn't be back until about one o'clock in the morning, and for her not to wait up for me.'

'I see. It seems like a long drive to make, especially since you were returning to Oxford the next day for the literary festival.'

'Yes. Normally when I'm in Oxford I stay with...' He stopped abruptly. 'I mean, sometimes I stay with a friend.'

'A friend? Who?'

Dearlove threw the end of his cigarette to the ground and crushed it angrily against the cobbles with his shoe. He reached into his jacket pocket for a replacement but found the pack empty. 'God, dammit! Where can I buy more of these?'

'There's a shop this way,' said Bridget, steering him in the direction of the High Street. 'Now, you were saying that you usually stay with a friend in Oxford. Do you want to tell me who that is, or shall I make a guess?'

He bowed his head. 'All right, I may as well admit it. I usually stay with Diane.'

Bridget recalled that during her previous conversation with Dearlove he had referred to Diane being "all alone in that big empty house of hers." Now it was clear that he had seen the inside of that house first-hand. And he had made no secret of the fact that he had slept with Diane when they were students.

'You were having an affair with her?'

'Yes,' he admitted.

'And did your wife know about it?'

'Of course not! That's why I didn't mention anything about it to you before. So you see,

Inspector, Diane meant a lot to me. She was far more than just a colleague. She was more than a friend. That's the reason I'm so keen to help you find out who killed her.'

'That may be so,' said Bridget. 'But you must understand that this also makes you a prime suspect for her murder.' They had arrived on the High Street now, close to a small independent newsagent that sold tobacco. Bridget indicated the shop. 'I think you'll find what you need in there.'

CHAPTER 28

Ffion had her head in a book. Several books in fact. A pile of Diane Gilbert's reference texts on code-breaking stood on one side of her desk. A book on steganography was propped open in front of her. And in her hands was a hardback edition of *A Deadly Race* - signed by the author herself.

Ffion was on the hunt for a secret message – Diane's password – and perhaps it was hidden right here, within the very book she held. After all, if Diane Gilbert wanted to use the art of cryptography to hide her password, where better to conceal it than within her greatest work, her first published book?

Steganography. Concealed writing. One message hidden within another.

Even better than protecting a message by use of a secret code, steganography went one step further and disguised the fact that a message even existed. Ffion imagined the pleasure that the academic might have had, knowing that her biggest secret was out in the open, on full public display. It fitted the profile Ffion had built up of

Diane.

Arrogant. Contemptuous. Presumptuous.

But these were qualities that could easily backfire.

It was late and most people had already left the office. But Ffion was going nowhere, not now that she had picked up the scent of her quarry. It was just a hunch, but she knew that her instincts were good. She had trusted hunches before, and they had led her to success. She was sure that this time would be no different. If only she could find the key.

She flipped through the pages of Diane's book. Nearly five hundred in total. Three hundred words to a page. And Diane Gilbert had never used a short word if she could find a longer one that meant the same. Ffion did the maths. Close to a million letters in total. It was like searching for a needle in a haystack. Or a grain of sand on the seashore. Or a drop of water in…

Come on, focus.

The principle of steganography was simple. Whereas in most codes – or ciphers, to use the correct term – a substitution method was used to replace each letter in a word or sentence with another, in steganography the letters that made up the hidden message didn't change, they were simply picked out of a larger text. The book that lay open on Ffion's desk explained it through examples.

One common technique had been invented by Francis Bacon, the English philosopher and adviser to Queen Elizabeth I. The principle of Bacon's cipher was to conceal a message using different formatting of text, such as letters emphasised in bold or italics. But Ffion had found no examples of irregular formatting. All the text in the book was of the same size and font face, apart from obvious exceptions like the table of contents.

Another method was to insert deliberate errors into the text – spelling mistakes in words for instance. By finding all the erroneous letters and arranging them in order, a message would be revealed. But Ffion had found no spelling errors in this book.

Perhaps she was overthinking the problem. The most ancient approach to concealing a message within a larger piece of text was to use the "null cipher" technique. In this method, a simple rule was used to select letters. Take the first letter from each chapter, for example, and arrange them to spell out a word or a sentence. This book had ten chapters. A ten-letter password sounded about right.

Ffion copied out the first word from each chapter onto a blank sheet of paper.

Never The Examples Military The Capitalism No Imperial What If

Next she wrote down the first letter of each word.

NTEMTCNIWI

It looked like nonsense, but a computer password didn't have to be an actual meaningful word. Any string of alphanumeric characters would do. She reached for Diane's laptop and eagerly typed in the string of letters, taking care to keep them in upper case as written.

No luck.

She tried them in lower case too, just in case.

The laptop remained firmly locked.

Never mind, Ffion wasn't beaten that easily. She opened the book again.

Her phone buzzed, and she checked to see who had sent her a message. Marion. She picked it up to read.

Just finished work. Do you want to go out for dinner or come over to my place? I can cook if you like. I have something important to tell you xx

Ffion's finger lingered over the message. It was a tempting offer and she was intrigued to find out what Marion's news might be. But she would never be able to relax knowing that her work here was unfinished. She would simply spoil the evening for both of them. She tapped out a quick reply.

Sorry, tied up at the office tonight. See you tomorrow instead xx

She felt a brief twinge of regret at declining the invitation, but it was over in an instant, and she put the phone back on her desk, switching it to silent.

Immediately her attention was back on the job

of cracking the password. If the first letter of each word didn't work (and that was really way too simple), then perhaps a variation on the theme might work. Perhaps the first letter of the first chapter, the second letter of the second chapter...

She started to write them out, double checking each one as she went.

Nhaifaklwi

Still no success.

The office was deserted now apart from her. Lights had been switched off, and only her desk lamp illuminated the darkened room. If she was going to be here all night she could really use some tea, and a pretty high-powered brew at that. But before going to the kitchen it was worth trying the third most obvious method. Take the first word of the first chapter: *Never*. Follow it with the second word of the second chapter: *establishment*. Next the third word of the third chapter: *abuse*. When she had written down her ten words, she took the first letter from each one. It didn't take long before a new word appeared before her, order coalescing out of seeming randomness.

Neapolitan

Ffion caught her breath. The secret word had been there all along, embedded within a book of ordinary text. Thousands of readers had read these same words and not one of them had guessed that a hidden message lay within them.

Her fingers reached again for the laptop and began to type. Seconds later she was in.

★

Jake entered the wine bar and peered around cautiously. He was looking for a woman called Lauren, with dark mysterious eyes and long black hair. He checked the photo on his phone for about the hundredth time. Lauren certainly looked very attractive, but after his experience with Tilly he wondered whether the real Lauren would bear much resemblance to her profile on the dating app. Would she, too, be almost old enough to be his mother?

He adjusted his shirt collar and ran a hand through his hair. Nerves. This wine bar really wasn't his kind of place. Far too showy. At least Tilly had chosen a nice down-to-earth pub on the Cowley Road as a venue. Maybe he should have stuck with Tilly after all. She'd been messaging him on the app ever since their first date, but so far he'd ignored her. Yes, he was desperate, but no, he wasn't quite *that* desperate. Not yet.

He swung his gaze around the glitzy venue, taking in the bright ambience close to the bar, and the dimmer, more secluded tables with their red leather seats. Most of the tables were for two.

It was obviously a singles bar. Young (and not so young) couples leaned into each other, gazing intensely into each other's eyes, clinking glasses together and murmuring sweet nothings. Or perhaps not murmuring – the thumping dance music that pumped through the speakers seemed to rule that out.

'Jake?'

He looked around and saw a woman aged about thirty smiling at him.

'Lauren.' To his astonishment she looked just as good as her photo. Better. Wearing a low-cut dress, with dark hair tumbling over her shoulders, her eyes were smouldering. 'I...' he mumbled.

She kissed him on the cheek. 'You get some drinks while I find us a table. I'll have a French Martini.' She drifted off towards a corner table and Jake made his way over to the bar. He tugged nervously at his sleeves. The clientele here looked like they had money to throw around. Perhaps he should have worn something smarter.

'Hi, what can I get you?'

Jake was distracted momentarily by the barman's haircut. Shaved to the skin at the back and sides, and clipped to a buzz cut on top, an abstract design of swooping lines and curves had been etched into the hair with a razor.

'Um... a French Martini' – Jake had no idea what a French Martini was, but he knew he didn't want one for himself – 'and do you have any beer?'

The barman reached into a brightly-lit fridge for a bottle. 'This month we're featuring a pineapple and mint sour beer from New Zealand.'

'Pineapple and mint?' The strange concoction sounded like one of Ffion's weird teas. 'What about a plain Yorkshire bitter?'

'No, sorry.'

Reluctantly, Jake accepted a beer and a cocktail in exchange for what seemed like a substantial portion of his month's salary, and carried them over to the secluded table where Lauren was waiting for him, all smoky eyes and plunging neckline. She looked very much at home, as if this place was a regular haunt.

He took the seat opposite her and tried a mouthful of his overpriced beer. In his opinion, pineapple and mint did nothing to improve the flavour, and Yorkshire had nothing to fear from an invasion of Kiwi beer.

Lauren sipped her cocktail, then slid her hands across the table to touch his. 'I've been so looking forward to meeting you, Jake.'

'Me you,' he said.

She rubbed her fingers lightly across his palm. 'So, go on. Tell me all about yourself.'

He wondered where to begin. 'I'm from Leeds originally, but I moved to Oxford about a year ago. I'm a police detective with Thames Valley Police.'

Lauren stroked her fingers over his. 'Mm. That's very interesting. Is that a dangerous job,

Jake?'

He turned the question over in his mind. Was his job dangerous? There had certainly been moments when he'd been in mortal peril. He remembered one occasion on top of a college tower, with only a low stone parapet preventing him from plunging to the ground below. And other times when he had grappled assailants armed with deadly weapons including a razor-sharp shard of Chinese ceramic and a ceremonial dagger. But just as often, he recalled, it had been Ffion who had faced the danger full on and made the arrest.

'It's not so bad, really,' he said.

'I think you must be very brave,' said Lauren. She gazed deeply into his eyes. 'You're a very handsome man, Jake. Has anyone ever told you that?'

'Um...' He tried to remember if Ffion had ever said anything along those lines. He didn't think she had. In fact, she had never said anything particularly complimentary about him during the whole time they were together. Somehow, that had been easier to handle than Lauren's outpouring of flattery.

He returned her gaze, losing himself in the dark pools of her eyes. It seemed expected that he should return her compliment. 'You're a very beautiful woman, Lauren.'

She leaned closer. 'Kiss me, Jake.'

He felt his own face move towards hers, almost like he had lost control over his actions. Lauren's lips parted and her eyes drifted closed.

They were about to kiss when a man's voice cut across the pounding music. 'Oi! Get away from her!'

Lauren's eyes flicked open and Jake felt the spell that had been cast over him break. He was on his feet in an instant.

A man was striding towards him, a look of outrage on his face, his hands bunching into fists.

Jake moved to intercept him. 'Hey, calm down mate. What's your problem?'

'You wanna know what my problem is?' The man jerked his head in Lauren's direction. 'You're having an affair with my wife!'

'Your wife?'

'Aidan,' pleaded Lauren. 'I can explain!'

Jake turned to her. 'Is this man your husband?' Ryan had given him plenty of dating advice, but he had never discussed this eventuality.

'I am,' said Aidan. 'And who the hell are you?'

'I'm a police officer.'

'You expect me to believe that? You cheeky bastard!'

A fist swung in Jake's direction and he dodged aside. Aidan was a big guy and he stumbled heavily into the table, sending drinks flying. Lauren screamed.

Jake reached into his pocket and pulled out his warrant card. 'I'm Detective Sergeant Jake Derwent,' he shouted as Aidan lumbered back to his feet. 'And you need to calm down right now.'

'Calm down? While you're sleeping with my

wife? I don't care if you're a bloody police officer or not!' He aimed another punch at Jake.

This time Jake caught it and spun the aggrieved husband around, gripping his arm behind his back. Aidan cried out in pain. Jake pushed him up against a wall and slipped a pair of cuffs over his wrists. 'Now then, mate,' he said, 'you can stay like that until you've calmed down. And then you and your wife can sort this out between yourselves in a civilised fashion. Otherwise, I'll be taking you back to the station with me.'

CHAPTER 29

At the team meeting the next morning, Bridget couldn't help noticing that Ffion was looking like the cat who'd got the cream, whereas Jake looked as if his milk had been snatched away from him and then he'd been shut outside all night in the cold.

So when Bridget asked whether anyone had anything to report, she wasn't surprised when Ffion's hand shot up. 'I managed to work out Diane's password last night, and got into her laptop.' Her excitement only made her Welsh accent more pronounced than ever.

'What have you managed to find?'

'I know where the payments to her off-shore bank account are coming from.'

Now Bridget felt her own anticipation mounting. Had they finally made the breakthrough she had been hoping for? Enough to keep Grayson off her back and Baxter at bay? 'Go on.'

'Diane wrote books.'

Bridget didn't know what she'd been expecting to hear, but it wasn't this. She could tell that the others in the room were feeling let down too. She tried to keep the disappointment from her voice. 'Books? Like *A Deadly Race*?'

'No,' said Ffion with a smirk. 'Definitely not like that.'

'What then?' asked Ryan.

'Well,' said Ffion, obviously enjoying being centre of attention, 'we already knew from Diane's phone that she enjoyed reading hot romance books. What I found from her laptop is that she wrote them too, and published them herself online.'

'She wrote romance books?' repeated Bridget agog.

'Hot romance?' queried Ryan. 'Do you mean _'

'Whatever your fevered imagination is picturing right now,' interrupted Ffion, 'then, yes, all of that with bells and whistles on. Not to mention whips, handcuffs and all kinds of other accessories.'

She opened up the laptop to reveal a screen packed full of book covers featuring half-naked men and scantily-clad women. The titles of the books were suggestive, to say the least. Jake's ears turned pink as he stared at the images.

'So it would seem that Diane had two sides to her personality,' continued Ffion. 'And two jobs that reflected them. By day she was a serious academic, writing papers for journals, attending conferences and seminars, and publishing a book about governments and their shady dealings. By night she devoured steamy romance books, and wrote and self-published her own titles under the pen-name of Lula Langton. Obviously, she went to great lengths to keep the two facets apart. She even went to the trouble of encrypting her laptop to stop anyone finding out. We assumed it was because of her investigations into the international arms trade, but it was to protect her academic reputation.'

Bridget wondered what Professor Al-Mutairi might say if he found out about Diane's flipside. Talk about bringing his department into disrepute. But she was still puzzled. 'So where did the money come from?'

'From sales of her romance books. She's published several series in total, and judging from the number of reviews on Amazon, she has a lot of fans around the world – far more than have ever read *A Deadly Race*. The payments into her off-shore company are from e-book retailers.'

'So, were her agent and publisher involved in this operation?'

'No. She published her e-books directly online.'

Bridget had no idea that it was possible to earn so much from e-books. And to do it single-handedly without an agent and publisher working on her behalf. So much for Diane Gilbert's socialist credentials – she had been a very successful entrepreneur.

Bridget thanked Ffion for her ingenuity and perseverance. But did this new information actually get them anywhere? Apart from clearing up the mystery of the off-shore company, Bridget wasn't sure that it brought them any closer to solving the case. If there was nothing sinister behind the payments into Diane's account, and if the denials of involvement by MI5 and the Saudis could be believed, then what remained? A hoax death threat by a down-at heel literary agent desperate to sell more books. Oh yes – and the persistent and unavoidable fact that a woman had been murdered in her own home while under police protection.

Who was it who said, *You can't go back and change the beginning, but you can start where you are and change the ending?* There was something about this case that had been bothering her right from the start.

'The broken glass,' she muttered, 'at the back door of the house.'

'What about it, ma'am?' asked Jake.

'Jake, you come with me. And' – Bridget searched the faces until her gaze came to rest on the youngest member of her team – 'Harry.'

'Me?' His eyes lit up.

'Yes, Harry. I think you'll be perfect for this job.'

★

The crime scene at the back of Diane's house looked much as it had the week before. The back door was still sealed off by crime tape fluttering in the breeze, but that wouldn't stop Bridget carrying out the experiment she had in mind. On the way from the station, they had stopped off at a local hardware shop in Kidlington to buy everything they needed.

Beside her, Harry seemed nervous. 'Are you sure this is a good idea, ma'am?'

'Yes. I want to get to the bottom of this, once and for all.'

Harry lowered the pane of glass he was carrying to the ground and propped it up against the brick wall of the house.

'Place it right next to the back door,' said Bridget. 'I want to try to reproduce the conditions on the night Diane was killed as closely as we can. Now where's that hammer?'

Jake was carrying it. He passed it to Harry, along with a pair of safety glasses.

'So,' said Bridget. 'Here's what we'll do. I'll go and wait in my car out the front. Jake, you go up to Diane's bedroom and wait there. Harry, we'll text you when we're both in place, and then you can smash the glass.'

Harry still looked dubious.

'Would you rather Jake broke the glass?' asked Bridget.

That seemed to make Harry's mind up. 'No, ma'am. I'll do it.'

'Good,' said Bridget. 'Now let's all get into position.' She left Harry at the back of the house with the hammer and the glass, and made her way to the front. The constable who had been guarding the house was no longer on duty. Jake let himself in with a key and disappeared upstairs. Bridget's car was parked immediately outside, in the exact spot that Sam and Scott had been parked on the night of the murder. She climbed inside, texted Harry to say she was ready, and then waited.

The street was probably almost as quiet by day as it was by night. Although the nearby Banbury Road was busy at this time, here on St Margaret's Road, screened by large houses, trees and hedges, only a faint murmur of traffic was audible. Bridget made herself comfortable, closed her eyes, and settled back to wait.

She was disturbed some while later by a sharp rap on the side window of the car. Harry. Bridget wound the glass down. 'What is it?'

'It's done, ma'am. Didn't you hear it?'

'No.' Bridget felt a thrill, knowing now that she had been right to trust Sam and Scott. Their version of events had been shown to be true. From inside a car at the front of the house, it was impossible to hear the sound of breaking glass at the back.

She left her car and followed Harry inside the house. Jake was just coming down the stairs. 'Did you hear it?' she asked him.

'Absolutely. Crystal clear.'

'And would it have woken you up?'

'I would say so.'

It was just as Bridget had thought. A light sleeper like Diane should definitely have woken

291

up when the intruder broke the glass. Yet she had been found dead in her bed. There was only one possible explanation that fitted the facts. Diane had already been dead when the glass in the back door was broken.

'Let's go back outside,' she said to the others.

Harry led them around to the back. There, where the pane of glass had been propped up, fragments splayed out across the flagstones, just like Bridget had seen on the kitchen floor when she'd arrived and discovered the break-in.

'Harry, can you walk across the broken glass for me.'

He did as she asked, a puzzled look on his face.

'Now show me the soles of your shoes.'

He leaned against the wall and lifted up his right sole.

'I see it,' said Jake, 'The broken glass gets trapped in the tread of the shoe.'

'That's right,' said Bridget. 'If the intruder had walked through the broken glass, they would have picked it up on their shoes and deposited some in the rest of the house. But the SOCO report didn't mention any glass in the carpets. Vik's always very thorough. He would have found it if there had been any.'

Jake scratched his head. 'What does that mean?'

'It means,' said Bridget, 'that the glass wasn't smashed by the intruder on their way into the house. It was broken by them as they left.'

'To make it look like a break-in,' said Harry.

'Exactly. Whoever killed Diane almost certainly had a back-door key to the house, but they broke the pane to conceal that fact.'

CHAPTER 30

Finally, like fragments of broken glass fitting back together, pieces of the mystery were beginning to slot into place. The killer had misdirected them by pretending to break into the house while Diane was asleep. In reality they had let themselves in silently through the back door with the key, crept upstairs and plunged the poisoned syringe into Diane's chest, killing her before she had time to respond. They had smashed the glass in the back door on their way out to conceal the fact that they possessed a key.

Now Bridget understood how they had gained entry to the garden. If the killer had a key to the back door, it was reasonable to assume they also possessed a key to the door in the back wall of the garden. They had entered the property that way, carried out the murder, and slipped away afterwards, locking the garden door after them and leaving no trace behind.

'So we're looking for someone who had a key to the property,' Bridget told Jake and Harry. 'In all likelihood, a family member. And the only relative with a clear motive to kill Diane is her son, Daniel Dunn. He inherits everything – the house, the royalties from her book sales, the lot.'

Bridget wasted no time in sending a police car round to Ian Dunn's house to pick up his son. She hoped he hadn't already left Oxford. Luck was on her side for once and soon after she returned to Kidlington the officers arrived with Daniel in tow.

He was clearly unhappy at having been brought into the police station under such ignominious circumstances. But Bridget didn't care about wounded pride. The time for the softly, softly approach had run out some while back.

Daniel insisted on his right to legal representation, arranging for a lawyer from the same firm that was handling Diane's estate. Once the lawyer had arrived and had spent ten minutes alone with his client, Bridget entered the interview room with Jake.

The lawyer was a sombre, self-effacing man in a dark grey suit who sat slightly back from Daniel as if to take a more objective view of proceedings. Bridget wondered if he'd already formed an unfavourable view of his client during Daniel's dealings with the firm regarding his mother's will.

She waited while Jake handed out plastic cups of tea – the best hospitality that the station could muster – and took a moment to observe Daniel Dunn. The man looked tired, as if he hadn't been sleeping properly. A muscle just below his left eye kept twitching, and when he reached forward to pick up his tea he knocked the plastic cup, spilling some brown liquid over the table.

'Sorry,' he said as Jake mopped up the spillage with a paper towel. 'Clumsy of me. This place makes me jumpy.'

'No need to worry,' said Bridget. 'You're not under arrest.' But Daniel did seem particularly nervous. Well, she could use that to her advantage.

The lawyer cleared his throat. 'Inspector, please could you explain why my client has been asked to come in today?'

'We have some further questions relating to the death of his mother.'

'Questions that couldn't have been asked at home?'

'Questions that may reveal new evidence or that might suggest new lines of enquiry.'

'I see.'

The lawyer appeared to have no objections, so Bridget turned to Daniel. 'Mr Dunn, do you possess a set of keys to your mother's house?'

He looked at her in surprise. 'I do.'

'And does that include a key to the kitchen door?'

'Yes.'

'And also the door in the garden wall at the back?'

'Yes.' He looked at her warily. 'Why is this important?'

'We have reason to believe that the person

responsible for killing your mother used a key to enter the property through the garden door, and then through the kitchen door.'

'I thought you said they broke in.'

'New evidence suggests that the glass in the kitchen door was broken on the intruder's way out, to make it appear as if they had forced an entry. That would explain why your mother didn't wake up. As a light sleeper she would almost certainly have heard the sound of breaking glass if she'd been alive when the glass in the door was smashed.'

Daniel's brow wrinkled as he processed the new information. 'That makes sense. But what does that have to do with me? You surely don't think I had anything to do with my own mother's death?' He looked to his lawyer for support but the man gave nothing away.

At a nod from Bridget, Jake took up the questioning. 'Where were you on the night that your mother was killed?'

'I was in London. That's where I live.' A surliness had entered his voice and Bridget sensed a growing reluctance to cooperate.

'Can anyone confirm that?'

He thought for a moment. 'I don't think so. No.'

'What about your girlfriend?'

'She was away for a couple of days on a training course.' He thought for a moment. 'But I was at work until late on Thursday. The end of the tax year is always a hectic time and I didn't leave the office until gone eight o'clock. I was back at my desk by seven the next morning. You can ask my boss.'

'We will,' said Bridget. 'But if you don't mind me saying, that doesn't account for your whereabouts at the time that your mother was killed.'

'And what time was that?' asked the lawyer.

'Between eleven in the evening and one in the morning.'

'Well, I went to bed at about eleven,' said Daniel. 'Who can possibly provide an alibi for the time when they were asleep?'

'Someone whose girlfriend wasn't conveniently away for the night,' suggested Jake.

Daniel shook his head angrily. He jerked out his hand and this time the rest of his tea sloshed over the desk.

Bridget waited patiently while Jake went to fetch more paper towels. When the mess had been cleared up, she asked, 'How long would it take for you to drive from your home in London to your mother's house in Oxford?'

'It depends on the traffic,' said Daniel, his arms now folded against his chest.

'In the middle of the night, with light traffic.'

'I'm not in the habit of driving to my mother's house in the middle of the night.'

'An hour and a half?' suggested Bridget.

'About that.'

'So a round trip of three hours.'

The lawyer leaned forward. 'Are you

suggesting that my client drove to Oxford in the middle of the night in order to murder his own mother?'

'I'm simply trying to establish whether your client can provide any evidence to exclude that possibility. And it would seem that he can't.'

'My client is not obliged to prove his innocence, as you well know, Inspector.'

'Of course.'

'So if you have no further questions, I am going to ask that you allow him to leave.'

Bridget glanced at Jake. 'No further questions for the moment.'

Daniel stood up, scraping his chair noisily against the floor. 'I have to say that this was a complete waste of time. Did you really learn anything useful from this interview, Inspector?'

Bridget regarded him calmly. 'I learned that you are in possession of a full set of keys to your mother's house, and that you are unable to provide an alibi for the time of her murder.'

He glared at her, fury etched on his face. 'You've had it in for me from the start, haven't you?'

'Not at all,' said Bridget. 'I'm simply following the facts.'

The lawyer took Daniel by the arm to try to lead him from the room, but he shook him off. 'You want the facts? Well, try this. My father's a fool when it comes to my mother. While she was alive, he was blind to her faults and always made excuses for her. Even now she's dead, he still refuses to believe what everyone else knows.'

'And what's that, Daniel?'

'That she was a selfish, self-centred woman who thought the whole world revolved around her, and was really only interested in other people if they could be useful to her or if they made her feel good about herself. All those causes she went after – her politics and her campaigns – they were just a way for her to bolster her ego and make her feel superior to everyone else. Well, in my opinion, she got what she deserved. She finally came up against someone who didn't think that her life mattered very much at all.'

He stopped, breathless. His lawyer once again tried to draw him from the room, but Daniel wasn't done yet.

'Louise was never fooled by my mother. Oh, I know she always did her best to be civil to her, for Dad's sake. But she saw right through her. She saw what a callous manipulative bitch my mother was.'

'How can you know that?'

'Because she told me! And do you know what else? Poor Louise has been trying to compete against my mother the whole time she's been married to my father. He talks about her all the time, you know. Diane this, Diane that. Do you know the real reason my parents got divorced?'

'What?'

'Dad always wanted more children, but after I was born my mother refused to have any more.

That's why he eventually left her and married a woman young enough to start another family.'

Daniel's claim wasn't too much of a surprise. It tallied with what Ian had told Bridget himself.

'Louise claims that being childless is a blessing,' Daniel continued, 'but that's just another lie! Why do you think she chose to become a paediatrician? She adores children, and she and Dad were desperate to have a family of their own. They even had fertility treatment. But it never came to anything. So there you have it. More lies. And yet another reason for Louise to feel resentful and inadequate.' He paused a moment to gather his breath. When he spoke again, his tone was more measured. 'I know you don't like me, Inspector. You think I'm nothing more than a spoilt brat and a money grabber. But let me tell you something. I would never do what my father has done to Louise. He may not have intended her any harm, but at times he treated her as if all that mattered was her ability – or her inability – to conceive. I would never put my own girlfriend under that kind of pressure.'

His words finally out, Daniel allowed his lawyer to lead him from the room.

CHAPTER 31

Bridget rose early on Friday, unable to sleep once the first light peeped around the curtains and the birds began their morning songs. So many things were bothering her about the case, and not just the fact that she had still been unable to solve it. There was something she was missing regarding Diane's family. Daniel's passionate declaration about his father's desire for more children, and the inability for him and Louise to start a family had set her thinking. She mulled her idea over in the shower, and decided to drive to Diane's house before going into Kidlington. There was something she wanted to check.

She parked in her usual spot just outside the house, exactly where Sam and Scott had been stationed on the night of the murder. Looking at the house and grounds, she could now read the sequence of events that had taken place that night. The door at the rear of the property opening silently at the turn of a key; the intruder walking up the garden path leaving no marks behind; unlocking the kitchen door and creeping upstairs; and then injecting the sleeping victim with the poisoned syringe. Diane's eyes might have opened briefly, taking in her killer's identity. But she was dead within seconds, leaving the murderer to retrace their steps, stopping just long enough to break the glass in the back door. It had been a meticulously planned murder – audacious, even – to commit the crime knowing that two uniformed police officers were on watch at the front of the house.

Bridget was confident that she had worked out the exact sequence of events. But she still didn't know whether this was a politically-motivated assassination or a personal matter. If the latter, had it been driven by hate, a desire for revenge, or greed? If she could unlock that mystery, the identity of the killer would surely be revealed at last.

In Diane's living room she went to the shelves and located the red photograph album that documented the road trip around Italy that Diane had taken with Annabel and their respective partners in April of 1983. It was clear from Diane's laptop password – Neapolitan – that the occasion held deep personal significance to her. What had happened during that three-week vacation that had been so important?

Bridget flicked quickly through the pages until she found the photograph of the two couples seated around the outdoor table in Naples, the great peak of Vesuvius glowering ominously behind them.

When she had first looked at this picture she

had been charmed by the palazzo-style villa and the allure of pasta and wine spread out beneath a fiery sun. Now she ignored the setting and concentrated on the four people in the photograph.

Two couples. Diane and Ian. Annabel and John. They would have been in their early twenties at the time, not long out of university, or in Ian's case, still only halfway through his long medical training to become a doctor. Diane and Ian had got married just two months after this picture was taken, Annabel and John the year after. Two of the four were now dead; one was widowed; one divorced and remarried. All had been touched by tragedy in some way.

The four people in the photograph were seated around a perfectly square table, the two sisters opposite each other and the two future husbands to either side. The photographer must have been standing diagonally to the table to fit everyone in the shot. Four young people eating, drinking and smiling in each other's company. A perfectly innocent moment captured in time.

And yet there was something odd about the picture. The more Bridget studied it, the more she sensed that she was right. She closed the album and took it with her to Kidlington. Before jumping to any conclusion, she wanted to get a second opinion.

It was no surprise to find Ffion already at her desk, a freshly brewed mug of herbal tea steaming beside her.

'I'd like you to take a look at this photograph,' said Bridget, opening the album. She pointed to Annabel's late husband, John Caldecott. 'Does he remind you of anyone?'

Ffion studied the photograph intently. She slowly nodded. 'You can see the similarity in the shape of the brow. The eyes are the same too.'

'I'm not just imagining it, am I?' said Bridget.

'No, I don't think so.'

The implications were already racing through Bridget's mind but she waited for Ffion to say the name out loud.

'Daniel Dunn,' she said at last. 'Daniel looks just like John Caldecott.'

★

Before long, the rest of the team had drifted in and the incident room was thick with the mingled scents of freshly brewed coffee, sweet and tangy bacon rolls and greasy jam doughnuts. Bridget took her place in front of the whiteboard, ignoring the smell of food, and quickly outlined her theory that Daniel Dunn might not be Ian's son.

She passed the Italian photograph around for everyone to see for themselves, hoping that it wouldn't come back to her covered in sticky fingerprints. 'The physical similarities between Daniel Dunn and John Caldecott,' she explained, 'suggest that John is actually Daniel's father.'

'It makes sense now you say it,' said Jake. 'Have you noticed how clumsy Daniel can be? When we interviewed him he spilled his tea not once, but twice. Could he have inherited Huntington's disease from his father?'

Bridget recalled the occasion when she had visited Ian Dunn's house in Headington and Daniel had dropped his leather document folder. Clumsiness didn't prove anything, but it was consistent with what Annabel had told her about the early stage of the degenerative disease. 'That's a very real possibility. Now, Diane and Annabel travelled to Italy with Ian and John during April of 1983. Daniel was born in January of 1984, nine months later. So, how does this change our view of the situation?'

'Temptation beneath the hot Italian sun?' said Ryan. 'Well, it gives Ian Dunn a strong motive. If Diane cheated on him during this Italian holiday, and Daniel is really John's son, then what might he do if he found out the truth?'

'Even though he and Diane had been divorced for ten years?'

'That wouldn't necessarily soften the blow of discovery. A lie is a lie. And it's not just about Diane's infidelity. The son he thought was his, turns out to be another man's. It would rock his entire world.'

'How might he have guessed the truth, though?' asked Bridget.

'The same way you did, ma'am' said Andy. 'You only have to look at the faces of the two men to spot the similarities.'

'I don't know,' said Bridget. 'If that was the case, surely Ian would have worked it out years ago.'

'Perhaps he had his suspicions,' said Ffion, 'but the first symptoms of Huntington's disease typically don't become apparent until your early thirties. So if Daniel's clumsiness is only just beginning to show itself, Ian might only recently have become certain of the facts.'

'And that would give him a strong motive for murder,' said Jake. 'Especially since he and Louise have been unable to have children of their own. Perhaps it isn't Louise who suffers from infertility, but Ian. That realisation would have fuelled his resentment.'

'Plus he's a doctor,' said Andy, 'so he would certainly recognise the symptoms of Huntington's.'

'And,' said Harry, looking chuffed to make a contribution, 'as a doctor, he would have easy access to hypodermic syringes and the chemicals he needed to poison her.'

'It's quite possible that he still has a set of keys to Diane's house,' said Ffion, 'given that he used to live there. Or he might have taken Annabel's set.'

Bridget put up her hands to stem the flow of information. 'I think that's more than enough to be going on with,' she said. 'It's time for another visit to Headington.'

CHAPTER 32

When Bridget rang the bell of the ivy-clad Georgian house this time, the door was opened by Ian's new wife, Louise Morton. Ian's Lexus Coupé was not parked outside. Neither, for that matter, was Daniel's Golf.

Louise didn't look particularly pleased to see Bridget. 'Is there something I can help you with? Only, I don't have much time. I'm just on my way to the gym.'

Louise was clad in tight-fitting gym shorts and a cropped top that did a great job of showing off her toned physique. Bridget had often been told by Chloe that the right clothing could make flab miraculously vanish. It never seemed to work for Bridget, but in Louise's case there didn't seem to be any spare fat for the clothing to hide.

'Actually, it was Ian I wanted to speak to,' said Bridget.

'I'm afraid he isn't here. He took a whole week off work to support Daniel, but he thought it was time he went back. After all, it wasn't as if he'd lost someone very close to him. He and Diane had been divorced for years.'

But married for twenty-five, thought Bridget. 'Don't worry,' she said. 'I'll find him at the hospital.'

At the John Radcliffe's main reception desk, Bridget flashed her warrant card and was given directions to the cardiology department. She followed the signs through the corridors and up various flights of stairs. The woman at the department's entrance desk informed her that Dr Dunn was currently with a patient but would be free to speak to her in about twenty minutes. Bridget took a seat in the waiting area and checked her phone for messages.

Inevitably there was a missed call from Vanessa. Bridget hadn't spoken to her since they had argued about their parents. Vanessa had driven down to Lyme Regis on her own on Wednesday and had stayed for a couple of nights, firing off a stream of rebukes to Bridget by text message – 'James is having to work from home so he can see to the children' – 'Mum could really use your support right now' and so on. Vanessa had been planning to return today, and no doubt she would be full of self-righteous indignation at the sacrifices she had made on Bridget's behalf. Bridget accessed her voicemail, bracing herself for the full impact of Vanessa's wrath.

'Bridget, I've just got back from Lyme Regis. Things are not good with Mum and Dad. Call me as soon as you get this. We need to talk urgently.'

Bridget's heart sank. Was Vanessa

exaggerating, or had the situation really deteriorated that much? When she'd spoken to her father the previous night, he'd sounded tired but upbeat. Was there really an urgent problem, or was this just her sister's histrionics? Bridget's thumb hovered briefly over the quick dial shortcut but then she caught sight of the receptionist approaching.

'Dr Dunn can see you now.'

Bridget put her phone away, feeling as if she had just been granted a stay of execution. She followed the woman into a consulting room where Ian Dunn was seated behind a large desk on which sat a computer, a phone and an in-tray of case notes.

He rose to greet her. 'Inspector Hart, this is a surprise.' His professional manner was polished, but Bridget detected a wariness behind his eyes. No one enjoyed a visit from a police officer, especially not at their place of work. 'Please, take a seat. Has there been a development with the case?'

'Possibly,' said Bridget. 'I have some questions for you that might seem a little indelicate.'

He gave her a resigned smile. 'I break difficult news to people every day as part of my job. I like to think that I'd be able to handle a little indelicacy.'

Bridget wondered if he'd already guessed what she was about to ask. Perhaps he had been waiting patiently for her to arrive at the obvious conclusion.

'It's about your son, Daniel. I've met him on a few occasions now and I can't help noticing that he seems a little… clumsy. He drops things. He spills his tea. Now, I realise he's just received a terrible shock, but he's a young man and this… clumsiness, for want of a better word, seems unusual.' She stopped and waited for a response.

Ian was gazing beyond her, as if lost in some distant memory. Then he nodded his head and shifted his focus back to her. 'I wondered if you'd notice. But you're a detective, so of course you have good observational skills. If you'd met Daniel just a year ago perhaps you wouldn't have seen it, but now it's becoming too pronounced to ignore.'

'Huntington's disease?'

'Early-stage. At least, that's my guess. He'll need to be tested to be certain.'

'How long have you known?'

'I noticed the earliest signs a few years ago, but I tried very hard to convince myself that I was wrong.'

'But now you don't think you are?'

'In my professional capacity as a doctor, no. But as a father, I would give anything to be wrong.'

'But that's the heart of the matter, isn't it?' said Bridget gently. 'Is Daniel really your son? Or is John Caldecott his biological father?'

Ian gave a prolonged sigh, perhaps in relief that the secret he had borne for so long was finally out. 'I've long suspected that John was Daniel's father. To be honest, I began to wonder almost as soon as he was born. His hair colouring, his appearance, his personality traits... Even the timing of his birth cast doubts in my mind. But I pushed all those misgivings to one side and loved Daniel as dearly as any father loved a son. I was the one who brought him up. I was his father in every sense that mattered.'

'And yet, if you had doubts about whether Daniel was really your son...' Bridget struggled to find a sympathetic way to phrase what she wanted to say, but couldn't.

Ian saved her. 'Then Diane must have cheated on me. With her own sister's husband – or boyfriend at the time. You think I was jealous of John? That I felt betrayed by Diane?'

'Yes.'

'It wasn't as simple as that,' said Ian.

'Would you care to explain?'

He looked as if he was battling with himself over whether to reveal some deep, dark secret. After a moment or two he seemed to come to a decision. 'We swapped,' he said abruptly.

'Swapped?'

'We swapped partners. On holiday, in Italy. The country of love and passion.' His voice was flat and deadpan, the antithesis of passionate. 'When we set out on that trip, I was dating Annabel, and John was with Diane. By the time we returned, Diane and I were engaged, and Annabel and John were a couple.'

Bridget's mind flashed to the photograph of

the two young couples seated around the dining table in the shadow of Vesuvius. Who was dating who when that photograph was taken? It was impossible to tell from the photograph alone. Naples had been the final stop on their grand tour of Italy. They had left England with one configuration and returned with another. It had all the hallmarks of one of Mozart's comic operas. But even comic operas had a dark vein running through their heart. In this case, a seed had been planted back then that would one day flower into tragedy.

'So Diane was already pregnant with John's child when you swapped partners?'

Ian spread out his hands. 'That would be the logical deduction.'

'But how did this swap happen?'

Ian gave a short laugh. 'You could explain it as a moment of madness, I suppose. Blame it on the wine and the sun. But the truth is more rational. All four of us got on very well, but as we travelled down through Italy, Annabel and John always wanted to go hiking up hillsides, whereas Diane and I preferred visiting churches and museums. It gradually became apparent that we were better suited with each other's partners. The swap was natural. We were all happy with the arrangement.'

'I see,' said Bridget. 'But how can I be sure you're telling the truth?'

'About what?'

'About you being happy with the outcome of

this romantic mix-and-match?'

'Ah, I see what you're getting at,' said Ian, amused. 'You think that I've secretly harboured a life-long resentment at being paired with Diane. Maybe you think that when I finally realised Daniel wasn't my son, I exploded with jealousy. Like a volcano simmering for years – decades even – before erupting with fatal consequences. You think I murdered her because of jealousy.' He was grinning at her now. 'The thing is, all this is ancient history. First of all, I've suspected for a long time that John was Daniel's father. Secondly, Diane never cheated on me. Daniel was conceived while she and John were still a couple. And thirdly, I split up with her almost ten years ago. So your theory really doesn't stand up to scrutiny.'

'Then what about Annabel?' asked Bridget. 'Might she have deduced that Daniel was really John's son?'

'I'm sure she has. In fact, I suspect that she's known it just as long as I have. Remember that she witnessed the onset of Huntington's disease first-hand with John. If anyone could spot the same symptoms in Daniel, it's surely her. But Annabel always treated Daniel as if he were her own child. Perhaps it was because she knew he was John's. Perhaps because she and John didn't have any children of their own.'

'But it seems like Annabel drew the short straw with this partner swap arrangement. She could have married you, but instead she ended up with

John who died from a terrible wasting disease.'

Ian shook his head. 'You're barking up the wrong tree. Annabel was devoted to John. You should have seen the way she cared for him when he was dying. She nursed him tenderly right until the very end.'

Bridget stared glumly across the desk. She had come here convinced that she had finally uncovered the dark secret that lay at the heart of this mystery. Now that secret had been brought out into the light and held up for scrutiny, yet once again her hopes of solving the case had been dashed.

'If anyone has grounds for complaint,' said Ian, 'it's Louise. I've treated her badly.'

'I don't understand,' said Bridget. 'How is Louise involved in this?'

Ian looked ashamed. 'I said before that one of the reasons I left Diane was that I wanted to have more children.'

Bridget nodded. 'Daniel mentioned it too.'

'Did he? Okay. Well, when I married Louise, I really hoped – we both hoped – to start a family of our own. But it wasn't meant to be.'

'I'm sorry to hear that.'

'We tried several rounds of fertility treatment, but none of it came to anything. In the end we gave up. It was all too upsetting for Louise. Believing that Daniel was my son, she blamed herself for her failure to conceive.' He put his head in his hands. 'I should have been honest with her.'

'Well, perhaps it's time to set the record straight,' said Bridget. 'Have you considered getting a paternity test?'

'It's crossed my mind. But sometimes we prefer not to know the truth. Isn't that so?'

'Maybe,' said Bridget, 'but Daniel has a right to know who his biological father is, especially given the possible implications for his health.'

Ian nodded his head slowly. 'You're right, Inspector. You're absolutely right. It's time for me to have some difficult conversations. I've put this off for far too long.'

CHAPTER 33

Bridget left the hospital deep in thought. She had gone there believing Ian Dunn to be a murderer, but on her way out he had shaken her hand and thanked her. Her intervention had been the catalyst he needed to start talking openly about what had happened, and to begin to repair the damage that had been done so many years ago.

Good news, but where did that leave Bridget? She turned over the facts of the case as she walked back to the Mini.

She remained convinced that whoever had killed Diane had possessed a set of keys to her house. Who could that be? The most obvious candidate was still Daniel Dunn. Daniel had freely admitted to having a set of keys to the house, and perhaps that made him less likely to be the true killer. But on the other hand, Daniel was a highly intelligent individual, who must have known that owning up to the fact would help to deflect suspicion away from him. The fact that he had no alibi for the night of the murder, and that he knew his way around the house and garden, including the gate at the back of the property, definitely counted against him. Plus, as the sole beneficiary of Diane's will, he was the only member of the family with an obvious motive to want her dead. A multi-million-pound motive.

Who else had a key? The only other person Bridget knew for certain was Annabel. But if Ian Dunn could be believed, Annabel had no feelings of jealousy towards her sister, and from what Bridget had observed, Annabel had been very fond of Diane. The regular messages and meetings that Ffion had uncovered on Diane's phone confirmed that. Annabel didn't benefit at all from Diane's death, and besides, the set of keys she owned had gone missing. Had someone taken them?

A family member seemed the most obvious candidate for the theft. Daniel already had his own keys. Might Ian Dunn have taken them in order to kill his ex-wife? As Harry had remarked, as a hospital consultant, Ian would have easy access to a hypodermic syringe and the toxins that had been used to stop Diane's heart. If so, he was a very cool customer, having just sat through a tough interview with Bridget. He had an alibi for the time of the murder, but it wasn't watertight. Perhaps he could have driven back to Oxford from the party he had been attending in time to kill Diane. But the timings didn't allow much room for that possibility.

Another obvious candidate was Professor Mansour Ali Al-Mutairi, Dean of the Blavatnik

School. He had openly confessed to the personal animosity between himself and Diane and their bitter professional rivalry. Their political views were diametrically opposed, and it was quite possible that the publication of her book had been the last straw. Bridget knew that when someone believed that their cause was just, they were capable of anything, even murder. The professor had described to Bridget the cold-blooded execution of his father by Iraqi soldiers. When political convictions were forged through bitter personal experience, the resulting fervour could become toxic. But how could the professor have got hold of Diane's key? Perhaps he had simply taken them from her office one day and had a copy made. It was as good an explanation as any.

Michael Dearlove, the journalist, had been Diane's secret lover. If he had been in the habit of staying with Diane when he was visiting Oxford, then it was possible that she had given him his own keys so he could let himself into the house unseen. He had been at the meeting at the White Horse until an hour or so before the murder. That gave him plenty of time to have stopped off at Diane's house, slipped inside, given her that fatal injection, and then driven home to his wife in London. But what was the motive? Bridget didn't know of one.

Also at that meeting was Grant Sadler, the disgraced literary agent. Of all the people involved in this case, Grant was the least trustworthy. He had lied repeatedly to Bridget, and only under intense questioning had he finally admitted to sending the death threat. Bridget only had his word for it that Diane was a knowing participant in a publicity stunt. It was just as likely that Grant had made the threat in all seriousness, and then proceeded to carry it out. He had a very strong financial motive, and plenty of opportunity, having lied about his alibi. But how had he managed to obtain the keys to Diane's house? That couldn't be explained.

Then there was Jennifer Eagleston, the publisher, always greedy for more money. Cynical, grasping, willing to hold secret meetings and break contractual obligations if it meant she could get what she wanted. She too had no alibi, having left the White Horse at the same time as Michael and Grant. Nobody had witnessed her return to her hotel. She could just as easily have walked to Diane's house instead. But, as with Grant Sadler, there was the question of the keys. How might Jennifer have got her hands on them?

There was always the possibility that Bridget had allowed herself to become fixated on the matter of the keys. If MI5 or someone working for the Saudi intelligence agency had carried out the murder, they might simply have picked the locks and entered the property without the need for a key. But then why bother to break the glass in the back door? Bridget's head was beginning to spin with all the unknowns.

One thing she knew for sure – just as Ian Dunn

could no longer postpone his difficult conversations about Daniel's paternity, Bridget couldn't continue to avoid Vanessa. It was time for her to face a tricky discussion of her own. She returned to her car and set off in the direction of North Oxford.

★

On arriving in Charlbury Road, Bridget was pleased to find Vanessa's Range Rover parked on the drive outside her house. She was by no means looking forward to seeing her sister, but it would be easier to do it face-to-face rather than over the phone. She strongly suspected that this would be a very one-sided conversation. Vanessa would do most of the talking, and it would be Bridget's job to listen attentively and take her sister's concerns seriously.

She rang the bell and waited. After a full minute there was still no answer. But with spring in full blossom and summer on its way, perhaps Vanessa was outside. She was a keen gardener and at the height of the season her herbaceous borders rivalled anything that the Royal Horticultural Society might produce.

Bridget made her way round the side of the house to the extensive garden at the back. The neatly trimmed hedges and perfectly edged lawn were a far cry from her own wild, untangled plot. There was very little chance of Bridget's tiny garden in Wolvercote improving any time soon.

But she had taken heart on hearing on the radio that leaving part of your garden to nature was good for the environment. Weeds were to be welcomed, it seemed. Perhaps she would redesignate a portion of it as a wildlife haven and abandon it to the whims of nature. Who was she kidding? She had basically already done that with the entire plot.

The barking of Rufus alerted Vanessa to Bridget's arrival. She stood up from where she had been kneeling, a trowel in her hand. From the look of it, she must have stopped off at the garden centre on her way back from Lyme Regis, because four bright-green potted plants were waiting to be assigned their place in the freshly dug border, and a watering can, a bag of compost and a brightly-coloured bottle of liquid fertiliser were on hand to give them the best possible start to their new life.

'Hi,' said Bridget. 'You're busy.'

'Weeding helps to calm me down,' said Vanessa. From the heap of dead weeds in the nearby wheelbarrow, Bridget guessed that Vanessa had needed a lot of calming. 'And Easter is a time for new beginnings.'

Bridget took that remark as a positive sign. 'Would you like to go inside and talk?' she asked. 'I've got time.' That wasn't strictly true but this conversation would flow a lot more smoothly if she could show Vanessa that she was making an effort. In any case, Bridget had run out of fresh ideas on the investigation. Every lead she had followed had run into the ground.

'We can talk out here,' said Vanessa. 'It's a beautiful day. Besides, I want to get these azaleas planted before their roots start to dry out.'

She knelt back on her gardening mat, scooped out a hole with her trowel, upended one of the baby plants, and struck the bottom of its plastic pot with what seemed like unnecessary force. The fledgling shrub popped out of its container in one neat movement, and Vanessa pushed it into its allotted hole, topping it up with compost. She firmed the dark crumbly material down with gloved hands, then started to dig a second hole before she spoke again.

'Mum's getting back on her feet now, and Dad's looking after her. I think they'll be okay for the moment at least. But I've said that I'll go back and see them again as soon as I can. I'm hoping that you'll be able to come with me next time.'

'I hope so too,' said Bridget. 'That is, I'll do my very best to get away. As soon as this current investigation is concluded, I'll be able to take time off.'

And, if as was looking increasingly likely she failed to conclude the investigation with a positive result, she would probably find herself with an abundance of free time. Grayson wasn't likely to cut her much more slack. He had made it perfectly clear that he would bring in Baxter if he lost confidence in her. Perhaps she should pre-empt the decision and suggest it herself. She couldn't claim that she was filled with confidence at her own ability to solve the case.

'Things are going to have to change, one way or another,' continued Vanessa. 'In the short term, we're going to have to spend more time down in Dorset helping out. Their house is just about manageable, but the garden is far too big for Dad to look after, especially now that Mum's taking up so much of his time.'

'How is she?'

'Not at all strong. She has too many underlying health conditions. Dad was already struggling, and this broken arm is merely the latest in a long line of issues. I'm worried about her, and I'm worried about how much of a burden she is for Dad. You and I are going to have to lighten that load, otherwise I don't know how he'll continue to cope.'

Bridget nodded. 'I hadn't realised things had got so bad. It's because we've seen so little of them since they moved to Dorset. They've been hidden away.'

'Exactly. You've put your finger on it. The fact is,' said Vanessa, 'they'd be much better off moving back to Oxford. We'd be close on hand to help out, and to step in if anything else happens. Or when it happens, I should say, because Mum's not going to get any stronger. They'd see their grandchildren regularly too, and they'd also be able to visit Abigail's grave whenever they wanted to.'

Bridget nodded. Her dead younger sister was

out of sight, but never far from her thoughts. 'But will they agree to moving back?' she asked.

The second plant was now in place. Vanessa moved her kneeling mat along the border and plunged her trowel once again into the neatly-weeded soil. 'Not without a fight.'

'Did you discuss that with them?' asked Bridget.

'Of course I did.'

'And what did they say?'

Vanessa freed a third shrub from its container and lowered it into place. 'They weren't exactly keen on the idea. They refuse to admit to themselves that they can't cope anymore. I think that for them, leaving Lyme Regis would be like an admission of failure.'

'So what's your plan?'

'The next time I see them, I'm going to insist that they move back to Oxford, and I'd like your support in this matter. If we both tell them the same thing, then they might start to listen.'

'I don't think I have any more influence with them than you do,' said Bridget.

'Nonsense,' said Vanessa. 'They expect me to make a fuss, but if you back me up, then they'll be forced to take the idea seriously.'

Perhaps that was true. Vanessa had always been the bossiest of the three sisters. But this was the closest she'd ever come to admitting it. Bridget savoured the moment.

Vanessa had now planted all four azaleas and was tidying up the edge of the bed where the soil met the lawn. 'Anyway, make yourself useful and pour some of that liquid fertiliser into the watering can, will you?'

Bridget picked up the green plastic bottle standing on the grass. 'How much should I add?' She scanned the label for guidance.

'Just one capful,' said Vanessa. 'It's strong stuff.'

But Bridget's mind was no longer on plants and gardening. Her attention was fixed on the bold letters on the label of the bottle.

Ericaceous fertiliser: Rich in phosphorous, magnesium and potassium for all acid-loving plants.

Phosphorous, magnesium and potassium.

The three substances that had been found in Diane's blood. She had been killed with liquid plant food.

'I'm sorry,' said Bridget, thrusting the bottle into Vanessa's hands, 'but I have to dash.'

Vanessa scrambled to her feet. 'Wait a minute! You can't just abandon me again. We need to talk about when we're *both* going down to Lyme Regis.'

'Call you later,' said Bridget. She was already halfway across the lawn, heading towards her car. She thought she heard Vanessa swear at her, but she was too far away to know for certain.

CHAPTER 34

Bridget still couldn't remember the Latin name for Professor Al-Mutairi's exotic pot plants, but that didn't matter. What did matter was that she had seen him watering his precious flowers with liquid feed. Phosphorous, magnesium and potassium. Seeing the deadly cocktail of ingredients listed on Vanessa's bottle of plant food had unlocked the final clue in the case.

The professor had never tried to conceal his personal and professional hatred of Diane Gilbert. He had even threatened to fire her just a day or so before her murder, and Diane had countered with a threat to expose the truth about him. Bridget had a good hunch she knew what that truth was. No wonder he had been forced to act when he did, even knowing that Diane was under police protection.

Bridget drove as fast as she could to the Blavatnik School of Government and dashed up the spiral stairs to the professor's office, bursting inside without knocking.

Professor Al-Mutairi looked up from his desk in surprise. 'Inspector Hart, what can I do for you?'

'I need to see the food that you give to your plants.'

He gave her a bemused look. 'Are you planning to take up horticultural pursuits? I can highly recommend it. Growing plants is an excellent way to counter the stress of modern life.'

He rose from his chair and walked over to the windowsill. A small bottle of plant food stood next to the dazzling display of yellow flowers. He handed it over to her and turned to study his beloved plants. '*Rhanterium epapposum* is a fascinating species. It's adapted for the harsh climate and the saline conditions of the shores of the Arabian Gulf. It flowers in spring and then sheds all its leaves as the desert heat grows in intensity. During the summer it has all the appearance of being dead. Then, when the first rain of late autumn falls, it returns to life and resumes its growth. When I first brought these specimens to this country, I didn't know whether they would take, but in fact they are thriving. I must say, I am rather proud of them.'

But Bridget didn't share the professor's interest in desert flora. She quickly scanned the bottle, searching for the proof she needed. Phosphorous, magnesium and potassium.

But the label on the bottle told a different story. *Rich in nitrogen.* She read through the rest of the ingredients, but none of them matched the chemicals listed in the toxicology report.

'Is that what this food contains?' she demanded. 'Nitrogen?'

The professor looked puzzled. 'Why? What were you expecting?'

'Phosphorous, magnesium and potassium!' yelled Bridget in exasperation.

Al-Mutairi shook his head. 'You are confusing these with ericaceous plants. Desert soils are strongly alkaline, so ericaceous plant food would be detrimental to their growth. That is not at all what they need.'

'Then do you have any ericaceous plants in your garden at home?'

'Sadly not,' said the professor. 'I really don't have time to maintain more than my little window garden here.'

Bridget returned the bottle to the shelf, her spirits deflated.

'I would love to spend more time talking with you about gardening and horticulture, Inspector,' said Al-Mutairi, 'but I do have other tasks to be getting on with.'

Bridget looked up at him, studying his features. Perhaps Al-Mutairi was innocent of Diane's murder, but she was confident that he was hiding one secret. 'I know what you did,' she told him. 'I know the truth about you that Diane Gilbert threatened to expose.'

A cold look spread across his face and she knew that she was right. 'Really? And what truth might that be?'

'That you work as an informant for MI5.'

Professor Al-Mutairi's expression gave nothing away. 'Is that a statement of fact, Inspector, or are you inviting me to confirm or deny your conjecture?'

'Is it true?'

He tugged gently at his beard before responding. 'Let me just say this. Diane Gilbert was a danger to the national security of this country, and also a threat to peace in the Middle East. Someone needed to watch her.'

'And you took it upon yourself to be that someone?'

He smiled broadly then, all traces of his earlier displeasure gone. 'It strikes me that if I tried to deny it, you would simply refuse to believe me.'

'I expect so,' said Bridget.

'In that case, Inspector, there is nothing more for us to discuss. Now, I really do have pressing matters to attend to, so I will wish you good day.'

★

Diane Gilbert had taken great care to conceal her second life as a writer of steamy romance. A secret pseudonym. An encrypted laptop. An off-shore company. She hadn't told anyone in her family or her professional world about this lucrative source of income.

Ffion, who knew a thing or two about leading a double life, was intrigued by the extraordinary lengths Diane had gone to in order to conceal her activity. And why? To protect her academic reputation. It might be the twenty-first century, but old-fashioned snobbery was still alive and kicking, especially in the world of academia where colleagues were often viewed as rivals. Ffion could well imagine the glee on Professor Al-Mutairi's face if he found out that Diane had stooped so low as to write commercial fiction, and romance at that. No wonder Diane had kept her secret so close to her chest.

But to her fans, Diane's alter ego Lula Langton was famous. She enjoyed a large global following, desperate to read the latest instalment from their favourite author. Lula had her own website where readers could discover her books and sign up to Lula's newsletter, ensuring they never missed a new release. But the *About* page, which would normally display a photograph of the author with an informative resumé, was deliberately vague. It featured a rear-view image of a woman walking barefoot on a beach – it could have been anyone – and a bio that focused almost exclusively on reviews of her books – *'sensual'*, *'scintillating'*, *'sexy'*, and *'seductive'* were popular adjectives – and on their bestseller status – *Lula Langton is the New York Times and USA Today bestselling author of red-hot, contemporary romance.* There was actually nothing about Lula Langton herself. But that was no surprise, since Lula didn't exist.

Diane's laptop had one of the best-organised filesystems that Ffion had ever encountered. Folders and files were all named so that it was easy to navigate the contents of the hard drive. A spreadsheet entitled *Writing and Publishing Schedule* provided insight into Diane's rigorous planning process, containing a detailed plan for the production of each book, with time allocated for plotting, writing, editing and publishing. It rather dispelled the myth that writing was a purely creative art which happened whenever the muse inspired you. Diane had treated it as a business, sticking to a rigid programme of work and hitting self-imposed and demanding deadlines. Ffion admired her self-discipline.

Diane – or Lula – had written three different series. There was the *Highlands* series set in Scotland, the covers of which featured rugged men poised on rocky crags and wearing nothing but kilts despite the inclement weather. A billionaire romance series featured images of men with smouldering good looks, and dinner jackets slung over their shoulders. To Ffion's way of thinking they all looked rather too young to be billionaires. But it was Diane's latest series, *Betrayed,* with cover shots of beautiful but wicked-looking women, that had proved to be the biggest hit. Each book was set in a different luxury holiday destination in Europe, and they had titles like *Betrayed in Barcelona, Seduced in St Tropez, Cheated in Cannes, Deceived in Dubrovnik, Abducted in Athens,* and the latest book, *Stolen in Sorrento.*

Stolen in Sorrento had been released a month before Diane's death. Ffion read the blurb.

Scarlett and Katie are sisters and the best of friends. Scarlett is engaged to Jamie, and Katie is engaged to Tom. A road trip around Italy seems like the perfect way to spend the summer before each couple marries and settles down.

But beneath the growing heat of the Italian sun, love and passion take an unexpected turn.

By the time they reach their final destination of Sorrento, loyalties and devotions will be tested to the limit. In the shadow of Vesuvius, lust and desire are about to erupt. But when the hot lava flows, which sister will come out on top?

A shiver ran up Ffion's spine. The plot of the story sounded as if it might be based on the Italian tour that Diane and Annabel had undertaken with their respective partners before they were married. It hinted at something dramatic happening on that holiday. What – or who – had been stolen? Ffion reached for the photograph of the two couples sitting around the dinner table, the threatening presence of Vesuvius clearly visible in the background. Could it be that Diane's romance books were not entirely fictional? Was that another reason why she had kept them secret?

Ffion clicked through the filesystem until she found the original manuscript of *Stolen in Sorrento*. It was only 50,000 words long, a fraction of the length of *A Deadly Race*. It wouldn't take her long to speed-read her way through the text, and maybe it would reveal something new. She settled herself in her chair and began to scan through the prose, delving into a world of *love and passion*, just as the blurb promised.

★

Bridget returned to her car, mired in frustration. Professor Al-Mutairi fed his plants the wrong kind of food! But what he had told her about ericaceous plants was correct. The food that matched the toxicology report was the kind that Vanessa used on her azaleas. Ericaceous plants loved acid-rich soil. So she was looking for someone who grew rhododendrons, camellias, heathers, magnolias and so on. She clapped her hands together and set off for Old Headington.

Soon she was pulling up again outside the Georgian house that belonged to Ian Dunn and Louise Morton. She stepped out of the car and paused for a moment to admire the glorious display of pink blooms on the magnolia tree in the front garden. Then she strode up the garden path and rang the bell.

The door was answered by Louise Morton. She had changed out of her gym wear and was wearing tight stretch jeans teamed with a sheer blouse over a camisole top. On seeing Bridget, she frowned. 'I thought you'd already spoken to Ian. He told me that you came to see him at the hospital.'

'I did,' said Bridget. 'May I come in?'

'Ian's not here. He came home from work and then went out again.'

'No problem,' said Bridget. 'It was you I wanted to see.'

She followed Louise into the lounge and sat down. No coffee was offered this time, and Louise gave Bridget the distinct impression that she would be glad to see the back of her. Bridget settled down in the armchair and made herself comfortable. 'I was admiring your garden as I came in. It's looking lovely. Is it you or Ian who looks after it?'

Louise eyed her suspiciously. 'Me, mainly. But I have a gardener who comes in once a week.'

'It must be a lot of work,' said Bridget. 'Especially the magnolia tree. Do you have a lot of ericaceous plants?'

'A few.' Louise looked pointedly at the smartwatch she wore on her wrist. 'Was there something in particular you wanted to ask me? Because if not, I have plenty I'd like to be getting on with.'

'I'm sure you do,' said Bridget pleasantly. 'Your job as a paediatrician must be very demanding. It can't leave you much time for hobbies like gardening. Personally, I can never find the time. My own garden's a complete mess. But working at the hospital does give you easy access to medical equipment, like syringes. And no doubt you would be fully aware of the effects of phosphorous, magnesium and potassium on the human body.'

Louise stared at her. 'What are you talking about?'

'That's how Diane was murdered. A concentrated solution of chemicals injected into her heart. She died almost instantly.'

'And why are you telling me this?'

'Because phosphorous, magnesium and potassium are the principal ingredients of ericaceous plant food, the kind you feed to magnolias.' She gave Louise a moment to digest the implication. 'I must say, it took me a while to make the connection. You appeared to have no reason to want Diane dead. There was no financial motive. There was no reason for me to suspect jealousy, since Ian divorced Diane so long ago. But then I discovered that you had lied to me the first time we spoke.'

'What do you mean?'

'When you said that you and Ian had no children of your own, you told me that it was a blessing. But in fact it was a source of great anguish to you.'

Louise shook her head angrily. 'You have no idea what you're talking about.'

'I think I do, though, Louise. I think that in reality you longed for a child, and that you married Ian believing that since he already had a son, he would make an ideal father for a child of your own. Then, when you were unable to conceive, you blamed yourself.'

A single tear began to roll down Louise's

cheek.

'I can only begin to imagine the sense of sadness you must have felt,' said Bridget softly. 'And then, when you realised that Ian wasn't really Daniel's father after all –'

'What?'

'You must have guessed,' said Bridget. 'The clumsiness, the trembling hands. As a doctor yourself, you must have spotted the symptoms of Huntington's disease and realised that Daniel was really the son of John Caldecott.'

Louise was staring open-mouthed, and Bridget began to have doubts. Still, she pressed on. 'You must have felt a sense of betrayal at the way Diane had cheated on Ian, then kept the truth about Daniel's paternity a secret. She didn't even appear to like her own son. Meanwhile, you had been trying desperately for a baby all those years, blaming yourself, and all for nothing. Diane's behaviour must have felt like a slap in the face.'

'No,' said Louise. 'It's not true. I didn't know any of this. How do you know?'

'It doesn't matter how I know,' said Bridget. 'But there was one final clue that made the puzzle fit together. Annabel's missing keys to Diane's house. I knew that the murderer must have had access to a set of keys, but I didn't know how they had got hold of them. But you could easily have taken Annabel's keys when you were at her house, couldn't you?'

'No,' said Louise. 'I've hardly ever been to Annabel's house. It's Ian who sees her most.

They've always been very close. He's known her even longer than he knew Diane. Anyway,' she continued, 'Ian found the missing keys.'

'What?' said Bridget. 'Where?'

'They were in one of our kitchen drawers. I have no idea how they got there, but Ian discovered them.'

'When?'

'When he came home from work an hour ago.'

'Can you show them to me?'

Louise shook her head. 'Ian's got them. He's taking them back to Annabel. You just missed him. He left about ten minutes before you arrived.'

★

Ian Dunn knocked loudly on Annabel's front door and was answered immediately by the sound of scampering paws and excited barking from within the house. Oscar. The small, yappy dog had always rather irritated Ian. He wasn't fond of dogs at the best of times, and the Jack Russell terrier that Annabel had chosen as her companion after her husband died was a particularly boisterous specimen. Always in need of a long walk, the dog was constantly barking, digging in the dirt, and jumping up to place its muddy paws on Ian's trousers. Not to mention trying to chew his shoes. He was glad that Annabel had the good sense to keep the dog on a tight leash.

According to Annabel, the Jack Russell breed was named after a nineteenth-century parson of that name, who had been an enthusiastic fox hunter and dog breeder. The young Mr Russell, while a student at Exeter College, Oxford, was said to have bought a terrier while out hunting one day in Marston. He regarded the bitch as the perfect fox terrier, and all Jack Russells were supposedly descended from that one animal. Ian rather wished that Jack Russell had fallen off his horse that day.

When Annabel opened the door, the dog rushed out, leaping up and yapping frantically as it always did. Ian bent down to pat the dog, hoping it wouldn't try to take his fingers off. It jumped up at him, licking his face with its pink tongue.

'Oh, hello, Ian,' said Annabel. 'You're lucky you've caught me. I was just about to take Oscar out for a walk around the field before it rains.'

Ian glanced up at the dark clouds gathering overhead. In his hurry to get to Marston, he hadn't thought to bring a coat with him. 'Do you mind if I join you?'

Annabel clipped Oscar's lead to his collar. 'Of course not. We'd love to have Ian join us for our walk, wouldn't we, Oscar?'

Ian regarded the woman before him almost as if she were a stranger, taking in the loose grey hair, the old, mud-splattered coat and walking boots. Such a contrast to Diane, who had always presented herself immaculately. And quite unlike

Louise, whose beauty and grace seemed so effortless.

I almost married you.

How different his life would have turned out, had it not been for that trip to Italy.

'There's something I want to talk to you about,' said Ian. He was glad he had caught her going out with the dog. It would be easier for him to do what he had come to do outside, with Oscar as a distraction, than sitting opposite her, face to face in her tiny front room. That's how much of a coward he was.

'As long as you don't mind a bit of mud,' she said.

He smiled.

'Wait here a second,' she said. 'There's something I need to do.'

He took Oscar's lead from her, and held it as the dog tugged vigorously. Annabel ducked inside the cottage but was back a minute later. She pulled the front door shut behind her and took the lead again. 'This way,' she said, as Oscar enthusiastically led the way down the garden path, sniffing at the gatepost as he went.

★

Bridget was already on her way to Marston when her phone rang. She answered it handsfree. 'Hello?'

'It's Ffion, boss. I've just finished reading Diane's latest romance book. I know who did it!'

'Me too. I spoke to Louise Morton. She told me that the keys to Diane's house that Annabel reported missing have turned up. Ian Dunn claimed to have found them in his kitchen drawer this morning. He told Louise he was going to Annabel's house to return them, and I'm driving there now. Get a response car round there and meet me at the house.'

'Okay, I'll organise a car. But listen. There's something you need to know...'

CHAPTER 35

Annabel didn't press Ian on the reason for his visit and he followed her and Oscar down the path, wondering how best to broach the subject he'd come to discuss.

He knew that by choosing to come and see Annabel first – under the pretext of returning her lost keys – he was really only doing what he'd done for many years. Postponing the difficult conversation he needed to have with his son. For despite everything, he still thought of Daniel as his own and probably always would. But a full and frank explanation was long overdue. Detective Inspector Hart's visit this morning had only served to drive that point home. If Daniel was really John's son, and Ian had little reason to doubt it, then Daniel was going to need all the help and support that Ian could provide, both as a father and as a medical man. It would come as a huge shock to Daniel, and a double blow to discover that not only was Ian not his real father, but that he was suffering from an incurable wasting disease.

Ian needed to explain and apologise to Louise

too for all the heartache he'd made her endure. She knew nothing about the swap that had taken place in Italy. It had happened so long ago and perhaps Ian had always been embarrassed by what, as the years crept by, looked increasingly like the folly of youth. Now he saw what a coward he'd been in not telling his new wife the whole truth about his past. He'd tried to bury it, but like a long-dormant volcano it had now erupted in spectacular fashion. The only decent thing to do was to try and sort out the mess he had helped create.

But before he embarked on those two most difficult conversations he needed to speak to Annabel. This involved her just as much as Daniel or Louise. He didn't think the news about John being Daniel's father would come as a great shock to her. As he'd explained to DI Hart, he was pretty certain she already knew the truth. But he was still nervous about tackling the subject. How would she feel about the matter? He had no idea, because he had never dared to raise it.

She had good reason to feel bitter towards him. If he had married her, as he had once fully intended, then she would never have had to endure the heartache of losing John. It was pretty clear that she had come off a lot worse than him in the bargain. Now the messy truth of their relationships was going to be exposed for all the world to see.

The one consoling thought was that she

couldn't possibly know the whole truth. For if she ever discovered that, the knowledge would surely kill her.

★

Bridget listened with a growing sense of disbelief as Ffion explained the plot of Diane's latest novel. Ffion had already dispatched a response car and promised to meet Bridget in Marston.

'So the book's called *Stolen in Sorrento* and it's about two sisters on holiday in Italy with their boyfriends, Jamie and Tom.'

'Got it,' said Bridget, negotiating the narrow, twisting lanes of Old Headington.

'When they set out from England, the two couples are very much in love, but it's obvious to the reader that not all is quite as it seems. The eldest sister, Scarlett, is the dominant one. She's a manipulative person who always gets her own way. She rather despises her younger sister, Katie, who has always looked up to her, and bosses her around all the time. Scarlett is ruthless and ambitious. She plans to become a journalist and change the world. Katie loves animals and wants to be a vet.'

The Mini bounced over a speed hump and skirted around the edge of Headington Cemetery. Bridget gripped the wheel tightly and pressed her foot to the floor. 'Can you just cut to the important bit?' she asked Ffion.

'I'm coming to it. Here's what happens. By the

time they reach Sorrento, which is their final destination, Scarlett has decided that Jamie is a loser – there are all kinds of reasons why he's unsuitable – and that she'd much rather have Katie's boyfriend, Tom.'

'Right,' said Bridget, 'and Katie prefers Jamie, and so they all agree to swap.'

'No,' said Ffion. 'That's not what happens. In the book, both sisters want Tom, and so Scarlett realises that in order to engineer a swap she's going to have to convince Jamie and Tom that it's in their best interests too.'

'How does she do that?'

'By telling them lies and being devious. I haven't got time to explain all the details. Anyway, to cut to the chase, Scarlett tricks the two men into going along with her plan, and so they sit down one night for dinner and bring it all out into the open. At first, Katie is upset, but because Jamie and Tom are both so keen on the idea, she gradually comes round to it.'

'So Scarlett gets exactly what she wants,' said Bridget, 'and Katie never finds out that it was really her sister who orchestrated the whole scheme.'

'Exactly.' By the sound of it, Ffion was now in a car herself and heading out of Kidlington at speed. Bridget heard Jake's voice in the background. 'So,' said Ffion, 'assuming that Scarlett is really Diane, and Katie is Annabel...'

'And Tom is Ian Dunn and Jamie is John Caldecott...'

'Then the upshot is that Diane tricked Annabel into exchanging partners. In the book, Jamie has a fatal flaw, and in real life, John had Huntington's disease. Back in the early 1980s there was no genetic test available, so John wouldn't have known whether or not he had it. But he would have known that his mother did, and there was a fifty per cent chance that he would inherit it from her. Now suppose that he proposed to Diane but told her about the risk. From what we know of Diane's personality, that would probably have been unacceptable to her.'

'But she would have had no qualms about dumping John on Annabel if it meant that she could get Ian instead,' concluded Bridget. 'When I spoke to Ian this morning, he told me that he and Diane were simply better suited to each other, but if what happens in the novel is what happened in real life, then he was lying to hide the fact that he was part of the plan to trick Annabel.'

'Precisely,' said Ffion. 'So Annabel never knew that there had been a conspiracy against her. Not until *Stolen in Sorrento* was published last month, and the truth was made public.'

'You're assuming that Annabel somehow knew about Diane's novels.'

'That's what I'm assuming. And if I'm right...'

'Then Ian Dunn is in danger too.'

★

The field was muddier than Ian had been expecting. Recent heavy rains and the constant toing and froing of dog walkers and their four-legged friends had churned up the ground, particularly near the entrance to the field which had turned into a quagmire. It was too early in the year for the grass to have started growing back properly. Always a fastidious dresser, Ian flinched at the prospect of walking through the mud, but he'd committed to the walk and was determined to talk to Annabel before he spoke to Daniel and Louise. He ignored the steady accumulation of mud on his expensive Oxford brogues and the hems of his dry-clean-only trousers, and plodded on gamely in Annabel's wake. So far, they'd discussed when the funeral was likely to take place and whether or not Diane would want to be cremated or buried. Uncontroversial matters. Now it was time for him to broach the subject he'd been putting off for far too long.

He cleared his throat before beginning. 'What I really wanted to talk to you about was Daniel.'

Annabel produced a muddy tennis ball from one of her voluminous coat pockets and threw it for Oscar to chase. The dog tore across the field as if he'd been propelled from a cannon. 'What about Daniel?'

'About whether he's really my son.'

Annabel said nothing and Ian wondered if she'd heard him properly. She waited for Oscar to return with the ball and drop it at her feet. The dog wagged his tail, eager for another go. Annabel obliged, picking up the ball and throwing it further this time. She didn't seem to mind the fact that it was covered in mud and dog spit. She had never minded anything that life had sent her way.

'It's taken you a long time to work that out, Ian,' she said. 'As a doctor I'd have expected you to realise it a lot sooner.'

Ian felt a sense of relief. She had already guessed. That would make everything so much easier. 'We don't always see what's right in front of us,' he said.

'You mean we don't *want* to see.'

Oscar returned again, his underbelly soaked with muddy rainwater. His legs and bottom half were almost entirely black. This time Ian picked up the ball and threw it with a powerful overarm to the far corner of the field. Undeterred, the little dog set off again, tail wagging with vigour. Life was so much simpler when you were a dog. 'When did you first realise?' Ian asked.

Annabel shrugged. 'I think I always knew. Because Daniel was born so soon after you and Diane were married there was always a good chance that he might have been John's. He looked like John too. And then he started to develop tremors. Even you must have noticed that.'

'Yes,' said Ian. 'I hoped it was just the stress of life in London, working too hard, worrying about money. But it's not. Daniel needs to be told the truth. Between us, we can do our best to help him.'

He was expecting Annabel to agree with him wholeheartedly. She was Daniel's aunt and had always loved her nephew. But she lapsed into a strange silence.

'We have to tell him the truth, don't we?' he prompted.

'How much truth do you want to tell him, Ian?'

'What do you mean?'

This time when Oscar returned and dropped the ball at her feet, Annabel ignored it. 'I thought you might be too ashamed to admit everything.'

'I don't know what you mean,' said Ian, although it was obvious what Annabel meant. Somehow, she must know everything.

'I think you do,' said Annabel. 'If not, let me spell it out. John asked Diane to marry him in Italy, but he explained to her that his mother had Huntington's disease and that there was a fifty per cent chance she had passed it on to him. He told her that Huntington's was an incurable disease, and that if he had it, he would expect to be dead before the age of fifty. He also explained that any children they might have together would have a fifty per cent chance of inheriting the disease. I think you know what Diane's answer was.'

'She refused to marry him.'

'Of course she did. An offer like that would never be acceptable to Diane. She had to win at everything. Marriage was no different. John was naïve if he imagined a different outcome.'

Oscar yapped, and Annabel kicked the ball away into the long grass.

'So then she came to you, Ian, with a proposal of her own.'

Ian blanched at the accusation, but it was useless to deny it. Somehow, Annabel already knew the truth. 'She told me that John had asked her to marry him,' he admitted, 'but she had turned him down because she had fallen in love with me.'

'And you believed her?'

'She seemed sincere.'

'Oh yes, Diane was always good at appearing sincere. So what did you say to her?'

'I told her I was flattered, but that I was planning to ask you to marry me.'

Annabel held his eyes, but there was little warmth in them. 'But you never did ask me.'

'No. Diane persuaded me that John would be a better match for you. I spoke to John, and he thought so too. And so we agreed to tell you what we'd decided.'

'Yes,' said Annabel. 'Poor little Annabel, no one thought to ask her what she wanted, she would surely go along with everyone else. Diane gave orders and you and John scurried to obey.'

'It wasn't like that,' protested Ian.

'It was! Diane tricked you into thinking you were in control, but she was always the one pulling your strings. She may not have intended to get pregnant by John, but she planned everything else right down to the last detail.'

Annabel was right. Ian knew it. But even now he tried to hide his shame. 'You didn't have to accept John's proposal,' he said. 'No one forced you.'

'What choice did I have? I thought you loved me, but suddenly you were with Diane. Besides, John was such a sweet man. He explained to me all about the risk of Huntington's, but that didn't matter to me. I was willing to take the chance. Diane knew that I would.'

Ian breathed hard, turning the facts over in his mind. 'Have you always known that Diane was behind the swap?'

'No. I had no idea. She made sure that she covered her tracks. But then a few weeks ago I found out.'

'How?'

'I read a book. *Stolen in Sorrento*. It explained everything.'

Ian shook his head. 'How can a book explain what happened almost forty years ago?'

'Diane wrote it.'

'What?'

'She wrote romance books and published them online using a pseudonym. You never knew? That was another of her secrets. She was really very good at keeping parts of her life hidden, wasn't she? But not quite good enough.'

A light rain had begun to fall, and Ian shivered, but it was less from the cold and more from the story that was unfolding before him. He had

351

come here thinking that he would be the one in control of this conversation, but Annabel had always been two steps ahead of him. He was struggling to keep up with her, just as he had stumbled across the muddy ground in her wake. 'I don't understand,' he said.

'It doesn't matter,' said Annabel, her voice cold and hard. 'All you need to know is that Diane underestimated me. She had no idea what I was capable of. I think you underestimated me too, Ian.'

*

When Bridget arrived at Annabel's house, the silver Lexus Coupé parked on the roadside told her that Ian Dunn had already arrived. A marked police car had pulled up behind it, and two uniformed officers were waiting for her by the front door of the cottage.

She strode up the garden path, noting the big hydrangea bushes she had seen on her first visit. *Of course.* Hydrangea plants flowered blue when planted in acid soil or treated with ericaceous feed. When summer came, these bushes would be covered in giant blue blooms, no doubt.

'There doesn't seem to be anyone here, ma'am,' said one of the waiting officers.

'Have you looked inside?'

'No. The house is locked, front and back.'

'Break down the door,' said Bridget. 'A man's life is in danger.'

When Bridget had set off from Old Headington, she had been in pursuit of Ian Dunn, but it was now clear that Annabel was the killer. The fictional story that Ffion had outlined to her matched the known facts so well that Bridget was certain the novel wasn't really a work of fiction but a thinly-veiled account of what had actually taken place in Italy.

The two constables exchanged glances, then one went to the car and returned with a red metal battering ram. It took him two attempts to break down the front door, and then he was in. The officers entered the cottage and Bridget followed. While one of the men went upstairs and the other checked the kitchen, Bridget put her head around the door to the front lounge. The room appeared much as it had when she'd visited Annabel to break the news of her sister's death. Copies of gardening magazines. Mismatched cushions and throws. A dog basket in one corner. Could this really be the home of a cold-blooded and calculating murderer?

The constable who had broken down the door came down the stairs. 'All clear up there.'

Bridget proceeded to the kitchen. 'Look at this, ma'am.' The second officer was pointing to a box of syringes that had been left out on the worktop.

Of course. Annabel had nursed John at home during the last days before he died. She must have kept hold of the syringes she had used to give him his painkillers. There was a plastic bottle next to them that Bridget recognised immediately. It was the same brand of plant food that Vanessa used. *Rich in phosphorous, magnesium and potassium for all acid-loving plants.*

But there was no sign of Annabel or Ian.

Jake's orange Subaru screeched to a halt in the road just as Bridget was leaving the cottage. Jake and Ffion jumped out. 'Any sign of them, ma'am?' asked Jake.

'They're not here. But I think I know where they might be.'

She turned to give instructions to the two officers. 'You two stay here. Call me if anything happens. The suspect is a woman in her late fifties with long grey hair, probably wearing a wool coat. A sixty-year-old man will be with her. Oh, and probably a dog too.'

'Come on,' she said to Jake and Ffion. 'I hope you don't mind getting muddy.'

★

'It was the death threat that gave me the idea,' said Annabel. 'After I read Diane's book, I was so angry that I went straight round to her house to confront her. But before I could say anything, she showed me the letter she'd received and asked me what she should do about it. It was almost like a sign from above. That's when I decided how I was going to pay back Diane for what she'd done to me.'

'But it was you who advised her to call the

police.'

'Yes. Because that was the sensible course of action, wasn't it? Good old Annabel, always dependable, always doing the right thing. But this time I decided to do something completely unexpected.'

Ian didn't need to ask what Annabel had done. He understood, and his blood ran cold. As cold as the rain that was now falling steadily, making the sodden field even muddier than it already was. Oscar returned once more, bedraggled and forlorn, tail no longer wagging. He dropped the soggy tennis ball at Annabel's feet, but even he didn't seem to expect any more fun and games. They were the only walkers left in the field. Everyone else had gone home when it first started to rain. Ian wanted to get away too. He wanted to run as fast as he could away from his sister-in-law but he seemed to be frozen in this godforsaken mud bath of a field, the rain pouring down his face.

'The keys,' he whispered. 'You didn't lose them at all.'

'No,' said Annabel. 'I used them to get into Diane's house. Then I put them in your kitchen and told you I'd lost them.'

'You planned everything,' muttered Ian.

'Yes.' She thrust her hand into one of the over-sized pockets in her coat and started to rummage around. What the hell did she keep in there apart from muddy tennis balls and doggie poop bags?

He didn't have long to wait before he found

out.

'Oh my God,' he cried. 'Annabel. What are you doing?'

'Putting things right.' She unscrewed the protective cap from the syringe she now held, revealing the sharp needle beneath. The syringe was filled with some kind of pale liquid. She looked up at him. 'Diane betrayed me, Ian. But she couldn't have done it without your complicity. Even John tricked me, although he never meant me any harm. Now they're both dead. So that just leaves you, doesn't it?'

CHAPTER 36

Bridget turned sharply into the field and swore loudly as her feet skidded in the mud, depositing her on her bottom. It didn't hurt much – she was well padded in that area – but it didn't do much for her dignity. How was she going to look, making an arrest with her backside caked in muck?

Jake reached down to help her back to her feet.

'I'm all right,' she said, wiping her muddy palms on her trousers. 'Now let's find them.'

The field was quite large, but virtually empty, so it didn't take long to spot two figures standing at the far end next to a line of trees. A small dog was running around them, sniffing the ground, as if looking for somewhere to do his business. What was the dog's name? Ah, yes. Oscar.

Ffion was already making strides across the field. 'Go with her,' Bridget instructed Jake. 'Don't wait for me.'

Jake set off and Bridget did her best to keep up in the rain which was coming down harder than ever. The field was becoming a quagmire.

Ffion was well used to running across Port Meadow in all weathers and was quite capable of making her way across a muddy field. By the time she was halfway to the distant corner where Annabel and Ian were talking, Bridget and Jake had fallen some distance behind. She turned to see them scrabbling around in the mud.

It looked like it was going to be up to her to make the arrest. No matter. Since she was the one who had found the truth buried in *Stolen in Sorrento* it seemed only fair that the collar should be hers. She approached Ian from behind, keeping Annabel clearly in view.

'Police!' she shouted.

Through the rain, she could see that Annabel held something in her right hand. An object made from metal and plastic. She realised what it was and called out a warning to Ian, but he seemed frozen in place, unable to move. 'Run!' she shouted, but it was only Annabel who moved.

★

Rain ran down Ian's face, seeping through his clothes, and drenching him to the skin. The water was falling in torrents, collecting in ever-widening pools of water on the sodden ground. He felt like he was standing in a lake. His smart shoes were sinking deeper into the mud with every passing second. He tried to lift one foot, but the mud sucked at him, holding him fast like the roots of a tree.

Annabel advanced towards him, those damned walking shoes of hers ideal for these conditions. She squelched across the grass, the needlepoint of the hypodermic syringe drawing closer with every step.

'Annabel,' he said, but quickly fell silent. The words he ought to have said to her had been firmly bottled up nearly forty years ago, and now it was far too late to say them. He remembered the hurt on her face back in Naples when he and John had first broached the idea of swapping partners. He might as well have plunged a dagger into her breast.

'You betrayed me,' she said now. 'You deceived me. You must have known that I would have done anything for you, Ian. We could have been happy together, but you threw my love back in my face.'

'I...' he didn't know what to say. Every word she spoke was true. He was a liar and a coward and a wretch.

The sound of a Welsh woman's voice carrying over the pounding of the rain was so unexpected that he was jolted out of his misery and back to the real world. 'Run!' shouted the woman, and Ian knew what he had to do. He might not deserve it, but he knew what he wanted – to live, to get away from this dreadful place and back into Louise's arms.

He tried to turn, but the mud claimed his shoe as soon as he took a step. He abandoned it, and staggered forwards, one noisy step after another. He might have got away, but suddenly there was a barking and a rushing of white fur and black mud. Oscar dived for his leg, and sank his tiny teeth through the fabric of his trousers.

Ian shouted and flailed his arms, trying to keep his balance, but there was nothing he could do to prevent himself falling forwards into the muddy water. The dog was anchored to his leg, shaking its head, teeth tearing through skin. Ian cried out again, and turned himself over.

Rain pelted down, driving into his face like a waterfall. He could barely see a thing. Then Annabel loomed over him, the hypodermic in her hand. She dropped to her knees and thrust it into his chest.

★

Ffion raced across the slippery ground as Annabel closed in on her prey. The dog was attached like a limpet to Ian's leg. No matter how much he tried to shake himself free, the animal clung on, holding him fast. Dog and captive had both turned a Stygian black as they rolled in the bog.

Ffion put on a final burst of speed just as Annabel caught her victim and plunged the needle into his flesh.

360

She had no need to think. Her Taekwondo training took over, and she flew into a flying side kick. Launching herself into the air, she closed the remaining few feet and kicked out with her left foot. Her heel connected with Annabel's jaw, knocking her away from Ian's prone form. By the time Ffion had landed on the ground, Annabel was lying on her back, moaning in agony.

The dog immediately left Ian's leg and ran to his mistress, licking her with his long tongue and whining urgently. Registering that Annabel would live, Ffion left them to it, and knelt down beside Ian.

He was gasping for breath, his eyes half-closed. The hypodermic needle was stuck in his chest, but the syringe was still up. Annabel hadn't had time to depress the plunger. Ffion plucked it out and stuck it in the soft ground where it could do no harm.

Ian opened his eyes. 'My God!' he exclaimed. 'You saved me!'

'Just doing my job,' said Ffion. 'But if you want to put in a good word on my behalf, don't let me hold you back.'

★

By the time Bridget reached the scene, she felt like she'd been dropped fully clothed into a swimming pool, and an unheated one at that. The torrent of rain had eased off now and was back to a normal spring shower. But everyone present was soaked to the skin, Oscar included.

Bridget was relieved to see Ian Dunn sitting up, apparently unharmed, and Annabel on the ground, incapacitated. The woman was clutching her jaw while the dog stood defensively at her side, barking viciously at anyone who tried to approach.

Jake went over to the dog and reached out a cautious hand. 'There, there, boy, no need to bite. I'm friendly.'

The dog yapped at him.

'His name's Oscar,' said Bridget.

'Oscar, is it?' said Jake. 'Good dog, Oscar. Good dog!'

Incredibly, the soothing words succeeded in winning the animal over, and soon the little dog was licking Jake's palm.

Bridget and Ffion helped Annabel to her feet. Unarmed and dazed, she posed little threat now, and there was no need to handcuff her. 'Annabel Caldecott,' said Bridget, 'I am arresting you on suspicion of the murder of Diane Gilbert and the attempted murder of Ian Dunn.'

CHAPTER 37

'DI Hart, you've done well,' said Grayson. 'I'd like you to know that I had complete confidence in you all along.'

'You did, sir? Thank you.' A hot shower, a change of clothing and a sweet cup of tea had restored Bridget to her usual self. With the perpetrator behind bars, she could afford to relax, even in Grayson's presence. 'So I assume there'll be no need for an enquiry now into what went wrong?'

'I don't think that would tell us anything useful,' said Grayson, 'especially since the death threat turned out to be a hoax. The two constables who were suspended from duty, PC Sam Roberts and PC Scott Wallis, have returned to work, and all complaints against them have been dropped. It would appear that they did nothing wrong, and told the truth throughout.'

'Yes, sir. I believe they did.' Bridget was pleased to hear that Sam and Scott had been vindicated, and gratified to know that she had been right to trust their account of their conduct. It was good to hear Grayson praise her too, but it would have been better if he could have expressed his support for her while the investigation was underway. 'Would you really have brought in DI Baxter to take over from me?' she enquired.

Grayson looked suitably sheepish. 'Not willingly, but sometimes certain actions become necessary. You'll understand that one day if you ever reach the lofty heights that I currently occupy.'

Bridget raised an eyebrow. Was the Chief teasing her, or did he really think she had the potential to step into his shoes and become Chief Superintendent one day? She had been a DI for less than a year. Ahead lay the ranks of Detective Chief Inspector and Detective Superintendent, should she ever make it that far. 'Sir? Does this mean that I can expect a promotion soon?'

'Baby steps, DI Hart. These things take time. In the meantime, is there anything you need from me?'

'There is one thing I'd like to request, sir. Time off. There are some personal matters I need to attend to.'

★

Bridget left the station with Grayson's blessing. But there were still a few loose ends for her to tie up.

Grant Sadler had been charged over the hoax death threat, and news of the hoax had inevitably leaked to the press. According to Grant, sales of the book would quickly dry up now that there was no juicy publicity to further them. Bridget spared a moment to think of all those freshly-printed books that would now be destined for the pulping machine. Such a waste of paper. But no doubt Professor Al-Mutairi would be quietly celebrating.

Grant himself was close to despair. 'That's it, then,' he told Bridget. 'My career as an agent is as good as over. Who will sign with me now? No one, that's who!'

Bridget refrained from reminding him that he had engineered his own misfortunes. Even though Grant had wasted a great deal of her time, it seemed unsavoury to gloat over his downfall. 'What about Michael Dearlove?' she asked. 'I thought you'd agreed a book deal with him and Jennifer.'

Grant's face turned sour. 'When Jennifer found out that I was behind the death threat, she cut me out of the deal and signed Michael directly. It's my own fault, I suppose, for acting on his behalf when I wasn't even his agent. So that's it. I'm finished.'

'I'm sorry to hear it,' said Bridget.

Now that the murder investigation was all concluded, it would be handed over to the Crown Prosecution Service. Annabel had declined the offer of legal representation and had made a full and detailed confession, explaining exactly how and why she had murdered her sister. She held nothing back, and seemed to find the process of unburdening herself a relief. Her only concern had been about her dog. 'Who will look after Oscar?' she asked anxiously.

'He's safe in the dog warden's kennels for the moment,' said Bridget, 'but I have an idea about what to do with him in the long term. Leave it with me for now.'

Daniel Dunn was very unsure about her suggestion at first. 'But I live in a small flat in London. And I have a demanding job. How am I going to look after a dog?'

Oscar was sitting next to him on Ian Dunn's sofa with his snout laid on his lap, gazing up at him with big brown eyes. Bridget was glad to see that the Jack Russell had been given a bath and was back to his usual white and brown colouring, his fur neatly brushed and dried. It was hard to believe that the creature had behaved so aggressively in defence of his mistress.

Ian Dunn stood on the opposite side of the room, eyeing the dog warily. He didn't look too happy at having Oscar in his house, and the dog narrowed his gaze whenever he made a movement.

Ian had spoken to Daniel before Bridget arrived, breaking the news that not only was he not his real father, but that Daniel had almost certainly inherited an incurable genetic disorder. It would be necessary to take a test to confirm, but from what Bridget had seen of Daniel herself, she didn't doubt that Ian's diagnosis would prove to be correct. Daniel, for his part, was clearly shaken after the day's events. It would take considerable time for him to come to terms with everything that had happened.

'What about your mother's house in Oxford?' Bridget asked him. 'What do you plan to do with it?'

'I was going to sell it,' said Daniel. 'And use the cash to buy a house in London. But now I'm having second thoughts. I need to rethink my whole life.'

Bridget nodded sympathetically. She may not have warmed to Daniel during the murder investigation, but she would never have wished on him the devastating news that he had Huntington's. Perhaps a dog was just what he needed.

'Oscar's a friendly dog,' she said, trying to dispel the image of the terrier's jaws clamped hard around Ian's ankle, 'and he knows you well. I think that you'd be good for each other.'

'You could be right. I'd like to look after him, for Aunt Annabel's sake.'

'I'm sure that she'd appreciate that very much.' The fact that "Aunt Annabel" had murdered Daniel's mother and done her best to kill Ian too didn't seem to have dented Daniel's affection for her. But Annabel wouldn't be around to help Daniel come to terms with the fact that he was dying. Bridget was sure that a dog would be a great comfort to him in the days ahead.

'I'll leave him with you then,' she said, standing up.

★

'Well done, Mum!'

When Bridget returned home, Chloe and Jonathan were waiting for her, with Alfie too. Jonathan wrapped his arms around her in welcome.

'Nice one, Bridget,' said Alfie.

Bridget had phoned Jonathan earlier to tell him what had happened, and to let him know that she was safe. Now, in his arms, she really did feel safe.

'You're a hero again,' Jonathan said with a smile.

'I think the credit needs to go to my team,' said Bridget, thinking about the way Ffion had tackled Annabel in the field.

'You're too modest.'

'Yeah, Bridget,' said Alfie enthusiastically. 'Take credit for yourself!'

'Come on,' said Chloe with a smile, looping her arm through his. 'Let's give the loving couple some time on their own.' She took Alfie upstairs, leaving Bridget alone with Jonathan in the kitchen.

'Wine?' asked Jonathan, pouring a glass of red without waiting for her reply. 'I have a casserole in the oven.'

'You are the hero,' said Bridget. 'I don't know how I'd survive without you.'

'Takeaway pizza, I expect. Or microwaved leftovers. I'm sure you'd get by somehow.'

Bridget took a sip of the wine. 'But I don't want to get by. I've been just getting by for years, and now I'm nearly forty!' She knew that she ought to be happy, but for some reason a tear was trickling down her cheek. 'After Diane was killed, I thought my career was over. I stared into the abyss and everything looked black. You were in New York, Chloe was in London. I didn't know what to do.'

Jonathan took her hands in his. 'But you did know what to do. You solved the case and caught the culprit. Now you're vindicated. Chloe's back home, and I'm here too. So what's the matter?'

'I don't know. It's just...'

He studied her carefully. 'Is this about Ben and Tamsin?' he asked. 'After everything you've been through, are you still worrying about the wedding?'

Bridget looked at him hopefully. 'Do you think we could get away with not going to the wedding ourselves? You could arrange another business trip and this time I could go with you. Paris, New York, Tokyo. We could go anywhere, except London.'

'You know we can't. We have to be there for Chloe's sake. It's important for her to know that her parents can still get along like civilised people.'

'Is it?' Bridget thought of Diane Gilbert and Ian Dunn and their so-called amicable divorce. That had turned out to be a seething mass of concealed resentment and bitterness. But perhaps that was what civilisation was for. To put a gloss over the surface and try to keep the bad stuff hidden. She only had to keep her feelings at bay for one day. For Chloe's sake. And for her own too.

'Don't give Ben the satisfaction of knowing how much he still rattles you,' said Jonathan.

Bridget nodded slowly. 'You're right. I can't let him think that he's so important. Because he isn't.'

'That's decided, then,' said Jonathan. 'See it as an opportunity to enjoy some good food and wine, at Ben's expense. And besides,' he added, 'I'll be there with you.'

★

Jake was running late. By the time they'd got Annabel back to the station, interviewed her – she admitted everything immediately – and charged her, it was already gone seven. He hurried home, had a quick shower, and put on a fresh change of clothes.

After his date with Lauren he had come to the realisation that although Ryan meant well his advice was hopeless. The problem was that Jake had allowed Ryan to write his dating profile for him, and he could see now that it wasn't authentic. There was far too much emphasis on his supposed good sense of humour and wanting to have a good time. No wonder it had attracted a woman like Lauren who just wanted a bit of fun on the side.

That wasn't what Jake was looking for. He wanted a steady, long-term relationship with a woman he felt comfortable with. And so he'd completely rewritten his profile on the dating app. Instead of simply highlighting his good points, he had tried to write a full and honest assessment of himself. There was no point hiding his true nature from a potential partner. If tonight's date turned out to be as bad as the previous two then he was going to delete his account and learn to accept his single status with stoicism.

Amy had agreed to meet him at a pub down the Cowley Road so at least he didn't have far to go this time. He checked the photo of her once more to make sure he knew who he was looking for – frizzy red hair and freckles. He wouldn't have looked twice at her if he'd passed her in the street, but after he posted his new profile on the app, Amy was one of only two women who contacted him. He was a little nervous, as she worked at the Bodleian. He hoped she wouldn't want to talk about books all evening otherwise it was going to be a very one-sided conversation.

The rain had stopped but the roads were still wet and were full of reflections of car headlights. Jake pushed open the pub door and stepped inside into the warm, fuggy atmosphere. It didn't take him long to establish that there was no one matching Amy's description anywhere in sight. He felt rather relieved. Now he could go home, stick a pizza in the oven, and watch TV. His safe routine.

He was just about to step back outside when the door flew open and a short figure in a bright yellow high-vis jacket burst into the pub. She removed her cycle helmet, and her frizzy hair sprang back to life. Her face was bright red from the effort of cycling. She looked at him for a moment.

'Jake?'

'Amy?'

She laughed a hearty laugh that showed off her front teeth. 'Sorry I'm a bit late! Bellringing practice went on longer than usual tonight.'

'Bellringing?' Jake had never before met anyone who rang bells.

'I've just come from Mary Mags.'

'Who?'

She laughed again as if he'd made a joke. 'The church. St Mary Magdalen. We call it Mary Mags.'

'Oh, right. If you don't mind me saying, that's a very Oxford kind of thing to say.'

'Is it? I expect it is. Where are you from?'

'Leeds.'

'Yes, I thought you were probably from Yorkshire. Do you play cricket?'

'No, sorry.'

'Never mind. I don't really like cricket anyway.'

Amy was quite unlike any woman that Jake had ever been out with. But he liked her down-to-earth manner and her forthright way of talking. Now that she'd cooled off a bit, her face was less red, and her freckles were starting to become visible. Of the three women he'd met via the dating app, Amy was the only one not wearing make-up. She didn't look like she'd gone to any special effort to make herself look nice for him. But despite that, she really was quite pretty. He found that he wanted her to tell him more about bellringing.

'So,' he said, 'would you like a drink?'

'Oh yes, please. I'm parched after all that ringing and cycling. I'll have an Old Speckled Hen. What are you having?' She pulled a rucksack off her back and reached inside for her purse.

'Thanks,' he said. 'I'll have the same.'

'Two pints of Old Speckled Hen, please,' said Amy to the barman. She turned to look at Jake. 'So, the most important thing you need to know about bellringing is this...'

★

Candlelight. Wine. Soft music. After being tied up at work for such long hours this week, Ffion knew she needed to make it up to Marion, and this restaurant was an inspired choice. French, of

373

course. No one did romantic dinners quite like the French. The Italians did passion, the Spanish did flamenco, and the Swedish did meatballs. But the French excelled when it came to intimate one-on-one dining, and Marion deserved Ffion's full attention now that the investigation was finally over.

Ffion was happy to let Marion choose the food and wine, knowing that she was in the hands of an expert. They had started with Mediterranean fish soup, moved on to a main course of pheasant served with chestnut and mushroom sauce, and were now awaiting their pistachio soufflés.

Ffion had divulged a few edited highlights of the case, and they had swapped anecdotes about their times travelling and dining around the world. Now a hush descended over them, pregnant with anticipation. Last time they had spoken, Marion had hinted at some big announcement she wanted to make. Ffion was itching to invite her to Wales, to meet Siân and the rest of her family. But it was only fair to allow Marion to go first with whatever it was she wanted to say. 'So,' she said. 'Do you have some news to tell me?'

Marion lifted her wine glass to her lips and sipped. 'Yes. Exciting news. I have been waiting all week to tell you.'

'Is it about work?' Marion was a junior research fellow in the Department of Engineering Science specialising in renewable energy. Ffion found it exhilarating to discuss her work and learn about the latest developments in wind and wave power, and to hear about the transformative effect they would have in preventing climate change. And Marion always took an intelligent interest in Ffion's own line of work, particularly the computer skills that enabled her to unearth so much information from a person's phone or laptop. Marion had been particularly impressed by how Ffion had worked out Diane Gilbert's password through the process of steganography.

Marion nodded her elegant head, a faint smile playing hesitantly on her lips. 'It's good news. At least, I hope you think it is good.'

'Okay,' said Ffion cautiously. 'Don't keep me in suspense.'

'So, I have been here at Oxford for three years now,' said Marion. 'My position will expire at the end of this year.'

'Right,' said Ffion. 'You told me you've been applying for vacancies.' Marion was hoping to get an offer of a permanent position at her college, but competition for faculty and college posts was fierce. Nevertheless, Marion had an excellent track record of research. She was always travelling abroad to present her work at international conferences.

'So,' said Marion. 'I've been offered a job. A full-time lectureship.'

Ffion reached across the table and squeezed Marion's hand. 'That's fantastic news.'

'Yes,' said Marion. 'The job is in Edinburgh.'

Ffion's smile faltered. 'What?'

'I will start there next term.'

'So you've already accepted?' said Ffion, her voice tight.

'I had no choice. An opportunity like that... it is too good to refuse. In Oxford, I might wait years for a permanent position.'

Ffion pulled her hand away in confusion. 'But what about us? You said that this was good news!'

Marion tipped her head to one side. 'Well, it is good news. For me, anyway. But I hope it can be good for both of us. Ffion, I want you to join me. Come to Edinburgh! I promise it will be a great adventure. What do you say?'

'Move to Edinburgh? And leave Oxford?'

'Why not?' said Marion. 'You have no family in Oxford. Nothing is keeping you here.'

'I...'

'I know this is a big surprise. But the university needed a quick answer. They want me to start in the summer term. Another lecturer is taking early retirement because of bad health. I tried to talk to you sooner, but you were always too busy at work.'

'I don't know what to say,' said Ffion. Only a few hours earlier, Bridget had praised her actions in apprehending Annabel Caldecott and preventing a second fatality. She'd strongly hinted that promotion to Detective Sergeant might soon be in the offing, given her good work in helping to solve the case. She would need to pass the relevant exam, but that would be easy for someone of Ffion's ability. Her career was just about to take off.

The waiter brought the soufflés to the table, depositing them with a flourish, but suddenly Ffion wasn't hungry.

'I hope you will say yes,' said Marion. 'Come with me to Scotland! You can get a job with the police there easily enough, can't you?'

'I expect so.' But Ffion knew that she didn't want to leave Oxford, even if staying meant that she would lose Marion. It wasn't just the prospect of promotion that was keeping her. She had good friends in Oxford, like her housemates, Claire and Judy. Work colleagues too – Bridget, Andy, Harry and even Ryan.

And then there was Jake. The two of them had been through so much together. First as colleagues, then as friends, then, briefly, as lovers.

The thought of leaving him and the rest of the team behind and going somewhere brand new felt like a punch to her gut. She pushed away her dessert untouched.

'What are you thinking?' asked Marion.

Ffion could hardly remember the last time she had cried. She hadn't cried when she left Wales. She hadn't even cried when she split up with Jake. But now tears were streaming down her cheeks.

'I'm sorry,' she said. 'But I can't go with you. I'm not leaving Oxford.'

CHAPTER 38

'I do think I deserve some credit for solving the case,' said Vanessa.

'Oh, really? What makes you think that?'

Now that the investigation was over and Bridget had been given some time off, she had made good on her promise to accompany Vanessa to visit their parents for a few days. The drive down to Lyme Regis was giving the two sisters some much-needed time to talk and to try to settle their differences.

'Well,' said Vanessa, 'if it hadn't been for me, you would never have worked out how the victim was killed. I think I made a rather decisive contribution.'

'I think I was the one who worked out that Diane Gilbert was poisoned with plant food,' said Bridget. 'I don't remember you telling me that.'

'Perhaps I would have done, if you'd given me the facts. I think that perhaps you overlook my usefulness.'

'You know that I can't discuss my work with you,' said Bridget. Vanessa had never previously paid the slightest attention to her work, and had always turned her nose up at any mention of the word "murder", so perhaps this newfound interest could be interpreted as a growing acceptance of her job as a police detective. As gratifying as that might be, Bridget certainly didn't want to encourage Vanessa to start poking her nose into her investigations. 'Let's just say that a serendipitous set of circumstances came together just at the right moment.'

'Well, all right,' said Vanessa. 'But it wouldn't hurt to say "thank you".'

'Thanks,' said Bridget grudgingly.

They lapsed into silence as the Range Rover swallowed up the miles on the dual carriageway.

'So, are you looking forward to the wedding?' asked Vanessa.

'Chloe is,' said Bridget, sidestepping the thorny issue of Ben and Tamsin. 'But she has her exams coming up in the next month or two. She ought to be revising, not thinking about weddings and clothes. And I don't think she should be spending so much time with Alfie either.'

'He seems like a very nice boy,' said Vanessa. 'And Chloe is more sensible than you give her credit for. She's growing up so quickly.'

'She'll be sixteen in June,' said Bridget. 'Sixteen!'

'What a lovely age. The whole world ahead of her! Do you remember what you were like at sixteen?'

'Barely.' At sixteen, Bridget had dreamed of travelling the world and marrying a wealthy Italian count. Or becoming a professor of History at Oxford, and discovering some long-lost ancient document in the depths of the Bodleian Library. She had done none of those things. Now she realised with a start that she didn't even know what Chloe's hopes and aspirations were. She couldn't even recall when she had last asked her daughter such a question. Time was slipping through her grasp and she was powerless to stop it.

'I'll be forty next year,' she said to Vanessa. 'How can that be possible?'

Vanessa snorted. 'Forty? Don't worry about it. At the grand old age of forty-two, I can assure you that birthdays are all in the mind.'

'Birthdays are not just in the mind,' said Bridget. 'And even if they were, that wouldn't make them any less worrying. If anything, I'd say it's all the more reason to worry.'

'Well, now you're just being silly.'

At the sign for Andover, Vanessa signalled left and turned off the A34 onto the A303. To either side, the road was lined with a thick layer of trees and shrubs. Ahead, the tarmac stretched straight as a dart towards the horizon.

'So,' said Bridget, turning finally to the purpose of their journey. 'What's your strategy for Mum and Dad?' She was sure that Vanessa would have one. Before leaving her career to have children and fill her time with domestic affairs, Vanessa had managed large projects for a big company. Strategy and planning had been as normal to her then as the school run and after-school violin lessons were now.

'Well, for now, we just need to make sure they can manage day to day. But long-term we need to move them back to Oxford, obviously. We can't keep driving down to Dorset every time there's an emergency. Besides, they need somewhere much smaller and easier to manage. A nice retirement home would suit them well, perhaps even an apartment. There's really no need for them to have to look after a garden at all.'

'I think Dad enjoys his gardening,' said Bridget.

Vanessa cast a scornful glance her way. 'That's all very well in theory, but he doesn't have the time or the energy any more. I had to mow the lawn and cut back the worst of the shrubs last time I was down there. Easter is the time of year when the gardening workload begins to get heavy, and so far Dad hasn't really done a thing. It's going to get out of hand very quickly.'

Bridget acknowledged the fact with a nod. She knew from first-hand experience just how quickly a garden could get out of control if you neglected it.

'I've also been looking into retirement homes that provide care,' said Vanessa. 'There's a retirement village in Witney that offers round-the-clock nursing. It even has its own spa.'

Bridget couldn't really picture their parents making use of a spa, but she let Vanessa talk enthusiastically about all the health and social benefits of such a place. She'd obviously given it a lot of thought.

'It would be nice to have Mum and Dad living closer,' Bridget acknowledged, 'but I think they're going to resist moving.'

'Of course they will,' said Vanessa. 'They're stubborn. Just like you.'

'Like me?' If anyone in this car was stubborn, Bridget felt pretty sure that it wasn't her.

'So I'll need you to back me up,' said Vanessa. 'Can I count on you?'

Could Vanessa count on her? The question went right to the heart of the two sisters' relationship. Although at times it felt to Bridget that she and Vanessa were pulling in opposite directions, they always had an instinctive understanding of each other. Unlike Diane Gilbert, who had kept an explosive secret from her own sister for so many years, Bridget and Vanessa had always been completely open with each other. Despite their obvious differences, perhaps they weren't too dissimilar after all.

Vanessa glanced anxiously across at Bridget, and Bridget smiled back. 'You can always count on me, Vanessa. You know that. Isn't that what sisters are for?'

Toll for the Dead (Bridget Hart #7)

A solemn funeral. A bitter schism. A brutal murder.

When the much-loved lord of the manor, Henry Burton, passes away, the villagers of Hambledon-on-Thames gather to pay their respects at his funeral. But the day is marred when the churchwarden is found brutally battered to death in the north transept of the church.

Called to investigate, Detective Inspector Bridget Hart soon unearths a tangled web of old grudges and simmering feuds beneath the tranquil idyll of this sleepy South Oxfordshire village.

Bridget and her team must look beyond the thatched cottages and rose-covered houses to uncover the truth and prevent another death.

Set amongst the dreaming spires of Oxford University, the Bridget Hart series is perfect for fans of Elly Griffiths, JR Ellis, Faith Martin and classic British murder mysteries.

 Scan the QR code to see a list of retailers.

The Bridget Hart series (large print ISBNs)
Aspire to Die (978-1-914537-01-1)
Killing by Numbers (978-1-914537-03-5)
Do No Evil (978-1-914537-05-9)
In Love and Murder (978-1-914537-07-3)
A Darkly Shining Star (978-1-914537-09-7)
Preface to Murder (978-1-914537-11-0)
Toll for the Dead – Due Oct 2021

Psychological thrillers
The Red Room

About the author

M S Morris is the pseudonym for the writing partnership of Margarita and Steve Morris. Together they write the Bridget Hart series of crime novels set in Oxford. The couple are married and live in Oxfordshire. They have two sons.

Thank you for reading

We hope you enjoyed this book. If you did, then we would be very grateful if you would please take a moment to leave a review online. Thank you.

Find out more at **msmorrisbooks.com** where you can join our mailing list.